WAIREKA

WAIREKA

a novel

SHEILA DONALD

Waireka

ISBN: 978-1-62020-614-0

eISBN: 978-1-62020-693-5

Cover background photo courtesy of Tracey Topp, Cosy Toes New Zealand. www.cosytoes.co.nz
Typesetting by Hannah Nichols

AE BOOKS

Greenville, SC 29601

www.ambassador-international.com

The colophon is a trademark of AE Books

I would like to thank my cousins Pam and Sally for their help in my research. I would also like to thank my family for their ongoing support and for the skills and patience of my editor, Lyndsey.

GLOSSARY OF SCOTTISH WORDS

Amiss – Wrong

Aye – Yes

Bairns – Children

Bonnie – Pretty or Fair

Canna – Can't

Cheel - Child

Dinna – Don't

Fair Flagging – Exhausted

Faring - Doing

Fret - Worry

Has the eye – Finds you attractive

Lass/Lassie – Young lady

Nay - No

No – Not

Tittle Tattle – Idle Gossip

Wee – Little

GLOSSARY OF MAORI WORDS

Paku – little

Waihaha river – noisy river

Waireka – sweet waters

Pakehas – white settlers in New Zealand

Anaru – Maori for Andrew

Mangapai - good stream

Chapter One

STAIR PARISH, SCOTLAND 1850

ELIZA YAWNED AS SHE LISTENED to yet another of the Reverend Reid's dull sermons. He was very large and brusque in his manner and either bored her to death nearly with his long drawn out Bible passages, which seemed to bear little relevance to her own life, or frightened her greatly with his sermons on sin and hellfire. Conscious of his own and his wife Jessie's place in society, he seemed to forget this when he chose to leer at any pretty young girl whatever her station in life. Eliza shuddered as she remembered how he had lately favoured both her and Kitty with his appraising glances.

Coming to the end of his sermon, Eliza was all at once alerted to him saying, "My wife Jessie and I wish to announce that we will soon be moving on from this parish and heading to one in Wellington, New Zealand. The new world."

Eliza found herself transported in her mind to that new land and the pioneering life. She and her beloved sister Kitty had often dreamed of travelling to far off places as they had poured over maps and books.

And then the Reverend was saying, "We do have need of a young nursemaid though to travel with us, so if any of you young lasses feel you would be able to consider parting from your own family to head out to the unknown with Jessie and me, we'd love to hear from you as soon as possible. We travel in just six weeks' time."

As the Reverend went on to announce the next hymn, Eliza dug her mother firmly in the ribs.

"Mama, don't you think it would be perfect for me? Please say yes, please, before some other girl takes my place. Say I can go."

"Hush, Eliza," said her mother sharply, her face registering her disapproval. "Have some respect. We're in church."

Eliza felt the looks of disapproval not only from her mother but also the other folk in the small rural community of Stair Parish, where everyone knew everyone else's business, and she bit her lip in anxiety. She just had to go. Her year as a nursemaid up at the Ballymore Estate had come to an end recently with the swift departure of the young lad to boarding school. Now the only future for her was to take up a similar post at the Purdy household in Glasgow, where her older sister Jean was employed as a housemaid. The position filled her with dread. She was no lover of big cities and had heard that the children were boisterous and unruly, with plenty of nursemaids leaving over the last few years, according to Jean.

As they left the church, Eliza again tugged at her mother's sleeve, "Mama, please won't you speak to the Reverend on my behalf. Say that I'm interested in the position with him and his wife to go out to New Zealand."

"Will you hush your fretting child, you're only seventeen yoursel' and if you think you can just go off into the unknown to look after someone else's children when you're no much more than a cheel yoursel', you're out of your mind."

"But Mama, I've always wanted to travel," said Eliza petulantly. "It's what I've dreamed of since I was a little girl. This would be such an opportunity for me. The posters say New Zealand is a land of opportunity and people have already been sailing there for the last ten years or more and I am good with children. Just think what an opportunity it will be for me. Only think that you won't have to worry about my upkeep anymore especially with me being out of work at present. I'm sure the Reverend and Mrs Reid will look after me well."

"Eliza, hold your tongue. I think you've said quite enough. I can't think the Reverend or his wife would approve of such unruly behaviour as suitable for their nursemaid. You're to go to Glasgow with our Jean and that's the end of the matter."

Eliza felt both angry and tearful at the same time at her mother's intractability. It wasn't just her age that concerned her mother, she knew, for Mama had put up a big fight against her oldest brother Joseph's joining the navy a couple of years ago when he was a year older than she was now. Her mother was afraid of the sea and the unknown and played out her own fears in the lives of others. Papa had intervened in Joseph's case and argued for the respectability of a good naval profession as a merchant seaman and her mother had been silenced. Maybe he was her hope now? Eliza didn't feel that confident. Her father was a strong disciplinarian who believed that women should know their place and be silent. She had often seen him silence her mother with just a look.

As they made their way home, Eliza and her sister, Kitty, just a year older than herself, tarried at the back of the little party discussing the Reverend's proposition. Kitty was fair haired like Eliza but by contrast, her long, blonde straight hair was beautifully obedient, and Kitty usually wore it in a neat compact bun on top of her head.

"I so want to go, Kitty," argued Eliza with feeling. "The thought of that nursemaid position in Glasgow fills me with dread and you know how I've always longed to travel."

"But with the Reverend Reid?" exclaimed Kitty in horror. "We all know of his reputation with young girls even though his wife seems totally oblivious to it, or chooses to be."

"I know but it's a risk I'll have to take if I'm to live my dream, may God help me."

"In that case you must face Papa. He will be your strongest advocate, I imagine, as he was for Joseph."

"Yes, but Joseph was a man and older than I am now."

"That's all true. But I don't see any other course of action for you."

Eliza realised with apprehension that Kitty was right. She usually was. But Eliza worried about how to approach her father without her mother knowing and how he would treat her request. He was so unpredictable, a hot-tempered man who kept largely to himself. On returning from his gamekeeper's role up at the Ballymore Estate he would choose to hole himself up in his study sorting out the estate's accounts and appearing simply for meals. Eliza rarely spoke to him except to exchange greetings in the morning or at night. He took no interest in their education, although her mother had seen to it that they could all read and write to a basic level, girls as well as boys.

Just a few days later Eliza found the courage to knock rather timidly on her father's study door. Indeed, she knocked so quietly she had to knock a couple of times before her father heard her and answered, "Come in," in an authoritative tone.

"What do I owe this visit to then, Eliza?" he said, turning to face her with one eye still half on his accounts.

He always appeared stern as he looked at her, maybe it was partly because of his thick woolly beard or the way in which he seemed to peer out at her from under his thick dark eyebrows.

"I imagine it is concerning the Reids' forthcoming trip to New Zealand. Your Mother tells me you are keen to travel with them to help look after their children?" It was half question, half statement.

"Yes, sir," said Eliza determinedly as she held her head of unruly golden curls high and tried to meet his dark brown eyes with her blue ones.

Andrew Renfrew was silent as he gazed at his daughter for what seemed to be an age but was probably no more than a few moments.

"Well, Eliza," he said finally, "I know your mother feels that you are too young, but I also know of her fear of sea travel. You may be young, but this is a good opportunity for you to travel if you've a mind to. There isn't a lot here for you in Stair Parish now that your services up at the Ballymore Estate are no longer required, and we can't really afford the luxury of one extra mouth to feed if you've no employment. First, I need to establish if you are so against the nursemaid's position in Glasgow? Jean seems to like the Purdy family well enough and they do say that Glasgow's becoming quite a Scottish centre with all the shops and businesses setting up there of late."

Eliza swallowed hard, looking nervously at her feet. She never liked having to defend herself against her father but defend herself she must or the opportunity with the Reids would be lost forever.

"Father, you know I'm a country girl at heart. I fear the sights, sounds, and smells of the city would not agree with me as readily as they have with Jean. Besides, I hear the children are a little boisterous and I've had just a year's experience in the role to date. I fear they would be too strong for me, Sir. I have seen the Reverend and Mrs Reid's children and they seem much more demure and amiable."

Eliza detected a slight smile and nod of acquiescence from her father.

"Well, there's no work to be had in this small parish, you know that. So, it seems that you either must be resigned to follow Jean to Glasgow or we must accept the Reids' offer. I dare say they would treat you fairly and give you a good wage, which is probably more than you could say for many in these times. And since those fellows, Stokes and Masters, have sent their reports back to Britain of New Zealand being a pleasant climate with friendly natives, many like you have dreamt of going there since the first settlers landed around ten years ago. Like Mama, I wouldn't have let you go either at your age unless it was with a respectable couple like the Reids but under their guidance I dare say you would come to no harm."

Eliza smiled nervously at this point as she thought about the Reverend Reid.

"Of course, the journey would be precarious, but like many others before you, you would just have to take your chances. Although your mother and I don't see eye to eye on this matter, I'm prepared to overrule in this case if it really is what you wish."

Eliza shook her head of curls vigorously as her father continued, "I'm sure your mother will soon come to see my point of view, by and by. We will make our decision over the next few days and then get back to you."

"Thank you, Sir," said Eliza curtseying and leaving quickly. There wasn't much more she could do, given that he had already turned his back to her, busy again on his accounts, which she knew was tantamount to a dismissal.

She couldn't wait to tell Kitty later that night. Kitty was a housemaid up at the Ballymore Estate and had been for the last two years. It had been a joy to work up there with her over the last year. There was just a year between them and they had always been close. They'd had such joy planning their days off together, but that was all over now.

"Kitty, Kitty," she shrieked in excitement as soon as she saw her sister come into the room they'd both shared since childhood. "I may be able to go to New Zealand with the Reids after all. Papa thinks it will be a good opportunity for me it seems. Isn't that great?"

Her joy all but evaporated as she looked at her sister's crestfallen face.

"Yes, of course it is, and I am wonderfully pleased for you, but New Zealand is such long way away, how shall I manage without you my dear Lizzie?"

"We . . . we can always write, and we will do so often," Eliza said hesitantly.

"But letters can take up to six weeks to get here, Lizzie. They have to wait for the next ship to depart which can take time."

A coldness came over Eliza. Up until this point her joy had been almost unbounded but suddenly she saw the reality. Separation from her dearest sister and best friend? That was a sadness she had not given a moment to consider.

"Maybe I'll tell Papa I shouldn't go after all," she said, biting her lip in anxiety, a note of uncertainty creeping into her voice.

"Oh Lizzie of course you must go. I'm just being selfish," said Kitty dismissively, but there was a slight tremor in her voice as she continued. "This is a one-off chance for you. Far be it from me to take it from you. I know how you would hate working with Jean in Glasgow."

"Indeed, the streets of smoky Glasgow would be a sore trial for me."

"Poor Lizzie. I know it is only fair of me to learn to manage without you. After all, I do have my Charles whom I hope may propose to me before long when his position as cowman is secured, and I owe it to you to make at least one of our dreams of travel become a reality."

Eliza went to her sister and hugged her. It was a hard price to pay leaving her behind, and she knew Kitty would miss her dearly too.

"Oh, my dearest Kitty, of course Charles will propose to you soon. Anyone can see he adores you and he is only waiting to secure his future. I am sad to be leaving you and most particularly to miss your wedding day which I will now only be able to imagine." Eliza's eyes filled with tears at the thought and she turned away quickly. She didn't want to upset her sister any more than she had to.

"Oh, Lizzie, I will miss you being my bridesmaid on that day."

"Let's not speculate yet," said Eliza quickly, seeing the look of loss on her sister's face. "We don't even know yet that I'm going any-where. Although I'm guessing if not New Zealand I'll be heading off to smoky Glasgow."

It was just a couple of days later when Eliza's father was leaving his office to head up to the estate with John, her second eldest brother and her father's newest assistant, when he called Eliza to him.

"I have discussed the possibility of your voyage to New Zealand with your mother and with the Reids. It turns out that they haven't had any other enquiries and so have agreed to your taking up the position of nursemaid to their children. Here is a list of the items you will need for the journey," he said holding out the list to Eliza which she took gladly. "I got a copy of it from the Reverend Reid. It's the list given out to all travellers by the New Zealand Company. Study it wisely and follow its dictates. But don't show it to your mother, for goodness' sake, it will only make her worry more. You're very fortunate that the Reids have already booked you a second-class passage on *The Adventurer* leaving from Glasgow docks. They did so as soon as I told them of our decision to allow you to go. You will be sharing a cabin with young Henry and Maria. Make sure you do us proud now so that they won't regret their decision."

"I will, Sir," said Eliza curtseying demurely although her heart was racing within her. She couldn't wait to show Kitty the list that very next Sunday.

Reading through the list of items together with Kitty, Eliza found herself greatly surprised by some items on the list:

> A strong pair of cork shoes that will withstand walking about on the ship's deck in all weathers, bearing in mind that the sea often washes over the decks in stormy or un-settled weathers.

> Strong and useful clothing both for on the ship and for the settler's new country. Something windproof is particularly useful in Wellington as it is prone to windy weather.

> Candles and matches.

Pictures, photographs, family mementos and books—the journey is long, four months or more, and passengers will need some occupation to pass the time.

Pens and paper. If passengers have any letters ready to send on their arrival in the new country, then these can follow them back on the next ship departing. Loved ones will be glad to receive notification of your arrival.

Soap, washing jug, bowl and chamber pot.

Eliza smiled as she considered that it would be impossible to travel without the latter item.

Furniture: All the items passengers wish for the voyage must be taken with them if they are to be in a cabin, such as beds, chairs, etc. and these items must be nailed to the floor in advance of departure.

"Furniture to be taken and nailed to the floor! Can you imagine that, Kitty?" Eliza said, incredulously.

"Yes, it does seem incredible, but I expect it's because ships move around a bit at sea, Lizzie," said Kitty laughing.

Eliza nodded her head solemnly at the thought before suddenly thinking of her sparse wardrobe with some alarm. "What shall I wear, Kitty? The list talks of strong and useful clothing but I have only one Sunday best dress and two fairly ordinary ones. Well, the ordinary ones will have to suffice. I can't spend too much money on this journey, I haven't much to spend, especially now that I have no work. Do you suppose that I really need those strong cork shoes?"

"I dare say you may have to put up with strong winds, even storms at times, so perhaps they might be a wise investment," said the pragmatic Kitty.

"Storms, goodness, do you really think so?" said Eliza a little alarmed.

"Yes, and heat through the tropics too, Lizzie. Remember the countries we studied?"

"Oh yes," said Eliza thoughtfully. "How funny it will be. I wish you could come with me and share my adventures."

"I shall do that though through your letters, if you remember to take the pen and paper the list suggests," said Kitty practically even though she looked rather sombre.

"Oh but of course I shall write, every day and then it will almost be like you are there with me," said Eliza sadly. "Meanwhile, let's not think of that. It will be such fun sharing all the preparations and packing with you, I do so value your good opinion, you know that."

Eliza was taken aback as her father turned to her at supper that evening and addressed her directly. "I hope you have studied the list carefully, Eliza. You've a lot of preparations to make in a very short time. So, make haste. Your luggage, all but a few clothes and personal items, must be sent on ahead of you where they will be dealt with in the appropriate manner for departure. Then you will take the mail coach as far as Falkirk where the Reverend Reid will meet you. You are to spend the first night with the Reids at their lodgings before leaving for the docks in Greenock near Glasgow early the next morning ready for an evening sailing. If you're lucky and the journey is good, you should arrive in Wellington in just four months. But it could take up to six or longer."

"Why then, Father," Eliza said, "if we arrive in just four months we would arrive in January. That will be cold. I'd better make sure I pack enough woollen clothes."

Eliza was surprised when her normally austere father suddenly threw back his head and laughed. She wondered if she had said something extremely foolish and wished she had kept her mouth shut. She looked across at Kitty who gave her a reassuring smile. Fortunately, her father didn't seem displeased with her as he answered, "You're thinking of Scotland and our January temperatures, Eliza. New Zealand is in the Southern Hemisphere, a long way from here. January will be mid-summer there."

How strange. The place sounded quite alien. To think of January being summer time. She could hardly get her head around the fact.

The next few weeks passed in a flurry for Eliza. There was shopping to be done, clothes to be packed, and her furniture and luggage to be sent ahead of her to be loaded on the ship.

As Eliza packed the last few items in her portmanteau on her final evening, she said, "Now remember, Kitty, I will write to you as often as I can, and you must write to me and tell me how things are progressing with Charles."

"Of course, I will dearest, Lizzie."

At this, each of the girls burst into tears and hugged and kissed each other as if their lives depended upon it.

Eventually drying her eyes, Kitty took a book from beside her bed and said, "You must take this book of my favourite verses with you to remember me by," and she held out her copy of poems by the fashionable Romantic Lakeland poets.

"But, Kitty," said Eliza horrified. "I know how much that book means to you. How could I possibly take it?"

"You must because it will show you that you mean much more to me than it. Every time you pick it up you will be sure to think of me." Her normally composed sister seemed to be speaking rather quickly and thrusting the book towards her as if her life depended on it.

"Indeed, I will. Here, take this copy of *Gulliver's Travels* from me and remember me by it," Eliza said, passing the book over to Kitty as an exchange for hers.

"But Lizzie, you love the tales of adventure in that book," said Kitty also looking slightly horrified and reluctant to take the book from her sister.

"I do. That is to say, I did, but you see I won't be needing those adventures so much now because I'll be living my very own. You shall need them instead as your comfort until you come to me." Kitty acquiesced and took the outstretched book.

"Oh, yes, I do pray that one day I will."

"Me likewise, God be willing," said Eliza and the two girls hugged again.

Dinner was a sombre affair as they partook of the family's favourite dish of haggis. Eliza was so full of emotion, both excitement and sorrow, that she found it very hard to eat anything, Kitty was also quiet and seemed to eat little, and Margaret was subdued, but John seemed largely unaffected by any tensions or strong feelings and tucked into his food as heartily as ever. The fresh air and physical labour always seemed to give him a hearty appetite. Her father broke the silence by reminding Eliza to do the family proud and to write to them regularly and let them know how she progressed. Her Mama then, having finished her meal, passed Eliza a small silver locket, which, upon opening, she saw contained a small picture of her parents on their wedding day.

"Thank you, Mama. It's very pretty," she said.

"Make sure you look after it, Eliza. It was a present to me from your father on our wedding day."

"Oh, then I cannot take it from you," said Eliza in horror, trying to pass it back to her mother. "It will mean much too much for you to part with it."

"Take it to remind you of us, please Eliza. We want you to have it," said her mother, handing it back in a determined manner.

Eliza's Father nodded solemnly. It was the nearest they had got to declaring they might miss her. And it was in that moment she realised that she probably wouldn't see them again and that if she should be fortunate enough to marry sometime in the future this might be one of the only photographs to show her children and grandchildren of her parents.

Her father then handed her a couple of bank notes, more money than she had ever seen in her life before, with the strict instructions that she was to keep it safe for emergencies only. Joseph and Jean had been unable to return before she left but her brother, John, with little ceremony, gave her a quick, awkward kiss on the cheek and wished her well. Her oldest sister, Margaret, who as a housemaid in a nearby village, had been given leave with Kitty for their last family meal together, made her own farewell giving Eliza a small handkerchief which she had embroidered as a keepsake.

As the carriage left the next morning with only her parents to see her off, the farewells took on a more formal nature.

"I've packed you some bread and cheese for the journey," said her mother. "Be good Eliza and write to us often," and then she kissed Eliza's cheek lightly and stepped back to give her husband room.

"Ay lass, be good," he said also kissing her cheek. This was the nearest Eliza had ever been to hearing a term of endearment from her father. "We'll be thinking of you," he added almost as an afterthought as the carriage pulled away. Eliza waved until her parents were mere pinpricks in the distance.

The sun was barely up yet but Eliza knew it would be almost dark before she arrived in Falkirk and the Reverend Reid collected her in his own simple cart. There was nothing to do but to sit back and enjoy the journey of around forty miles.

The conditions in the public stagecoach were fairly cramped as Eliza was seated between two ladies of large proportions, one of whom had an equally large brood of children who were very noisy. The two gentlemen travelling with them travelled on top, as Eliza half wished she could do. The springs of the coach had clearly seen better days and the journey was very bumpy making sleep impossible even though Eliza had risen at dawn and was very tired. However, she was also excited and wasn't sure she'd be able to sleep even in more fortuitous circumstances. She felt a little tearful as she gazed at the fields ripe for harvest, seeing some of the stalks already sitting upright waiting to be gathered in. She would not be there to see them gathered in this autumn or sing out her praises to God at the annual harvest service followed by the supper. That was always one of the biggest events of the year in Stair Parish. Certainly even better attended than Christmas, if that were possible. Eliza could see from the coach that the skies were grey and a little overcast today. She knew she would miss the changeable Scottish weather and the mist over the hills. She had heard there were hills in the new country, but they wouldn't be the hills of her childhood.

The coach made several stops before its evening arrival. One was at a coaching house, where Eliza sat with the other ladies and took a dish of tea and one for a light lunch of soup and bread. Eliza only took some of the soup after having eaten her own bread and cheese on the coach. A further stop was made during the afternoon for another dish of tea.

Finally, the coach arrived at Falkirk and Eliza climbed down in relief with the aid of the coachman to be greeted by the Reverend. He shook her hand and pulled her to himself to kiss her cheek, his familiarity making her feel slightly uneasy. He then loaded her small packing case on to the back of the cart which was pulled by a single pony, as he said, "Good journey, my dear?"

"Not too bad," said Eliza, not wishing to go into detail though the Reverend had so kindly paid for her passage.

"Mmm, I can't imagine it was the most comfortable from the number of passengers I saw alight from the coach but never mind that now.

My Jessie has prepared us a good supper and then we must try to get an early night, as we've an early start to make tomorrow morning," he said helping her up into the small cart beside him. "We must set out on the road to Glasgow as soon as it grows light, making only a few stops on the way before reaching the docks by late afternoon."

Eliza nodded. She already felt travel weary and another journey with its various stops made her feel too weary to contemplate. She also could not even begin to contemplate the long sea journey, although she hoped there would be entertainment on board to distract them all. She was largely silent on the journey to the Reids accommodation. She could hear the Reverend's voice droning on in the distance but didn't hear the gist of what he was saying—partly because she was very tired and partly because she so felt excited. But she smiled in all the right places and if the Reverend noticed her preoccupied manner he made no comment.

Jessie Reid, a small dumpy lady of motherly appearance, was full of smiles and warmth as they alighted at the small cottage an hour's drive from Falkirk. They ate a simple meal of boiled mutton, potatoes, and greens followed by an apple pie, before Eliza helped to put the children to bed and then settled herself in the small bed beside them. This was to be her life from now on, looking to the needs of the children, putting them first. But it was also to be a grand adventure, and they were overall good children with no more than a share of the usual naughtiness. With a smile of satisfaction Eliza undressed quickly, lay down on her bed, and blowing out the candle beside it, she was soon asleep.

Chapter Two

THE VOYAGE

THE JOURNEY NEXT MORNING WAS long and tiring. This time Eliza
was conscious of her charge of the children and didn't feel that she
could allow herself to succumb to sleep. Henry and Maria would hardly
have let her anyway, so full of excitement were they that they chatted
almost excessively, pointing out every small detail along the route. They
could hardly contain themselves as the coach they travelled in finally
reached the port of Greenock. Eliza couldn't blame them. She felt quite
excited herself as she saw the dimensions of the huge vessel they were
to travel in to New Zealand. She could hardly believe its incredible size,
it seemed bigger than any ship she'd ever imagined. Her eyes travelled
up from the bow of the ship with its figurehead of a painted lady with
long flowing locks to the large furled sails towering above them.

The family stepped down from the coach to the port to be greeted
by the deafening noise of the various vendors shouting out their wares
for sale, anything from simple soaps and candle wax to wash bowls and
chamber pots, whatever they seemed to believe the travellers might
have forgotten to purchase. Eliza's nose wrinkled at the stale body
odours of the crowds flocking around the port. There was everything
from sweat to stale urine and vomit as they pushed and shoved one
another in their haste to purchase the various items needed before
making their way to the awaiting ship.

The Reid children added to the general cacophony as Henry tried
his best to annoy his sister, Maria, and baby Flora cried heartily for
her mother's breast.

"Come, come Henry," said Eliza. "I know you're tired but pulling Maria's hair isn't going to help her or you. It's simply making her cry. Please try to be less noisy."

"Yes, do be quiet children," Jessie Reid said putting her hand to her head. "My poor head is quite throbbing with the noise of you children amidst all the other chaos." Then, turning to Eliza, she said, "Hand me the baby, Eliza, quickly. It's more than time she was fed."

As Mrs Reid sat on a nearby bench with the Reverend beside her, Eliza tried to keep Henry and Maria amused by pointing out various things for them to see on the ship.

"Why are those grand ladies and gentlemen being hoisted up on chairs on to our ship?" queried Henry.

"I'm not really sure, Henry," answered Eliza honestly.

"Will we be hoisted up like them then?" asked Henry, genuinely excited at the thought.

"Maybe, I don't know, although they do look much grander than us. We will just have to see what happens when it does," answered Eliza practically.

But when it was time for Eliza and the Reids to climb aboard, they were requested to mount the gang plank themselves. Eliza wasn't entirely surprised by this. The grander ladies and gentlemen were probably travelling in a better class she supposed. Eliza and the Reids were about to step on to the gang plank when Eliza spotted the figure of her sister, Jean, running down the quayside with her hair flying wildly behind her.

"Lizzie, Lizzie," she shouted breathlessly. "I was hoping I might catch you before you boarded. I managed to get the afternoon off to say goodbye and to give you this."

Mrs Reid, who after returning from feeding little Flora and had promptly placed her in Eliza's arms prior to the boarding, was now forced to reclaim her as Eliza reached out to take the little lavender potpourri proffered by her sister.

"I made it for you," said Jean shyly. "A sort of keepsake."

"Thank you, Jean, it's lovely," said Eliza putting it to her nose and breathing in the fragrant smell which at least helped to somewhat mask the putrid smells around her. "I will treasure it. What a lovely surprise to be able to see you after all. I am only sorry I won't be able to take up the position of nursemaid at the Purdy's house with you."

"I never thought in my heart that you would, Lizzie. You are too much of a country girl for the position to suit you greatly."

"But I do wish them well in securing some other to the post."

"Oh, don't you worry about that. Work is short here. They've already had plenty of applications for the post and have a long list of candidates to interview."

"Good, I am pleased," said Eliza, giving her sister a quick hug before taking the baby once again from Mrs Reid. She would have loved to bide her time with Jean a little longer and find out how she was getting on and talk about her own feelings about the journey and her fears and expectations for the future, but the crew were shouting at the passengers to make haste as the crowd of passengers behind them pushed forward. Eliza was able to catch only a brief view of her sister waving her handkerchief madly before she saw her swallowed up by the crowds surging around the port and lost sight of her altogether. Eliza's eyes filled with tears as she followed the crowds in front of her blindly, and she had to gaze out towards the sea in order to gain her composure. Jean had been her last contact with home, and she was suddenly painfully aware of how alone she really was. As they reached the top of the walkway, she felt a tug at her sleeve which brought her back to the reality of her role as she heard little Maria ask, "Are we going soon, Lizzie?"

Forgetting her sadness, Eliza smiled down at the young girl. What a huge adventure it was for the youngster, even more so than for herself. "We need to find our cabins first, dearie, and get all our things stowed safely. Then I dare say we shall be off."

The cabin seemed rather cramped considering it would have to house herself and two noisy boisterous children for four months and up, as well as their furniture. Baby Flora's cot was going to be in the Reverend and Mrs Reid's cabin next door. In Eliza's cabin, there was simply her own bed, a twin bunk for the youngsters fixed against the cabin wall for safety, a small wash stand, her little writing desk and chair, and a small porthole window. Eliza realised at once that the set up wasn't going to afford her much privacy to collect her thoughts or to simply fulfil basic human needs.

After all their possessions were safely stowed in their cabin, Eliza took the two excited children on deck while their parents rested. Departure, she learnt, wouldn't take place for a bit as the sailors and dockhands busied themselves with getting the ship ready and provisions for the journey were loaded aboard with much shouting and excitement. The supplies seemed to be endless but then the ship was full of people and these supplies had to last them all for months. To the children's delight, they saw the live animals begin to be loaded aboard in crates. The smell of manure and animal flesh was so pungent that, although used to animals and animal smells at Ballymore, it caused Eliza to reach for her newly acquired potpourri to mask the smell. She guessed the poor animals might have been stacked in these same crates for quite some time.

"Pigs and hens. We shall have some grand pets on board, shan't we Lizzie?"

"Yes, Henry, we shall," said Eliza smiling but knowing full well many of the animals would come to an early end as provisions before they ever became pets or farm animals to stock the newly acquired land, but such information was best kept from the young lad.

As they wandered about on the deck amongst the many passengers, Eliza's eyes were drawn towards a young man leaning over the side of the boat looking out into the distance. He stood out from the crowd not only because of his tall, handsome form with light brown hair, fashionable mutton chops, and equally fashionable rim beard, but mainly because he was alone. Most other passengers seemed, like herself, to be either in couples or small groups, and Eliza found herself wondering why a young man would want to travel such a long way alone, although it was true that many single young men had travelled to the new world in recent years in the hope of making their fortunes.

As she was lost in her thoughts, suddenly there was a great commotion and before Eliza knew what was happening she spied a large pig running towards them. Anxious to protect the children, she had just enough time to shout, "Run Henry, Maria," before she was catapulted off her feet and lay stretched out on the deck with her petticoats on view to all. As she looked up she saw that a small crowd had gathered around her, and the young man who had so recently occupied her thoughts pushed himself to the head of the crowd proffering her his hand.

"Madam, please let me help you up. I hope you aren't hurt. Don't worry though, your children are fine."

"No," said Eliza quickly, exceptionally embarrassed by the show she was making in front of such a fine-looking gentleman. "I . . . I'm fine, thank you, Sir."

She could have stayed and explained to the handsome young man with the dashing sideburns that she wasn't the children's mother, but she felt so humiliated at having been laid out by a pig of all creatures and the spectacle she had made of herself. It certainly wasn't the way in which she would have chosen to make his acquaintance.

"Come children," was all she said, marching them back to their cabin at a smart pace, as she felt the eyes of the young man boring into her back. She suddenly realised that she must have seemed rude and ungrateful to him. She hadn't even said "thank you" properly in her rush to get away. No wonder he was staring at her.

"Why didn't you explain, Lizzie, that you're our nursemaid and not our mother?" asked Henry as they marched swiftly along.

"I need to get back to our cabin and check that I haven't grazed my knees or elbows," said Eliza as a quick explanation to cover her shame.

"But I don't see how that's possible," argued the astute young Henry, "seeing as you landed on your bottom."

"Henry," said Eliza, pretending to be shocked, but secretly smiling to herself, "you should never mention that word in a lady's presence."

"Sorry," said Henry, a little shamefacedly. "I didn't mean any harm."

"I know you didn't," said Eliza reassuringly. "Everyone is fine anyway. Probably best not to let your parents know anything about it though just in case they worry. Our little secret," she said as she gave the children a mischievous wink, much to their delight.

After this Eliza was keen to stay with the children in the cabin for the last hour or so before departure. She didn't feel she could go back on deck with the risk of coming face to face with the young man again. Instead she sat the children down on her bed and began to read to them from a large book of *Aesop's Fables*. Mrs Reid had told Eliza that she would like her to read to the children from this as she believed that the morality of the stories was good medicine for their souls. The little group had become so absorbed in their study of the stories and appreciation for the beautiful coloured pictures that it was only the sudden jolt they experienced that made them realise they were sea borne at last.

"We're off, Lizzie," said Henry excitedly rushing over to their small porthole window.

He and Maria jostled for space in the small enclosure.

"Henry, I want to see, let me see," said Maria in a whining, frustrated tone.

Eliza moved over to the small porthole to take charge of the situation.

"Henry, Maria, there's just enough space for us all to see if we're careful and share the little we have. Remember the story we read of the Greedy Dog? None of us must be greedy dogs, must we?"

"But it's so exciting isn't it, Lizzie? I don't want to miss anything," breathed the young Henry.

"Nor me," declared Maria.

Eliza wondered if the two children would still be so enamoured of the sea in a month or two when it would be the only view day after day. But at least they were getting some pleasure from the experience now. Although she tried her best to calm the situation, Eliza could see that things were getting a bit out of hand with the two children as they were in such high spirits.

"We could get a better view if we were go up on the deck to see the ship moving out from port," she suggested slightly nervously, still all too aware of her last visit there but not sure what else to do. "Would you like to go?"

"Oh yes please, Lizzie," they both breathed excitedly.

Indeed, they were so excited by the prospect that as they made their way carefully up to the deck, Eliza had to tell them more than once, "Henry, Maria, please keep hold of my hand. You've already seen that space is limited on the decks and we must take care."

She desperately hoped that she wouldn't glimpse the tall, handsome stranger again, but he was nowhere to be seen as the three of them stood on the deck looking down at the crowds of people on the docks, some waving, some crying, some shouting out. She wished again that Jean could have spared a little more time to have come to see her off but knew that even a lady's maid had to be grateful for the leave she got and ask no questions.

All too soon it seemed, the harbour was behind them, as the waving figures got smaller and smaller before eventually disappearing from view altogether.

Soon after they had returned to their cabin, Jessie Reid knocked on their door informing Eliza it was time to prepare herself and the children for dinner. It seemed that she was to dine with the children and other families at a slightly earlier hour than the majority of the passengers. As Flora was only on breastmilk as yet, Mrs Reid could feed her in their cabin at the same time, and then it would be up to Eliza to settle all three children whilst the Reids went for their meal.

Therefore, at her dinner Eliza was surrounded by lots of other nursemaids and young children so there was no chance of her coming across her handsome stranger again. As the ship had just put out from port, the food was fresh and they all dined on a delicious meat stew with lots of vegetables, potatoes, and dumplings followed by a simple lemon flavoured junket. Eliza, who had eaten an early breakfast and hadn't had a lot to eat since, was surprised at how hungry she was. The children must have felt the same too because their plates were soon clean. She passed the time making polite conversation with some of the other young girls and struck up a companionship with a young nursemaid called Morag, slight like herself but with dark curls. She was also heading for Wellington with a Scottish family. Unlike herself, it wasn't a family that Morag was on familiar terms with, having just joined them weeks before setting sail.

"They seem like a nice family though, "she told Eliza, "and the children are passing good."

Eliza laughed. "Little Henry and Maria are passing good too but I'm not quite sure how I'm going to fare with sharing a cabin with them for four months or more."

Morag nodded. "Aye for sure. Would you mind keeping company with me and mine a little to pass the time, Eliza? It'll be very lonely otherwise with just a couple of wee ones for company."

"Why not indeed?" answered Eliza. "I've only got the children most of the time for my company too. The Reverend is a prodigious reader and his wife, Jessie, is often taken up by young baby Flora, so I can't be sure I'll see a lot of them. It will be marvellous to have a friend and confidant in you, Morag. It might help me to forget my dearest friend and sister, Kitty, just a little." And she proceeded to tell Morag about Kitty and how their plans to travel had helped in some way to bring her here.

The children were utterly exhausted that night and although still excited by the start of their voyage, on return to the cabin, sleep very easily got the better of them and Eliza had a peaceful bedtime.

In the growing dusk Eliza was able to watch the ship pass by the tip of a large land mass which she later discovered had been the tip of Northern Ireland before it finally made its descent into the North Atlantic Ocean. They had finally left all traces of land behind them. The landscape of the sea would be their only view for a while now, a landscape they would have plenty of time to familiarise themselves with over the coming months. At least at the moment the passage was steady and the sea calm. Eliza wasn't sure how they would all fare in choppy seas and stormy weather which they would have to expect sometime in the crossing. After a quick wash, she then found her own eyes growing heavy due to all the excitement of the day, and, despite the movement of her bed, she was soon asleep.

The children woke her early the next morning just as the sky was growing light.

"We're at sea properly now, Lizzie," said Henry in an excited tone.

"Yes, indeed we are," said Eliza. "And what a lovely blue, cloudless sky we have. It's sure to be a good day ahead," she said, much to her own relief. There would be plenty of chance for walking and fresh air. But what if she should come across the stranger again on the decks? They had just been fortunate last night. On a ship holding around three hundred passengers the likelihood of her bumping into the stranger again was very high.

After dressing and washing herself and the children, they were all able to breakfast together for this meal, herself with the Reids, and the other adults. The adults dined on fresh herrings while it was boiled eggs for the children.

The Reverend and Mrs Reid then suggested a walk out on the deck after breakfast which seemed a good opportunity to take advantage of the early morning sunshine and peacefulness of the decks. Many folks were still breakfasting, and Eliza hoped with all her heart that this included her stranger. Unfortunately, as they rounded the next corner, Eliza spied her young rescuer making his way towards the family group, and she coloured as he lifted his hat in recognition.

"And how are we this morning?" he asked. "Mrs . . . ?"

"Miss Renfrew," said Eliza quickly. Then she hastily provided an explanation of their meeting to the Reids before the young man did. "This young gentleman and I met yesterday afternoon on deck when I was out walking with the children."

Something in Eliza's look or tone must have warned the young man to say no more about the circumstances of their acquaintanceship as he simply held out his hand to the Reverend Reid and said, "Alister Douglas at your service Sir."

"Reverend George and Mrs Reid, our children Henry, Maria, and baby Flora, and our nursemaid Miss Renfrew," the Reverend said by way of explanation.

Eliza felt the eyes of the young man focused on her with both puzzlement and interest and wondered if it might be anything to do with her change of status. She still felt appalled by how rude she had been to him on their first meeting. He had been so solicitous of her welfare and she had been short with him.

Alister, however, didn't seem to be acting as one who had been offended by her. He was certainly not averse to joining the family on their morning stroll on the deck at the Reverend's invitation.

"I am a farmer's son from Kincardine. I'm the youngest of a family of thirteen so there wasn't a lot of future on the farm for me," he said as they walked.

"You travel alone, Sir?"

"William, one of my brothers was to have travelled to New Zealand with me to look out some land but unfortunately he got married in the interim and that put paid to the plan. Now I must farm alone."

The Reverend smiled and chortled gently. "I've never considered marriage that unfortunate before, having married a number of couples and had a happy marriage myself."

Now it was Alister's turn to look embarrassed. "I meant no offence, Sir. Marriage is indeed a great institution and William has married a lovely girl in Rachel, but she is in the family way and in no fit state to undertake such a hazardous journey as this. The only misfortune I elude to Sir, being the fact that I now have to procure and farm the land on my own without my brother's help."

The Reverend nodded seeming to take in this explanation of Alister's.

Alister looked towards Eliza. Aware of his glance, she averted her gaze, both in embarrassment and in experiencing the pleasure of the eyes of a young man being fixed upon her. This was a new experience for her, any lingering gaze before this having been only attributed to her brothers or the leering ones of the Reverend.

"We do hope that you won't be lonely on the journey, Mr Douglas," said the Reverend. "We would be delighted if you wished to keep us company."

"What a kind offer, Sir, and one I'll be glad to take you up on," said Alister, again looking towards Eliza and giving her a warm, friendly smile. "I'm sure Miss Renfrew and the children would also benefit from an escort around the deck. At times, it can get busy and in addition littered with various obstructions." Eliza thought she detected a slight twinkle in his eye, and she blushed.

Alister then went on to explain to the Reids that he was also a carpenter by trade. He felt that the carpentry would help to supplement his farming, being an invaluable skill in a new land where many properties were still required for the settlers.

Later that evening when the children were settled in bed, Eliza began her first letter of many to Kitty.

September 8, 1850

My dearest Kitty,

She wrote, explaining all about the pig incident and her meeting with Mr Alister Douglas, describing him as,

> Tall, and very handsome, taller even than the Reverend Reid with light brown hair and a very fashionable rim beard with mutton chop sideburns. I do not know what you or Mama

or Papa would think of him but the Reids, and young Henry and Maria, seem to like him well enough.

And she also told Kitty of the nice surprise meeting she had with Jean, finishing her letter with,

I hope you are well and working hard. Missing you already.

Your, loving Lizzie

Over the next few weeks, Alister often joined the Reid family for a stroll on the deck after breakfast. Lunch times and evening times Eliza dined with the children and her new friend Morag, so it was only at breakfast time that she had the chance of dining with the other adults. But as they walked together on the deck with the Reids, she gradually found herself becoming less awkward with him as she chatted more freely about her family, especially her beloved Kitty, and also began to learn something of his.

Morag said at tea one evening a few weeks later, "I think that young man has the eye for you. He seems attentive. Hanging on to your every word."

Eliza shook her head, swallowing her tea rather quickly in astonishment. "I imagine he is just lonely and we are pleasant enough company to wile away his time with," she said dismissively.

As the ship passed near the tip of Africa the temperatures became more intense and Eliza struggled to cope with the heat which was like nothing she had experienced before. She found her many layers of clothing unbearable, and often felt uncomfortable and breathless. Her dresses were fairly thick and more suited to the Scottish than the African climes. She noticed the children also becoming more argumentative and irritable as they struggled to cope with the high temperatures and they fought each other much more frequently. They all walked out on deck a lot less and the daily meetings practically ceased. The temperatures could be unbearable even first thing in the morning. There was no let up from them anytime of the day.

A couple of weeks in, the heat brought with it a tropical storm. And, Eliza, who had up until this point considered herself to have fairly strong sea legs, began to be affected by sea sickness. Henry and Maria, who had generally gained their sea legs by now after a few bouts of sea sickness in the early days, began to be similarly affected as the winds picked up towards the evening. The sea seemed to change all at once from its gentle undulating ripples to a hungry tempestuous giant about to swallow them up. Eliza was due to take the children to the dining room for their evening meal but neither they nor she felt at all hungry.

A message was then sent around the ship by a member of the crew that everyone was to remain in their cabins until further notice. The command also went out to batten down the hatches. Eliza shivered as she thought of the steerage passengers who she had heard would be stuck down below in the airless heat as the ship above them pitched and rolled violently.

She tried unsuccessfully to read to the children from their favourite *Aesop's Fables*, but they were having none of it. They refused to be comforted by her, demanding their mother. At her wit's end, she felt there was nothing for it but to take them next door.

Eliza knocked on the Reids' cabin door a little hesitantly and as the Reverend opened it she could see Mrs Reid lying prostrate on the bed looking rather pale.

"I'm sorry to disturb you, Sir," she said, "but little Henry and Maria won't be comforted by me. They want their mother."

"I'm sorry, Eliza, but you'll just have to manage somehow," said the Reverend rather brusquely, looking over at his wife. "My Jessie is none too good either, as you can see."

Eliza, feeling rather overwhelmed by the situation and the Reverend's distinct lack of support, tried to grab the hands of both the children and march them back next door, despite their protestations and yells. But, before she knew what was happening, little Maria had slipped out of her grasp and run upstairs towards the deck. The Reverend, then sensing the obvious danger of Henry following suit grabbed him quickly by his collar at the same time shouting to Eliza, "Go after her, Girl, she'll be swept away up there on the deck."

Eliza ran as fast as she could under the circumstances with the ship lurching back and forth and finding it difficult to maintain her balance. She felt sick and frightened. The Reverend had sounded cross with her. What if something should happen to Maria? It would all be her fault.

Keeping her head down against the strong winds and waves, Eliza didn't see the figure of Alister, until she had bumped into him.

"Miss Renfrew, stop," he shouted, catching her wrists. "Where on earth are you going in these conditions, you should be in your cabin. It's not safe to be up on deck."

"I know that full well, Mr Douglas," she said in exasperation. "Truly, there's nowhere I'd rather be, but I how do you explain that to a terrified child?"

"Oh no," he said quickly, seeming to realise the seriousness of the situation. "Where has Henry or Maria gone?"

"Unhand me quickly, Mr Douglas," Eliza said in fear, "or Maria will be up on deck and washed over the side, and I don't know what I'll do then." She felt dangerously close to tears.

"We'll go up together to find her," said Alister putting an arm around her and gently escorting her up the narrow steps to the deck. "Forgive me, I didn't mean to judge you, I'm only anxious for your safety. I wouldn't have left my cabin either except I'd been feeling a little queasy, but now I thank God that I can be of service to you."

They reached the deck to find the small child retching and crying out in pain and distress. Alister quickly grabbed Maria, momentarily losing his grip on Eliza at the same time. With the unsteadiness of the ship, Eliza stumbled a little and vomited in fear, but then, in sheer relief at seeing the young child safe and unhurt, she was suddenly overcome with the whole situation and felt her feet give way beneath her. When she finally came to herself, she found she was on a small bench at the edge of the deck beside the dining room with Mr Douglas and the small, white frightened face of little Maria beside him. She realised that he must have carried her there.

When she saw that Lizzie had opened her eyes Maria began to sob uncontrollably. "Lizzie, I thought you were dead."

She saw Alister reach a hand out to reassure the little girl and say, "Don't worry, Maria, Lizzie fainted that's all. She's going to be fine now, and so are you."

It was the first time he had called her by her name, especially the familiar one the children called her by, and he was so gentle and tender towards the frightened young child that Eliza's eyes filled with tears once again in spite of herself.

His hold on her tightened, and she found herself also being comforted by him.

"Shh don't distress yourself, Eliza. Let me take you both back down to your cabin. You feel cold and wet through and could do with a hot drink I'll warrant."

Very carefully the small party made their way down the steps with Eliza holding on to the handrail and Alister holding on to her and Maria.

She had enough presence of mind to direct him towards their cabin but by this time her teeth were chattering uncontrollably. Alister sat her down on the bed before he offered to take the small girl next door to her parents while she recovered. Eliza had managed to slip out of her wet things and wrap herself in a thick, warm nightdress before he knocked again on the door and she quickly wrapped a blanket around herself before calling out, "Come in."

"Mrs Reid is much recovered herself now," he said, entering her cabin a little uncertainly, "and has said she will bring you a drink to help you sleep. I'm afraid a hot drink is difficult to arrange but I believe she is bringing you some sweetened water instead. It might help with the shock."

Then having played his part in the little drama and anxious, it seemed, to get away quickly, he bid her "Goodnight" and was gone.

A few minutes later, Mrs Reid knocked on the door and came in. She was all sympathy for Eliza.

"My poor dear, Eliza," she said. "I'm sorry for how you must have suffered on account of our Maria, but we are so grateful for her safe return. "I'm sorry too that I was so incapacitated myself as to be of little use. Here, take this drink," she said as she proffered the cup towards Eliza. "It may not be the most palatable of drinks, but it will help you to sleep. I have slipped in a little sleeping draft into it too. I am not fully myself yet either and must resort to the same sleeping draft, I think."

Eliza dutifully took the cup and swallowed the concoction of the sweet sugared water with lime juice and added sleeping draft. It made her practically gag as she imbibed it, but it was all that was available, the quality of fresh water having deteriorated much by this stage of the journey.

Then as Mrs Reid left bidding her good night, Eliza lay down with her blankets around her as the waves of sleep quickly overtook her. Her last thoughts were of Alister and of how kind and attentive he had been to her. Her heart felt more kindly disposed towards him than it had before. *Perhaps his care and attention did denote a sense of caring as Morag had suggested?* She drifted off into a deep sleep with these thoughts uppermost in her mind.

Next morning Eliza woke early to see the children tucked up in their beds as the sunlight streamed through the porthole window, the intense heat giving way to a refreshingly pleasant breeze. She lay there for a moment or two thinking that her vague recollection of the evening's events must have been a dream. However, the children soon opened their eyes and confirmed the reality of the happenings.

"You were poorly last night, Lizzie. And so was Maria after her little adventure. Oh, how I wish I could have been there," said Henry wistfully.

"I don't think you would have wished to, really," said Eliza. "It was far from being a pleasant adventure with the ship bobbing and weaving about under our feet."

And Maria, still slightly overcome nodded her head vigorously. "And I thought Lizzie was dead," she added as an afterthought.

"Well, do you know, Father had to put Maria and me to bed. He's never ever done that before, so we had to help him, but Mother wasn't too well either."

"Oh Henry, I'm sorry," said Eliza. She felt as if she had failed them.

"It's alright really," said Henry. "Actually it was quite good fun to help Father, and before I went to sleep I heard Mr Douglas come back again and enquire after you."

"I didn't," complained Maria.

"No, you were already asleep, but I can stay up longer than you, being the oldest," Henry boasted.

Eliza was glad in the pale light of the morning that the children couldn't see she was blushing at the thought of a young man whom she hadn't known that long bringing her to her cabin. She also had some vague memory of vomiting before she passed out. What must he think of her? Did he think her foolish or a bad nursemaid to the children? It was hard to tell what he thought, and she was too afraid to ask him.

The next few weeks passed without any further dramas and without any mention of the events of the previous evening excepting a polite enquiry from Alister the next day as to her health. Alister was politeness itself in everything, talking after this mainly to the Reverend and Mrs Reid about his plans for the new country and seldom engaging Eliza in conversation.

"I do not think he has any regard for me except as a friend," she said to Morag as they walked around the ship with their charges. "He hardly seems to speak to me these days. It's like the whole episode on the deck a few weeks ago never happened. Maybe I just let my imagination make a simple act of kindness into something more."

"Perhaps Mr Douglas is just shy," Morag said. "His special regard for you that night of the storm seems to suggest a certain partiality if you ask me."

"I think we both have far too fertile imaginations," said Eliza dismissively. "It can be dangerous to enter into too much speculation."

Her firm and dismissive tone at once silenced the quiet Morag with a blush and the subject was closed.

It did however occur to Eliza that Alister might simply be embarrassed about what had happened on the deck between them and this had silenced him, but she didn't want to say this to Morag. She felt that she hardly knew the young nursemaid and certainly not well enough to share confidences with her. She wasn't sure what she'd share anyway. Sometimes Alister seemed to dominate her thoughts, especially after one of the dances on deck, but at other times when she was busy with the children her mind was so occupied she hardly gave him a thought.

The scenery as they rounded the Cape of Good Hope at the base of Africa was spectacular, and they moored here briefly to take on fresh supplies. They had been at sea by now for nearly three months. The children had become fractious and bored of the sea, and Eliza was struggling to keep them amused on a daily basis. *Aesop's Fables* was on its second read through. But everyone was grateful to taste fresh meat and vegetables and fresh water again. It was just a pity that they couldn't take on enough fresh water to forfeit the need for the dreaded salt baths they all had to take.

Eliza had written all about the episode of Alister's second rescue of her to Kitty, adding,

> It seems to be becoming a bit of a habit for Mr Douglas to rescue me with this being the second incident after the pig! At least the sea is all calmness again after that dreadful night. Sometimes I wonder if his careful attentions then showed a special regard for me, but he is a very kind and polite gentleman who may just have felt he was doing his duty.
>
> The weather is still hot, so we don't generally venture out on deck except in the early morning or later in the day. But just before my early dinner with the children we have taken to having a little dancing on the deck as one of the emigrants plays a very good violin. I mainly dance with the Reverend but once or twice I have even been bold enough to venture out on to the deck with Mr Douglas. Of course, this dancing continues long after I have to leave with the children for dinner, and I understand it even continues after the main dinner with the whale oil lamps supplying the light for them, but I must be in the cabin then putting the children to bed so am not a part of it.
>
> I cannot believe that this weather accompanied my birthday rather than the usual December chills of Scotland. I passed it pleasantly enough yesterday, even though it seemed strange to have a birthday without a card or present from you or Mama and Papa. I must say however, I was very touched by the little card Morag, my friend made for me. Reverend and Mrs Reid wished me "Many Happy Returns" and Henry and Maria had attempted to make a sweet little card for me. I didn't say a word about it to Mr Douglas but the Reids must have because he wished me "Many Happy Returns" that evening and lamented his lack of a suitable gift or card insisting on dancing with me twice before dinner instead, saying it was "probably more for his benefit than mine." Imagine!

You will never guess, but after these few casual dances with Mr Douglas, Mrs Reid is now suggesting that he has a partiality for me too, adding to my own and my nursemaid friend, Morag's speculations. I for my part cannot decide what to think of him. He is very friendly and courteous certainly and most thoughtful towards myself and the children but when Mrs Reid suggested to me the other day that he would make a good husband, I really didn't know where to look, I felt that embarrassed. I hadn't considered Mr Douglas in that light before. I cannot even write this letter without blushing at the very thought of it. I am sure that his carpentry skills will be sought after in this new land and make him very eligible. But for me?

Mrs Reid even suggested the other day that she and the Reverend might have to look for another nursemaid on our arrival in New Zealand. But I told her quite categorically that I was committed to the children and to staying with the family and had no plans of going anywhere else for the meantime.

Thankfully we took on new supplies in Africa, so we have had a rest from the dreaded salt meats for a while, thank goodness. I only hope we may now reach New Zealand without any further storms or bad weather.

Your, loving, Lizzie

But then they entered the Tasman Sea at the base of Australia. There were reports of a recent large earthquake under the sea between Australia and New Zealand and everyone began to imagine the worst. Eliza felt quite sick at the thought of there being any further stormy seas ahead. She had hoped and prayed that the storms off the African coast were the last she would have the misfortune to experience but these reports of more made her feel uneasy. She kept her thoughts to herself though, not wishing to alarm the children.

The storms began first thing in the morning just before Christmas day and didn't let up for nearly a week. Eliza had never spent such a miserable Christmas before. She had heard from various people that the Tasman Sea was particularly treacherous ordinarily but with the added pressure of a recent earthquake, nothing could have prepared her for the violent onslaught of these storms. They magnified the previous storm several times over with the ship not only pitching and rolling this time but tossed about like it was made of matchwood and no competition for the waves that seemed feet high. Indeed, these storms were so violent that even the crew members were suffering from sea sickness. Holed up in their cabin, Eliza and the children were sick until they were no longer able to be and then just lay on their beds feeling like death. They heard other reports of dysentery and scarlet fever being rife on the ship too, especially amongst the steerage passengers. Eliza had seen many bodies dispatched over the edge already, particularly those of young children and she feared for the health of the young Reids.

Meals were on hold for the passengers, most of whom had no desire to partake of them anyway and even Alister's company was scarce. Eliza could only imagine he was also overcome by the sickness himself this time. But despite her apprehensions she still tried to keep the children's spirits up by telling them stories—her head hurt too much to read—that she made up on the spur of the moment and singing familiar little songs and ditties. None of the ship's incumbents seemed to care that Christmas day came and went in these conditions and certainly none cared to celebrate it.

"Will the storm stop soon, Lizzie?" complained Maria on the third day.

"I'm sure it will, dearie," said Eliza with much more conviction than she felt. It was hard to comfort the children when she herself felt comfortless. She kept her thoughts to herself however and dared not tell the children that she feared for their very lives and could not now imagine ever seeing the coast of New Zealand.

Finally, on the sixth day the storm seemed to wear itself out. The children appeared to recover remarkably quickly so that by lunch time Henry declared that he was, "hungry enough to eat a horse."

"Well I don't think there are an awful lot of those on hand," said Eliza laughing in relief. She felt a little more cheerful now that the storm seemed to have spent itself and her only fear was that it might suddenly ignite again. Of one thing she was sure, she would never ever go anywhere on the water again in this life.

She sat with the children at lunchtime gladly enough, but her own appetite had all but deserted her. After their meal, they decided to venture up on deck once more along with Morag and her children and were surprised at how many other folks seemed to have the same idea as themselves. Eliza guessed that they were all bored with being holed up in their cabins. It must have been unbearable for those in steerage she imagined. After walking for just a few minutes, the person of Alister came into view. He had met Morag before in Eliza's company and lifted his hat to acknowledge them both. Eliza was grateful to see a familiar face and smiled warmly.

"Alister, how grateful we are to see you again," she said impetuously. Then realising her over familiar use of his name she blushed.

"I . . . I'm so sorry, Mr Douglas, I . . . I didn't mean to sound familiar. The children and I are just glad to see a familiar face again. We have all been so bereft of company these last few days."

Alister, who seemed equally delighted to see Eliza once again and to hear her use his first name, said, "Indeed I have as well. There's no need to apologise, Miss Renfrew, Eliza, I think we know each other well enough now to feel that we can use first names, don't you?"

"Of course, Mr Douglas," Eliza started, and then realising her reversion to the formal she smiled. "Alister. Oh, how bored and fearful we have all been these last few days and so sick too."

"Yes, indeed. I even succumbed this time I must admit. I think we have all felt very poorly. How are the Reverend and Mrs Reid and baby Flora?"

"The Reverend and Mrs Reid are tolerably well but baby Flora hasn't fared so well. She is quite a colicky baby anyway and the sea sickness has meant she hasn't kept anything down despite Mrs Reid administrating regular doses of Epsom salts and Syrup of Figs to her. She is rather thin and pale and has been screaming a good deal and Mrs Reid is afraid that she might have succumbed to the dreaded dysentery."

"I'm very sorry to hear that. Let's hope it isn't the dysentery anyway. I think there are a few notable doctors in Wellington. It may be that she needs to see a good physician."

"I think that is highly likely if she is to thrive."

After a significant pause, where Alister seemed to collect his thoughts, he continued, "I do hope that I may have the pleasure of calling upon you and the family once we reach Wellington?"

"Oh yes, Lizzie, say he may," pleaded Henry.

"I . . . I'm afraid it's not really up to me, Alister. You should ask the Reids," said Eliza, feeling a little unsure about his continuing intimacy with the family. In some ways, it would be nice to see a familiar face in a strange land, but on the other hand she didn't feel ready to commit herself to any relationship yet, whatever the Reids thoughts. She was only just eighteen and she wanted time to experience a new land and new adventures. She was much keener to stay in touch with Morag—they had already exchanged addresses with a promise to write to each other and possibly visit.

"I will certainly ask then," said Alister. "Good day to you, Miss Renfrew, Eliza, Henry, Maria, and Miss Fitzwilliam," he said, raising his hat again as he walked quickly away from them.

"Well," said Morag. "I think that shows some definite partiality, Lizzie."

"What's partiality?" asked the inquisitive Henry.

"Being friendly," said Eliza quickly.

"Well, Alister is very friendly to us, isn't he?" said Henry.

"Yes, dear he is," said Eliza blushing as Morag gave her a knowing smile.

It was with immense relief that Eliza finally saw the first land come into view just a day later—the first since leaving Australia. She couldn't wait to feel her feet on dry land again and was anxious to explore the new country that she had heard so much about, the country she felt she might never live to see. The four and a half months they had been at sea suddenly seemed like a long time. The January sun felt warm and reassuring on her face, promising better times, as the ship slowly made its way towards the small harbour.

However, as they neared the harbour entrance, Eliza was alarmed at how narrow it seemed, making it difficult for their vessel to navigate, and it took several attempts before they were finally able to draw into the walls of the harbour. She breathed a sigh of relief when they got the all clear to let down their anchor and she could finally allow herself to take in her new surroundings. She was at once surprised by the number of bush clad hills that still surrounded the narrow harbour, a sign of rather less development than the New Zealand Company had given them to believe, and she hoped that the Reverend's living would prove a reality and not just a distant promise.

Chapter Three

KARORI, WELLINGTON

ELIZA NEEDN'T HAVE FEARED CONCERNING the reality of the Reverend's living. In fact, the house to be occupied by the Reid family was one of the most established and well-built houses in their area of town. It was a wooden structure with wood lined walls on the inside and a roof covered by wooden tiles. This already denoted a sense of wealth, they soon discovered, as the available wood in New Zealand was still somewhat scarce.

Inside it was more basic with two main rooms, a living room with a small stove and a bedroom which was divided into two by stretches of calico. The toilet was housed in a separate building at the back of the house and consisted of a simple hole in the ground surrounded by a four-walled wooden structure. The entire set-up was hardly luxurious and less than Eliza was used to, but compared to most of the houses in the surrounding area which were either tents or simple raupo or bull-rush constructions she knew they had a lot to be thankful for. At least there was the simple divide between the bedroom that the Reverend and Mrs Reid were to occupy and the one she was to share with the children, for which she was thankful. Until the furniture arrived from the ship in a few days' time, the family had to make do with packing boxes in the place of a table and chairs and bracken for bedding

The children, full of excitement, were at once keen to explore their new surroundings. Eliza was happy to take them as she was also keen to find her bearings. The children were particularly intrigued by the sight of the tents, which made Henry feel like he was on a real adventure. For her part, Eliza was grateful that the Manse at least provided slightly more comfort than some of the basic homes of the settlers. A further exploration revealed a general store selling everything from food and basic clothing to hardware supplies, a blacksmith, a bank, four saloon bars, and several churches. The whole place appeared more rural to Eliza than her home in Scotland, although this was called a town. She quickly swallowed her sadness at the memory of the village and the family she had left behind. She must instead get used to this simple set up which she must now call home. But she was heartened by the friendly greetings of the settlers, which seemed warm and welcoming. Their young children appeared particularly pleased by the sight of Henry and Maria as two new potential playmates.

After a couple of days their furniture and belongings were delivered in large barrels by horse and cart. Unfortunately, on arrival, some of the furniture was scratched. This was due to it having been rolled off the ship into barrels and then driven by cart over rutted, unmade roads. However, Eliza was certainly glad to substitute her bed of springy bracken for her own proper bed and to be reunited with her photographs, clothes and furniture. The items carried with them a smell and feeling of home, which was such a comfort to Eliza. And now having her small writing desk once again she had the opportunity to share her first impressions of the place with Kitty but continued to be surprised by there still being no answering letters from her sister, which she had half expected to be awaiting her as they docked. She could only imagine that they had been held up somewhere on their journey. It was unimaginable that Kitty hadn't written to her in all this time. It would be completely out of character.

January 6, 1851

My Dearest Kitty,

I cannot believe I still have no news from you but nevertheless I wanted to write and share my first impressions of the new country.

Firstly, I must say what a relief it is to have my feet on firm ground at last after being at the mercy of winds and waves these long months.

We passed through the Tasman Sea during Christmas and though I thought of you all and imagined the home scene, we were too ill to celebrate ourselves, or indeed to write and send you greetings, the storm here being worse even than that over Africa and continuing for six long days.

However, when I had time to be sensible, I saw in my mind, Jean arriving on Christmas Eve and you and Margaret packing up work at the big house at Ballymore to have those precious hours together celebrating Christmas day.

Did Ballymore estate furnish Mama with some sprigs of holly for decoration as the previous year, and a chicken? I am sure Papa and John will have managed something with all their hard work. I do hope so and that you all made merry despite mine and Joseph's absence. Now I am here and able to think clearly, I feel sad that I missed something special.

The Reverend's house is near the coast in an area of town known as Karori. It is passing good, indeed. We see this house is one of the best in an area which is furnished chiefly by tents and unfinished houses, although I think you would turn up your nose at our simple toilet, a small hole surrounded by four wooden walls at the back of the house!

Everything here is wood which seems strange, even the various churches, a Baptist, Anglican and our Church of Scotland, plus the local store. However, I believe that they build in wood because we are now in an earthquake zone and wood is lighter and more flexible than brick. I shudder to think about earthquakes at all, although it was reported that our last storm in the Tasman Sea was caused by a recent earthquake under the sea between New Zealand and Australia. Well, if they have had a recent one, all I can say is that I hope that will do us for a very long time!

Before we arrived in the new country, Alister promised to visit us before long but I although I enjoyed his company on board, I feel unsure as to whether or not I wish to see him again. Isn't that strange? On the contrary, my parting with my nursemaid friend Morag was more of a wrench, although we may write to each other from time to time. What about my feelings for Alister though? I don't know. I can only assume that my feelings for him are not of the marriageable sort although everyone else seems to believe to the contrary.

Talking about marriage, how are things progressing with you and Charles? Do let me know as soon as anything accrues, I am wild to hear. To be honest I am wild to hear anything from you at all. Your long silence is a torture to me. Please write soon.

Your beloved sister,

Lizzie

The Reverend and his wife were still concerned about little Flora. They had discovered that the nearest physician was a good ride from their home, and being without transport, the same cart that had delivered their belongings to the Manse was now to take the Reverend and Mrs Reid back towards the harbour so that baby Flora could be seen by the doctor.

The Reids returned a few hours later with some encouraging news.

"I'm glad to say that after her days of sickness on the ship," Mrs Reid confided in Eliza, "Baby Flora has at last started to put on weight. But I feel a little less certain of the doctor's prescriptive diet of a thick, wholesome gruel to supplement her milk. I had hoped to keep her on a purely milk diet for another three months until she turns a year old. It's what all the experts recommend."

Eliza nodded encouragingly as the Reverend interrupted his wife, "But we live in different circumstances to those experts in Great Britain, now my dear," he said authoritatively. "I dare say we will be forced to make some changes in our children's diets in order to meet the demands that a much more basic lifestyle dictates. The gruel might be just what she needs to help to fill her out a little."

"Perhaps you are right," Mrs Reid agreed with obvious reluctance. "I just hope it is for the best."

Little Flora wasn't a scrawny baby, but Eliza felt she could do with being a bit bonnier.

The Bethel Presbyterian Church was, like their home, a simple wooden construction and just across the road from where they lived —if *road* could be the description given to the simple dust track that ran through the town. The church was painted white and covered with a red corrugated tin roof. Some concessions had been made to its form with a pointed roof and a tower at one end. It was reached by a small path just off the main road.

A few newly dug graves, mostly child size, surrounded the narrow strip of land beside the church, a reminder of the harsh conditions of the settler life, especially on the young children. Eliza shivered with apprehension when she saw them, wondering about the stories behind these little tragedies.

She was surprised at how full the church was on the first Sunday after their arrival nearly a week ago. There wasn't a bench or seat left in the simple, plain wooden interior and every person from the youngest to the oldest got to their feet as their family entered the church. They took their seats on the bench at the front of the church which had been left vacant for them, all, that is, except the Reverend Reid who made his way to the small pulpit at the front of the church, the people falling into a respectful silence as he did so. He was introduced to the church members by one of the professed church elders, a Mr Matthew Hunter.

"Good morning to you all," the Reverend said, clearing his voice after the brief introduction. "I am the Reverend George Reid the new minister at Bethel Presbyterian Church as your own Mr Hunter has declared. It will be both an honour and a privilege to serve you all. I have with me my wife Jessie, our children Henry, Maria, and baby Flora, and our nursemaid Eliza," he said pointing to each member of the family in turn. "We have come here all the way from Glasgow in Scotland to serve the needs of this parish. I do hope that you won't hesitate to call upon us, if we can help you in any way. For we are all in the same position here as pioneers in a strange, new, unfamiliar land."

Eliza's own worship that Sunday was particularly heartfelt. She was grateful to God for bringing them safely through the storms especially the one on the Tasman Sea off Australia and sang the hymn "For Those in Peril on the Sea" with real conviction.

"We're heartily glad you and the family have come to us, you know," confided tall, dark, bearded elder, Mr Hunter to Eliza after the service. "We've been without a minister here now for nearly a year since the young Reverend Cleverly left us. Never settled, that one. Perhaps with him not being wedded and all that. Some . . . " He leant in closer to Eliza at this point. "Some took it to there being a young lassie on his mind back at home, but we never did find out for sure."

"Fancy," said Eliza blushing slightly and not knowing what else she could say on the subject.

"I dare say he also found the settler life too hard and demanding for his like. He wasn't of the strongest constitution. You have to be out here you know."

Eliza nodded fancying that Mr Hunter was assessing her suitability for the harsh conditions and hoping that she passed his scrutiny. Right now, she wasn't at all sure that she would, home still seemed so close to her thoughts and the grip of loneliness still haunted her in her quiet moments.

Breaking into her thoughts, Mr Hunter continued, "Anyway, he returned to his native Scotland which has left us without a minister for months and having to share with the ministers from the other churches even attending the Anglican or Baptist churches at times."

His last words were delivered with a sense of mild revulsion as if they might somehow be sullied by their contact with Christians of different faith persuasions, and Eliza, despite her somewhat gloomy thoughts, had to put her hand up to her mouth to hide the smile behind it, fearing that he might associate her with the same lightweight believers in his mind.

Eliza later overheard Mr Hunter having a similar conversation with the Reverend Reid whom she overheard assuring him that he was made of hardier stuff than the Reverend Cleverly, and she only hoped that he would be able to live up to his words.

As for Alister, none of them had heard anything about him for many weeks, not even a letter. Eliza was glad though to have received a letter from Morag just a couple of weeks after they parted. She and her family had settled in a spot known as Oriental Bay. It sounded very grand and exotic to Eliza. Morag wrote about the area, their simple wooden abode, just one room, which made Eliza heartily grateful for theirs, and the natives she had met. Eliza by contrast hadn't seen any Maoris yet excepting their housemaid Paku, who was always smiling and seemed genuinely keen to serve.

Life settled down into a routine for Eliza, teaching the children in the mornings, washing her own and the children's clothing (Paku was employed to take care of the laundry only for the Reverend, Mrs Reid and baby Flora) at a spring on the edge of town and shopping for provisions at the local store while the children played. Then it was stories and prayers at night before bed, when she would occasionally dash off a letter to Kitty before her own retirement. Her week was simply punctuated by the family's church attendance twice on Sundays.

She wondered about Alister from time to time but surmised that perhaps he hadn't found himself quite so keen to maintain contact with the family and herself as he had made out towards the end of the voyage. She couldn't decide whether she was sad or glad by his absence.

She had been out at the local spring doing the afternoon washing as usual, one day, when Paku came to tell her, "Missy, gentleman Alister up at the house. Mistress sent me to tell you to come quick."

This was difficult however, as the basket was heavy containing her washing and that of the children over several days. It was also a good distance from the spring to the house, with the added task of hanging the garments out on the rudimentary line the Reverend had managed to erect outside, and when that ran out, the nearby bushes. Therefore, Alister had been at the house a while before she arrived.

She was taken aback to see him seated in the small living room with the two children sitting on his knee. Seeing her he gently lifted the children down from his knee and rose, taking hold of Eliza's hand and kissing it.

"How are you, Eliza?" he asked, looking down into her eyes.

The new climate, she gauged, seemed to have agreed with him and already his face had browned in the sun.

"I'm well enough thank you, Alister," she said. "You look well too."

"Yes, it's been a time since we last met. I realise that I might look a little different to you now since we last saw each other. I'm afraid my complexion is due to all the time I've been spending out of doors," he said somewhat sheepishly. "I'll soon be looking more like a native, but with so many houses to be built, my skills have been in demand."

She nodded, feeling suddenly overcome with shyness, not knowing what to say in return. She needn't have worried though, he seemed to have more than enough tales to entertain them all with of his escapades in the bush, searching to clear land which might be deemed suitable for building.

"I have to admit to feeling both disappointed and frustrated," he said bitterly. "The acres of building and farmable land that the New Zealand Company promised us are nowhere to be found. Instead, the area of land north of Wellington known as the Hutt Valley is a quagmire. It also doesn't boast the large river we were given to believe it did and the hills, although green, are covered by dense bush and swamp rather than the fertile land we expected. Even the quality of some of the wood is variable."

Eliza was amazed at how despondent he sounded. And then, as if noticing the general feeling of malaise that seemed to have crept over them all, he at once lightened his tone.

"But of course, there is still lots of useful timber for building, as this house itself is testament to, and I dare say we will find fertile land fit for building and farming before too long if we clear some of the bush."

Finishing up the last gulp of his tea he seemed reminded of the chief reason for his visit.

"It's lovely to see you all again indeed," he began, "but I was wondering if it might be possible to have a word with Miss Renfrew, Eliza, alone?"

"But of course, you may," said Jessie Reid sending a knowing glance towards the Reverend, as she continued with, "I am sure you two young people have a lot of news to catch up on. Come Henry, Maria, Paku needs your help."

"Must we go, Mother?" asked Henry disappointedly. "Alister has got so many interesting tales of adventure to tell us, I could listen all day."

"I dare say you could, Henry, but as I've explained Paku needs your help at this moment," said Mrs Reid resourcefully.

Eliza was left alone facing Alister, her heart quickening in anticipation at what he might say. He had certainly been favouring her with frequent glances as he related his adventures to them all, and she began to suspect that Mrs Reid was correct in her surmise about his partiality.

She detected a sudden flush in his cheeks as he came closer to her and took her hands in his.

"Eliza, you cannot be unaware of my feelings for you over the last few months of our voyage together. Feelings of warmth and friendship which have gradually developed into something stronger. I know that my circumstances at present are not especially favourable but if I was fortunate enough to secure myself a few acres of land and a house, I wondered if you might consider joining me as my wife and life partner?"

Eliza felt a sudden rush of emotion detected by the flush of her own cheeks.

Noticing her hesitation, Alister spoke again. "I . . . know I don't have a lot to offer you at this moment, Eliza, Lizzie, but if you were able to remain here with the Reids for just a little while longer until I was able to secure some sort of living then I would return for you. Say you'll consider my offer at least. I promise I would always take good care of you."

Eliza knew him to be a sincere man of his word but still she hesitated. He was a good man and would make any girl a caring and considerate husband. But for her? She still wasn't sure.

At last after another pause she found her voice, which came out decidedly low and a little squeaky so that Alister had to lean in closer to her to hear her response.

"Alister, I am aware of the great honour you do me in singling me out to be your wife. You are a good, kind and considerate man and I am very grateful to you for asking me. Could I possibly consider your offer until you return next?"

If Alister was surprised by her response he didn't show it but instead pressed her hand again to his mouth warmly, his eyes holding hers and said, "Of course, Eliza. Don't let me rush you in your decision which I know isn't easy, especially considering our strained circumstances here. It is understandable that you should be pragmatic and take time to make the right decision. I will return as soon as I have secured some land and built a house and then you can let me have your answer. Please give my regards to the Reverend and Mrs Reid and the children."

"Aren't you going to stay to give them yourself?" asked Eliza in surprise, feeling her response to his proposal was the cause of his swift departure.

"No, I must be going. Goodbye." And grabbing his hat and coat he turned and headed for the door.

It had hardly been the most romantic of proposals that was for sure, but then it was equally true that Eliza was none too sure that it was romance she was seeking with him.

The Reverend and Mrs Reid seemed also surprised by his sudden departure and even more surprised by Eliza declaring that Alister had proposed to her and she was going to take time to consider her response.

"We thought you were all for accepting him, lassie," said the Reverend, nonplussed. "Jessie and I thought you liked him well enough, and he always seems very attentive to you. He's a good man. I doubt you'll do better than him."

Eliza was surprised by the forcefulness of the Reverend and attempted to state her case with an equal amount of conviction. "I know that, Sir, but without a house or land yet, how should I accept him? Besides, I need time to think and pray about it. Marriage is a big step."

The Reverend and his wife seemed to accept this explanation, but Eliza still felt she was being unduly forced into a decision she didn't yet feel ready to make. She was only just getting used to living here at the Manse and seeing to the needs of the children and had grown quite fond of little Henry and Maria and Jessie Reid, although the leering looks of the Reverend still unnerved her. She wasn't sure yet that she wanted to change a familiar situation for an unknown one when she was practically alone in a strange, new country. It felt too soon to contemplate another move. *Why were the Reids so determined that she accept him anyway?* They all knew so little about him in many ways.

Over the next few months whilst she was teaching the children and going about her tasks, she agonised over her decision concerning his proposal.

"Dear God, what should I do, should I marry this man or not?" she prayed at night, at church and at frequent moments during the day. But God seemed silent to her demands and the answer didn't readily come.

How she wished she had Kitty here to ask her opinion. Instead she set about writing to her soon after the proposal, knowing that she probably wouldn't receive an answer back until Alister's return or even later.

Then she discovered that Mrs Reid was expecting again, and the pregnancy wasn't going well. She was continuously tired and pale and seemed lacking in energy. Eliza could tell that the Reverend was concerned about his wife and she didn't want to add to their worries by seeking Mrs Reid's advice about Alister.

God must tell her what to do. She opened the little Bible she had brought with her, examining all the entries concerning the subject of wisdom as she prayed. The clearest reference she found was in the book of James. In the first chapter, verse five, it told her that if "any of you lack wisdom, let him ask of God, that giveth to all men liberally." *Where was her wisdom, then,* she asked herself. Or did the passage with its reference to God being liberal in the wisdom He would give to men therefore exclude women? She didn't know and there was no one she felt she could ask. In the end the decision was dictated to her by circumstances.

* * *

One day when Eliza was taking an evening stroll along the high street, having put the children to bed, the Reverend came across the road from the church and asked Eliza if he might join her. Surprised by his request, which was unusual and made her feel uncomfortable, Eliza felt that there was little she could do except to acquiesce with a gracious nod of her head. They walked along exchanging a few pleasantries about the weather until the Reverend asked, "What about little Henry and Maria, Eliza, do you think they're settling in?"

"Oh yes, Sir, I think so," she replied. She began to tell the Reverend about what they had learnt about the new country and how Henry had been particularly interested in the signing of the Waitangi treaty, thinking he would be interested in their progress, when he interjected, "Enough. I didn't join you to discuss my children or their education. Hasn't young Alister told you how pretty you are?"

Eliza didn't like the new twist this conversation had taken and felt uneasy by such an intimate question from the Reverend but replied, "Yes, Sir, I think he may have mentioned it once or twice. Why?"

The Reverend smiled in a rather menacing way, saying, "I've been thinking it myself a bit of late."

Eliza felt embarrassed. How could he be thinking of such things when his pregnant wife needed all his attention at the moment?

"It's such a pleasure to have you all to myself for once," he said moving closer to her side and taking her arm in his.

Eliza could feel herself growing frightened and very unhappy.

"Perhaps we could cross again towards the church for a moment, there's something I need to share with you," he continued.

The street was all but deserted in the growing dusk and Eliza hesitated.

"Could you not tell me whatever it is another time, Sir, it's a little dark to see much anyway without lighting."

"We know each other well enough not to need lighting surely my dear."

That was exactly what Eliza feared as she found herself pulled across the road by his strong grip into the dark recesses of the churchyard in the gathering gloom. She didn't feel she could object, after all he was her boss and a Reverend, and he was much too strong anyway for her slight form. Maybe he needed her help and she was just being foolish to fear?

"I'm not surprised young Alister wants you for his wife, you're that bonnie, young Eliza," he said.

"That can't be what you wished to say, Sir! If there's nothing of real import for you to say to me, I would be grateful if you would unhand me and let me go back to the house," she said terrified.

"Aye, by and by you will go back there. But for now, come here you young hussy. I've a mind to kiss you first."

"Please Sir, I've asked you to let me go. You should be attending to your wife, Sir, especially in her delicate condition."

She felt shaken and looked around desperately for someone to call, but the place was deserted.

"I need to go, Sir. Please let me go," she asked again in an increasingly desperate voice.

Her entreaties were lost upon him. Grabbing her and thrusting her against the church wall, he lifted her skirts as he undid the buttons on his trousers and forced himself upon her. It all happened so quickly it was over before Eliza had time to recollect that her virginity had been stolen from her in a moment. She felt sick as well as bruised, battered and sore. She had never felt so alone, so betrayed. Shock robbed her of speech, but the Reverend seemed to have no desire to speak after the event either. She watched him move away from her and enter the church.

"Oh God, what am I to do," she sobbed. "How am I to face Mrs Reid or Paku in such a state? What will they think of me?"

She was shaking violently and felt cold. Her petticoats were torn and bloodied, and she felt a mess. She must go back to the house, she had nowhere else to go and she couldn't let anyone see her like this. She would have to say she had a headache and she was unwell. She made her way slowly back towards the house hoping and praying no one would see her. Slipping in through the back door she made her way quickly to her side of the room. Thankful that the children were both sleeping soundly, she stripped herself of the offending garments and threw them into a pile beside her, too shocked to think of the consequences of them being discovered, as she attempted to wash away the blood staining her flesh with the water in her wash bowl. Then she heard a soft voice calling to her. Frightened that it might be the Reverend again, she answered in a whisper, "What?"

"Missy, it be Paku. Mistress wonders if you care to take a drink with her?"

"No, Paku," her voice wavered, "I'm not well, please, I'm not well."

"You want help, or anything, Missy?"

"No, no, please, no help. I'll be fine in the morning. I'm off to my bed."

"Okay, I tell Mistress Reid."

Rolling the blood-stained garments under her bed, Eliza got into her nightgown and lay down on her bed sobbing quietly into her pillow in fear that someone might hear her. Perhaps she had been a fool to come to New Zealand with this man. They all knew what he was like, but now it was too late to undo what had been done. And where was God when she needed Him? She felt more alone than ever. She doubted that she would be fine in the morning or ever again.

Chapter Four

THE WEDDING

ELIZA WOKE EARLY THE NEXT morning hoping that the events of the previous evening were some horrible nightmare, but as she glanced under the bed and saw the pile of blood-stained clothes lying in a heap, the reality came back to her. She could even smell the stale stench of the Reverend's garments and recall his sweaty, fat hands on her bare flesh. The memory was so vivid that she got up quickly and vomited in her wash bowl. Her only thought was that she had to get out of this house now as soon as she possibly could.

She realised she would have to take the soiled clothes down to the spring to wash them as soon as possible. No one must discover them or her guilty secret. At least no one came into her space except the children and Paku and if she kept them well hidden, all might be well. But she didn't feel well anymore, only different. Dirty and sullied. If Mrs Reid knew what had happened to her she wouldn't consider her a fit companion for her children anymore, although she was pretty sure that her secret wouldn't be revealed by the Reverend. In many ways, he had more to lose than her. But what had occurred still necessitated that she leave the house as soon as she could. Meanwhile, she would have to keep out of the Reverend's way as much as possible. As soon as Alister returned she must then make plans for her departure. There was nothing for it but for her to marry Alister. Another nursemaid's position was out of the question after what had happened, especially if, God forbid, she was now in the family way. She would be a disgrace to any respectable household. She only had to hope that by marrying

Alister soon, if there were a baby, he would just assume it was his. This had to be her best course of action in the circumstances.

"Did George talk to you about our little problem, Eliza? I did ask him to," Mrs Reid said to her that morning.

"Problem?" said Eliza paling.

"Oh dear, don't fret yourself about my health," said the unsuspecting Mrs Reid as she noticed the pallor of Eliza. "As you know, I am with child again, and George will probably have told you too that the pregnancy isn't progressing as well as we would like."

Eliza knew that but guessed this was the official sharing of that information. This was surely the message the Reverend must have been sent to tell her. Instead he had used the opportunity to his advantage instead of sharing the news his wife had asked him to. Eliza felt sick. *How could he even think of taking advantage of her in such a way with his wife struggling with her pregnancy?*

Mrs Reid, unaware of Eliza's thoughts, continued, "I expect George told you of Susan, too?"

"Susan?" said Eliza puzzled.

"Oh, no doubt he didn't give you all the details I told him to. Typical man I'm afraid."

Typical man indeed. Especially in the way his thoughts had turned to self-gratification rather than concern for his wife's health, thought Eliza with disgust.

"Well, it has come to our attention that there is a young lady in the neighbourhood, called Susan, who is not only a nursemaid like your good self but in addition has been a governess and has had some experience in delivering babies. With my delicate state of health at present, we could do with someone who could care for me up to the delivery and then through it, as well as looking after the other three children, especially with the lack of doctors nearby. Susan is also looking for work at the moment and she seems perfect for the role. We have no wish, of course, to rush you in your decision regarding Alister, we are all very fond of you and feel a natural obligation to your parents, for your continued wellbeing." Eliza doubted this in the Reverend's case. "I'm just making you aware of our circumstances that is all. Of course, any decision you make must be the right decision for yourself. Should you decide to stay on with us, it may be that we can still secure Susan's services at the right time even if she is not in our full employ or alternatively secure the services of one of the doctors near the harbour."

"You have been most kind to me and I am very fond of you and the children, naturally," said Eliza quickly, hoping that Jessie Reid hadn't noticed she omitted to mention the Reverend in this universal kindness. "But I would like you to be one of the first to know that after careful consideration, I have decided to marry Alister."

"Bless you my dear, I'm sure you'll both be very happy."

Happy, how could she be happy under the circumstances? If, please God, there was no baby because of what had happened, she just had to hope that she might grow to love Alister in time as she got to know him better. At least this Susan had given her a reason to leave, for which she would be forever in her debt. Although Eliza feared for Susan's safety as far as the Reverend was concerned, if she were at all young or good looking. She believed that any woman in that category would be easy prey to the Reverend. How could Mrs Reid really be so ignorant of the monster her husband was or be so kind and well-disposed to her when he was anything but? Marriage truly was a mystery. At least she was reassured that she wouldn't be leaving Mrs Reid in such a delicate state of health without assistance.

Consequently, when Alister came riding back to the family home a few days later with the news that he had gone into partnership with a Mr Byatt at a sawmill in Taita whilst he looked for some suitable land to purchase, Eliza was ready to receive his proposal with some relief. He explained that he had not only established this partnership with

Joe Byatt, but he had also laboured at the same time to build a suitable house for Eliza in the hope that she would accept his proposal.

"Thank you, Alister. I would be glad to receive your offer," said Eliza with feeling. This, anyway, was certainly true.

He seemed pleased by her response and pressed her hand to his lips. Eliza, after her recent experience drew back a little reticently at his touch and taking her response as being one of timid inexperience he was emboldened to lean forward and plant a simple kiss on her cheek.

Eliza was relieved by his gentlemanliness and suitably impressed by his care for her well-being in having built a house and secured a stable job. Important considerations in this new land.

They were to be married by the Reverend Reid at Bethel a few weeks later, after which, Eliza was glad to know, she would be rid of him. She straightaway sat down to write to Kitty to tell her of the forthcoming marriage.

November 2, 1851

My dearest Kitty,

Just think of it, I am now an engaged woman and soon to be a married one! I dare say you haven't yet received my last letter asking you for your opinion as to if I should marry Alister, but in the end, it was as if the decision was made for me.

Eliza then went on to explain about Mrs Reid's pregnancy and the concern for her well-being and that of her baby. She couldn't mention the Reverend's forceful behaviour though, even to her dearest sister. She was too ashamed. She continued,

Doctors are very short in number here, and if Mrs Reid were to have complications and no doctor to be found in time she could lose the baby or even die. I would never forgive myself if either of these things happened. I do feel that perhaps this is the divine wisdom I sought. I'm sure that Alister will make me a good, kind husband and that I may come to love him in time as he assures me that he loves me.

The chief thing that mars my happiness is that you will not be here as my bridesmaid to walk behind me and support and comfort me. I will just have to make do with young Henry and Maria as my helpmates instead. Also, the chief elder, a Mr Matthew Hunter has agreed to give me away in place of Father. This will seem strange but not as strange as the loss of you my dearest. Please send me your blessing instead.

Write soon. I cannot understand how it is that I haven't received any letters from you yet. I am sure you must have written and only hope your letters haven't got lost. I will need them more than ever now, dearest, when I am cut adrift from all those I have ever known and go to make a new life with a man I am only just beginning to be acquainted with.

Your ever loving,

Eliza

The sun heralded a good day for the wedding which was to be a simple affair with Eliza wearing her best blue skirt and Alister just a simple suit.

A bundle of Kitty's letters arrived that very morning which Eliza felt must be a good omen. It seemed that they had all been held up. But now it was the nearest thing to having Kitty with her on her wedding day.

September 8, 1850

Dearest Lizzie,

I am already missing you exceedingly even though it is just over a week since your departure. Mama has been boring us all with tales of drownings at sea and has already had you as a lost cause which I do not believe for one moment.

I hope your voyage is proving interesting and that the children are not being too troublesome. I long to hear of all your adventures and when I read them I will feel as if I am living them too, through you. Longing to get your first letters.

Your loving, Kitty

January 2, 1851

Dearest Lizzie,

We received your first letters recently from your berth in Africa. How interested I was to read of your acquaintanceship with Mr Alister Douglas. He sounds like a handsome and skilful man and I long to hear more about him. The manner of your meeting was intriguing though, and I must admit the story about the stray pig did make me laugh. What adventures you are having already!

Your loving, Kitty

Dear Lizzie,

I was shocked to receive your letter telling me of how Mrs Reid has all but married you off to Mr Douglas. What a thing! I was concerned though to read about your awful adventures in the storms and Mr Douglas' rescue. Don't worry, I haven't told Mama how bad these storms were, or we'd never hear the end of it!

Your loving, Kitty

April 28, 1851

Dearest Lizzie,

We were so glad to hear of your safe arrival in New Zealand and to read the details of the Manse and its surroundings. My opinion about Mr Douglas' proposal is don't accept him if you have any doubt at all in your heart. You and I are very alike. We are both romantics and in touch with our own feelings. Once these feelings are engaged they are till death. I know mine are for Charles and I guess yours to be likewise.

How do you know that you will grow to love Mr Douglas, Alister? That is just a surmise, dearest. Far better to give the relationship time until you are sure of your feelings. Please consider waiting. You could always find another position nearer to him and give the relationship time. It is what I would tell you if I were there with you, although the news has been greeted here with joyful acceptance. Mama thinks you would be a fool to turn down this opportunity and I think Papa agrees with her, but he doesn't give an opinion much on these women's matters.

By the way, Charles and I were married earlier this month at Bethesda Chapel, nearly a year since you left us. I missed you exceedingly all day and had to make do with just Margaret and Jean as my bridesmaids when there should have been three of you and now I'm not there to advise you about Alister. It is only because of Charles being here for me now that I can abide your absence. He says I shouldn't interfere in this matter of your marriage and must let you make your own decision, but I do fear for you, dearest. Charles doesn't know you like I do or how vulnerable you can sometimes be. Please take care in this instance, won't you? Praying for you in this.

Your loving, Kitty

June 21, 1851

Dearest Lizzie,

It is commendable that you have Mrs Reid's welfare at heart but for goodness' sake, don't accept Alister just because of Susan's possible employment. Surely your friend, Morag, would be able to help you secure another nursemaid's position? She must have some contacts. I'm sure that in a country where there are new arrivals daily there must be other families on the lookout for a nursemaid of your experience. Only consider, if you take some time over your decision, you may indeed come to feel for Alister what it seems he feels for you but if not, then you may meet someone else whom you can love better. Someone like my Charles. Don't be hasty my dearest, Lizzie, but bide a while. Praying for you to find another position.

Your loving sister, Kitty

Eliza cried as she read Kitty's letters, the last of which had been written but a few weeks ago. If only Kitty knew that she didn't have the luxury of waiting or securing another nursemaid's position, especially if she might be pregnant. There was no option for her but to accept Alister's offer and get away from the Reids or rather the Reverend as soon as she could. As for contacting Morag, the nursemaid who had become a friend to her on the voyage out, she realised that all correspondence must now cease forthwith. Although she wouldn't be surprised Eliza had married Alister, Eliza worried that any further contact with herself might sully Morag.

"All women feel a little nervous and tearful on their wedding day," Mrs Reid said reassuringly, as she dressed Eliza's hair in ringlets. "And you have even more cause than most with your family miles away."

Eliza felt tearful as this thought and at having to hide the truth of her situation even from her beloved sister, Kitty. She remembered how as children they had played together dressing up and imagining their princes coming to take their hands in marriage. And then when she met the man she was going to marry she had always dreamed of Kitty following her down the aisle as her bridesmaid and yet here she was marrying without even securing Kitty's blessing in circumstances not of her choosing and the thought scared her.

"There, there," said Jessie Reid, patting her arm affectionately. "Everything will go smoothly don't you worry your pretty little head. George will give you both a good send off, I know."

Eliza nodded. A send off from him was exactly what she needed. At least in her best powder blue spotted skirt teamed up with a simple white blouse and matching blue spotted bonnet, she felt she had done herself proud and hoped Alister would notice.

The church was full of all the settlers in the area who had come to wish them well. As Mr Hunter led her down the church to the altar, Eliza was overwhelmed by all the flowers decorating the small church, all the colours of spring supplemented by the simple seasonal flowers the settlers had managed to grow from the seeds they'd brought with them. Alister was looking as smart as she had ever seen him in his suit and he turned around at her approach and smiled reassuringly, but Eliza still felt fearful as she stood beside him.

As they both knelt at the altar for the blessing, Eliza wondered if God would condemn her for marrying when she was no longer a virgin and in addition marrying a man she didn't love, and her hand shook as she gripped the rail. Alister reached out and covered her hand with his although she imagined he would be surprised by her thoughts at that moment.

Please forgive my cold, hard heart God, You know the circumstances aren't entirely of my making, she prayed. *And please smile upon Alister and I this day and give us Your blessing. Help me to learn to love my husband. He's a good man, God.*

The Reverend Reid prayed for God's continued presence with them as a couple. Eliza wondered how he could pray in such a way after what he had done. But she nevertheless managed to add a tremulous "Amen" to his prayer.

The wedding breakfast had been prepared for them as a big celebration in the street with every household supplying their own table and chairs and a large combined meal of lamb and fresh vegetables, including the indigenous roasted kumara, or sweet potato, that Eliza was already gaining a taste for.

The Reverend stood up to make a short speech—Jessie Reid had already had to retire early—singing Eliza's praises and welcoming Alister into the family. Eliza found this speech entirely hypocritical on the Reverend's part with his having all but forced her into this marriage. As for them being her family, in truth she hoped she would never see him again, although she felt very sorry to have to part with Jessie Reid, who had been good to her and little Henry, Maria and Flora.

The Reverend then presented Alister and her with a cart to carry away their belongings, which was more than Eliza had expected or wanted.

"Thank you, Sir," she said stiffly, recoiling as the Reverend pulled her towards himself and kissed her on the cheek. "But I don't think we can accept such a generous gift from you."

"Nonsense, my dear, you have been a part of our family for a while now and we are all very fond of you."

Some more than most, she thought with disgust. Then, Alister intervened and shook the Reverend's hand vigorously and gratefully. "We are most grateful, Sir, for your care of Eliza and for this token of your esteem. Indeed, we will have need of something to transport all our goods in, so it is most welcome."

The Reverend's esteem? Eliza felt like laughing out loud. He hadn't thought of her esteem when he had disgraced her. *Wretched man.*

Then one by one she and Alister were presented with the various gifts the settlers had brought for them: candles, a whale oil lamp, potatoes, four laying hens, a simple rug, an axe and some home brewed beer for Alister. This generosity was astounding, and Eliza knew heart felt, especially as the settlers had so little themselves.

"Thank you so much," she said more than once. "Both my husband (*how strange the word sounded*) and I are so grateful to you all."

Leaving the children was one of the hardest things Eliza had to do.

"Please write, Lizzie and come back and see us soon," said Henry struggling to hold back his tears and act like a man. "Yes, please do," echoed Maria, making no attempt at all to hold her tears back.

Eliza kissed and hugged them tightly, feeling choked up inside as her own eyes filled with tears but she didn't want to upset the children more than she needed and said as cheerfully as she could, "Just think what grand times you will have with Susan."

"Susan, isn't you," said Henry. "We didn't know her in Scotland or travel so far on a ship with her."

"No that's very true but we must all move on for your Mama's sake," said Eliza turning her back on them quickly and making her way to the cart before they could see the tears glistening in her own eyes. She had said she would come back to see them but in her heart of hearts she knew she couldn't come back, however much she wished to, with the risk of meeting the Reverend again. She was fond of them and it was true, they had been through so much together that the parting was painful to her.

Alister lifted Eliza carefully up on the new cart. It was to be pulled by the horse that he had managed to purchase from the Maoris. And in this way, with all her possessions beside her and Alister up in front guiding the horse, they waved until the Reids and townsfolk were well out of sight.

As soon as they were a little down the road, Eliza's tears spilled over on to her cheeks, despite her trying hard to hold them back.

"Cheer up, my dear," said Alister. "I know it's hard leaving your family here, but we will soon have our own."

"Yes indeed," she said falling suddenly silent with the worry that it might be sooner than he had anticipated. Whatever happened, Eliza was determined that she would love any children of hers with a love that would never part them from her.

After a short time of travelling along in silence each consumed with their own thoughts, Alister suddenly said, "I cannot think what my Mama and Papa would think of our very simple nuptials or the simple presents we received."

Eliza smiled as she thought of her own parents. "Yes indeed, my folks would certainly look askance at our wedding arrangements too, I fear."

"But remember we're a couple now, man and wife," said Alister with conviction. "Other folks' opinions, even those of our respective families need no longer bother us."

Eliza nodded. They were a couple indeed. Wedded for better or for worse. But how would Alister react if the worst should occur? She didn't know him well enough yet to surmise. Best to make sure he never found out the truth about her past.

At least the first part of her life in the new country was ending, for that she was full of relief. Now she was happy to embrace a new chapter and a new beginning.

Chapter Five

TAITA

THE JOURNEY IN THE BULLOCK cart, jostled around with her possessions, was far from comfortable for Eliza. It was quite a journey from central Wellington in Kaori, the home of the Reids, to Alister's house in Taita in the Hutt valley. They had set out in the early afternoon when the celebrations were over, but it was well into the evening by the time they arrived at the small wooden shack that Alister had built. Eliza felt both bruised and exhausted from the emotional events of the day as well as the bumpy ride.

The wooden dwelling which was to be her new home was not as large or imposing as that which she had left behind and although made of wood, like the Manse, the roof was made of tin rather than wooden tiles. As Alister lifted her gently down from the cart and carried her inside, her first view was of one single, large room with no divisions. There was no stove gracing the main living room as there had been at the Reids' but a simple fireplace with pots and a large black kettle hanging suspended from hooks inside the chimney.

Alister, after carrying Eliza over the threshold, placed her carefully down and then shifted about nervously waiting for her opinion on the house. "I know it's not as big as what you're used to," he began.

"Well I was just thinking that the smaller space should be easier to heat," said Eliza truthfully, "and I'm sure the fire will send out a good heat on a cold day."

"Lizzie, ever the pragmatist," said Alister admiringly. "Err . . . like the Reids' bathroom facilities," he said a little awkwardly, "ours will be of a similar nature, housed in a separate building at the back of the house."

Eliza blushed, thinking they would have to learn to share much more in the way of intimacy than just discussing the toilet arrangements. A glance towards the one and only large bed in the corner of the room reminded her of her marital duties and filled her with a sense of alarm as she tried to put the thought out of her head. Alister followed her glance and she saw him smile as a shiver went through her own body.

"Let's unpack first and have a simple meal," he said, to her relief. "It's already getting late. The hens must stay in their coop for a day or two before I can fashion them a proper house. There's not a lot of food here but maybe we can get a fire going and bake a potato or two in there. I do have a little butter too, to make them taste nicer."

"That would be fine," said Eliza, glad to put her mind to practical matters. "I'm not that hungry anyway after that more than adequate bridal feast, I must say."

"Still, a little food would warm us both up I'm sure," said Alister. "It may be nearly summer but the nights can still feel a little chilly."

For the next hour, the young couple busied themselves with unpacking and organising their home. Alister put the hen coop out the back, unpacked all the larger items and lit the fire. Eliza saw to the arrangements for their meal and the unpacking of her own personal items—she had been able to bring her small writing desk and her chair but had to leave her own bed behind. However, she was glad she had been able to bring her books and photographs, especially the one of her dear Kitty. These small things helped her feel a little more at home. And the wooden packing boxes that housed her things would have to do for seats and a table for the meantime.

After enjoying their buttery potatoes, the night was already drawing in. Alister said it was time to go to bed and Eliza blushed as she took in the full implications of his words. She wanted this time to be different for her from the last, but she felt nervous as she slowly and self-consciously undressed by candlelight with her back turned away from her husband. She was also aware of how little she knew this man both physically and emotionally. It would be the first time she had seen a man fully undressed before and she didn't know quite what to expect. But when she turned around she was glad to see that Alister was attired in a long, white nightgown and cap as she had managed to pull her cotton nightdress over her own head.

At first, she was glad to be able snuggle up to him in the bed as the embers of the fire were slowly dying down. Her reticence at first seemed to be matched by his, but gradually he became more physically demanding with his mouth finding hers and his body cleaving ever closer, as night clothes were slowly pulled up and then divested. All the time Eliza felt insecure, half holding her breath and waiting for it to be over and trying not to think of the last time. She wondered nervously if he would guess that she wasn't a virgin but although she did see him briefly hesitate, he said nothing. Then suddenly it was all over, and he had fallen asleep. The experience wasn't as unpleasant or forceful as previously, but Eliza felt only indifference, not any great romantic feeling. As she listened to Alister's gentle snores she swallowed her bitter disappointment. She and Kitty had both had such high hopes of romance, but maybe these had simply been the musings of two silly, sentimental young girls and married love was made of a different calibre. Eliza knew she would have to live with her disappointment as surely as her previous violation. She would also have to get used to the fact that this marital encounter would be only the first of many.

True to his word, in a couple of days, Alister had built the four hens a splendid house, but they both agreed they could do with two or three more hens. In addition, the few food provisions Alister already had, coupled with the few that the Reids and the old townsfolk had given them had almost all run out and a food shop and the purchase of some rudimentary furniture was also necessary.

The Taita area of Wellington was more inland and densely forested than Karori with fewer dwellings. There was a small store not far from their cottage, but it wasn't as well stocked as the one in Karori, stocking only very basic supplies. The local weekly market near the harbour was, therefore, a necessity and not to be missed by any of the residents in the Taita area. Eliza alighted again onto the cart with her husband driving up in front but as they made their way to the market she felt a very different woman to the young, frightened girl that had travelled on the cart just a few days earlier.

At the end of their first week, Eliza and Alister went along to the local Presbyterian Church in Taita, known as Knox Chapel, which was a short walk from their cottage rather than a cart ride away, like the market. Like Bethel in Karori, the church was a small painted wooden structure with a tin roof. The simple wooden interior of the church reminded Eliza of the one in Bethel and the people seemed friendly enough, welcoming in the young couple with smiles and nods. Eliza and Alister had heard that a new minister had arrived there in the last few months, by the name of Robert Yate. Eliza regarded the young minister carefully as he got up to the pulpit to speak. He wasn't as tall as her Alister but there was something prepossessing about him that drew him to her gaze. His features were more finely painted than the rugged ones of her husband's and in place of Alister's light brown hair, a crop of thick, dark curls framed his beardless face. It wasn't an especially handsome face in the same way as Alister's, but a face which looked as if it could understand the griefs and joys of the world in equal measure and could empathise with both. It was a face that drew her, mesmerised her. She had to be careful not to stare too much.

Robert's wife by contrast had mouse coloured hair and very pale skin. She looked frail and not at all suited to the harsh pioneering conditions as she held out a thin, wan hand to Eliza in greeting after the service, "I am so pleased to meet you, Mrs . . . ?"

"Douglas," Eliza supplied. "My husband of just a week, Alister, has recently gone into partnership with Mr Byatt at the local sawmill. You might have seen Alister here before?"

"Ah yes, I do believe we have met him briefly. Congratulations to you both. Robert and I have been married only just under a year ourselves. I'm Mary Yate."

"Eliza Douglas, and I'm pleased to make your acquaintance. Please call me Eliza or Lizzie. I hope we shall be friends."

"Indeed. Please do visit us and take a cup of tea with us. The houses are so scattered here that we don't see many folk, especially those of a similar age and circumstance."

"How kind," said Eliza. "I should like that."

"Good. Shall we say next week then?"

"Fine. What day?"

"Tomorrow?"

"That would be very nice. Thank you," said Eliza smiling warmly.

Robert Yate, who was preoccupied speaking to his parishioners at the door, saw Mary talking to the young woman with the pretty blonde curls. He had noticed her from the moment she entered Knox Chapel with the man he assumed must be her husband. But handsome though the husband was, there was something ill-matched about the young couple, although he struggled to know exactly what it was. Robert couldn't help but be drawn to the young girl and he felt a little jealous of Mary being able to engage her in conversation when the prattle of some of his more talkative parishioners kept him. When he was finally free of them he looked up to see her and her husband walk off down the path and out of sight.

Eliza could see she had no chance of meeting the young Reverend Yate who seemed preoccupied with parish matters. Reluctantly she followed Alister out of the small church for the walk to their cottage. She was left hoping that she would be able to meet the young minister properly in the future weeks.

However, she was to meet him much sooner than she expected. On reaching the small Manse the next afternoon to take tea with Mary Yate, she was greatly surprised to be met at the door by the young minister instead.

"I'm sorry that you've had the bother of walking all this way, Mrs Douglas, but I'm afraid Mary isn't up to seeing you. She has one of her bad heads and has taken to her bed. She's not very strong I'm afraid."

Eliza nodded. She had certainly noticed that.

She then she heard the young minister hesitate for a moment before he said, "Err . . . but I can't have you walking all this way without taking some form of refreshment. I was about to take a cup of tea myself, will ye no join me?"

Why not? He was the minister after all. What harm could there be in taking a simple cup of tea with him?

As they drank their tea, the young minister explained about his wife, Mary, that she had suffered polio as a child which had left her weak and exhausted and prone to frequent headaches.

"I know she's not really suited to these harsh conditions," he said seeming to notice Eliza's surprise. "But we were childhood sweethearts and our families expected us to marry. I felt I couldn't disappoint . . ."

His voice trailed away as Eliza swallowed her curiosity. It almost sounded as if he was reluctant to marry her but felt pressured by the family ties. She would love to know more but felt it wasn't her place to ask as a newcomer to the area. She was surprised he had shared quite so much in a first meeting.

As if he realised that he had said more than was wise, he got up quickly.

"Anyway, I mustn't detain you any longer, Mrs Douglas. It was my wife you came to see and not me. I'm sorry she wasn't well enough. Do call again. I know Mary would like it. She gets out so little you see—her health does not allow it."

Eliza nodded. She felt a little awkward as if she they had shared confidences that they ought not to have shared and she was nearly as eager to get away as he seemed eager for her to go.

"The minister, Robert Yate, has an invalid wife," she later told Alister.

"Aye, well I had noticed the lassie didna look that bonnie," he said as Eliza continued to tell him of her polio as a youngster. She also told him that Mary and Robert Yate had been childhood sweethearts and that it was the wish of their families for them to marry.

"It doesna seem wise though that he would bring such a frail lassie out here to face these harsh conditions," Alister said.

Eliza nodded. She had been thinking the same thing herself. It was a bit of a mystery to be sure.

As far as Alister was concerned the subject was closed. He had no real interest in the young minister's background as long as he preached the word of God and did his duty to his parishioners, he was minded to just let him get on with it. But the mystery of the Yates filled Eliza's thoughts and she was determined to get to the bottom of the mystery. She didn't have to wait long.

Mrs McMann, a known church gossip, regaled Eliza with the facts just the next week. Eliza fancied that she had probably extracted the story from the young minister almost under duress.

"Poor Reverend Yate," Eliza had said. "What a shame about his wife, Mary and her polio. I only wonder that with her frail condition they have taken this position."

"Oh, my dear," said Mrs McMann. "Had you not heard? We understand that towards the end of his training he had applied for a number of positions in Scotland but on hearing that his wife was barren and not able with her poor health to perform the duties of a Presbyterian wife adequately, he wasn't able to find such a position."

"Oh, I see. But perhaps we shouldn't be discussing their personal circumstances quite so openly," Eliza said, both annoyed by her own speculation and the way in which it had opened the opportunity for idle gossip.

But her determined statement appeared to have alienated the woman, who on hearing her response, had stuck her nose in the air and walked off with a, "I'll say good day to you then, Mrs Douglas."

"Let's go home, Alister," said Eliza not wishing to engage either Mary or the Reverend Yate in conversation now, after she had been so indiscreet. Alister who was more than willing to get off home, not being one for small talk, gladly took hold of his wife's arm and marched her off.

Eliza decided to write to Kitty, being keen to share her feelings about the Reverend Yate, Mary and the dreadful Mrs McMann. She knew Kitty would be all sympathy.

December 21, 1851

My dearest Kitty,

Well, I am now a married woman like you, dearest, and am daily expecting your letters to catch up with me with the news of how you are finding married life. I enclose my new address with this letter. Hopefully the Reids will forward any of your letters before you receive my new details, but I do not expect to have any further contact with them.

I have heard so little of how you and Charles are getting on together, although I did enjoy reading all about your wedding, imagining myself there.

I don't know about you, but I am finding I enjoy my new status. Alister seems very kind to me and our cottage, although much smaller than the Manse—just a single room—I expect will be easier to heat and clean when the cold winter winds arrive, and Alister has built it very securely. At least we don't have to think about this at the moment as we enjoy a good summer. Alister has also built a splendid house for our hens, we have six. In addition, he has built me a small washing line which is infinitely better constructed than that built by the Reverend Reid. It is much larger meaning that I hardly need to recourse to using the nearby bushes as lines like before, and of course there is only the two of us. Between us both we have started to make a small garden at the front of the house, Alister digging and me deciding what we might grow. I think we must have herbs or seasonings of some kind, both to stop our food becoming too bland and in addition for medical use, as the usual tonics and medicines are in short supply here.

We have been along to the small local church of Knox Chapel. The young minister there is called Robert Yate and he has an invalid wife called Mary who suffered with polio as a young woman. She is pale and sickly looking but quite friendly. I did go to have tea with her one afternoon, but she was too unwell to see me. It was then that the Reverend Yate explained her condition to me. I wondered at them being out here in New Zealand in such harsh, basic conditions but a woman from the church, Mrs McMann, a real gossip and busybody, seems to put it down to him not finding a position anywhere else with such a sickly wife. Imagine! I am quite ashamed of myself having listened to such idle tittle tattle outside the church of all places. Poor man to be the subject of such speculation. I look forward to making better acquaintance of him and his wife though in the near future.

I pray that I may hear news of you and Charles very soon. I send you both my love.

Your, Lizzie

After a week of setting up their new home together, Alister had to return to work at the sawmill and life established itself into a regular routine with Alister leaving home early in the morning with the simple packed lunch that Eliza had prepared for him of home baked bread and a piece of cheese.

Eliza met the Reverend Yate and Mary only once more at the church after this, when Mary renewed her invitation for tea but this time it was Eliza who had to renege, having found herself suffering from bouts of morning sickness. She soon discovered herself to be pregnant. This seemed so early on in their marriage that she feared that Alister might be suspicious but was relieved to find that he seemed truly delighted. This, unfortunately, put an end to her visits to the Knox Chapel for the foreseeable future as she was largely confined to the house as Alister attended the small church alone. She did manage to continue making his lunch, feeding the hens and sweeping out their cottage and was able to provide a nourishing hot meal for his return in the evening, but Alister had to maintain the small garden on his own. Eliza found tilling and weeding the hard soil too difficult in her present condition. With more time on her hands, Eliza felt she should sit down and write a letter to Jessie Reid telling her of their new life in Taita and the news of their expected little one. She was also keen to hear news of Mrs Reid's own confinement.

She received a letter back from Jessie Reid within a few weeks telling her of the birth of another son, Graham. Apparently with Susan's expert help and plenty of bed rest during the pregnancy, the birth had gone well. Mrs Reid went on to praise Susan highly, detailing what a treasure she was with the children and the baby. She finished her letter by congratulating Eliza on the good news of her forthcoming birth, extolling her good sense in choosing Alister as a husband. She hoped that they would come and visit soon after the birth. Eliza felt sad as she knew the impossibility of this. She also felt somewhat peeved at how Mrs Reid had made so much of Susan's abilities. She had never praised her so profusely and yet she knew that the children were fond of her, as she was of them. She still missed the children, but a visit was out of the question and Eliza expected that Mrs Reid's offer would probably soon be forgotten. If Henry and Maria were as fond of Susan as Mrs Reid made out, they would also soon forget her, she was sure of that.

When the sickness bouts ended, Alister considered it inadvisable for her to make the walk to Knox Chapel and so it was a while before she was able to meet the Reverend Yate, his wife or the locals again.

The birth of her first baby was long and tiring and with the help of a local lady well versed in deliveries and her Maori helper, baby Alister finally made his entry into the world in the midst of winter. Although small in stature and not of the strongest constitution, he was a good feeder and easily contented and Eliza considered herself very fortunate after baby Flora. He soon established himself into an easy sleeping pattern only waking briefly in the night for his feed and then falling asleep quickly. Alister also seemed satisfied that Eliza had given birth to a boy, although once or twice he observed, "He is so like his mother but I canna see much of myself in him."

Eliza had noticed that too but strove to reassure Alister.

"Oh," she laughed nervously, "don't they always say that the first son takes on his mother's likeness and he does bear your name, dear."

Life, however, was largely good and Eliza was happy, pouring all her love and devotion into the young life.

Then at just three months old following an abnormally cold winter, baby Alister caught a nasty cold. Eliza nursed him vigilantly day and night until she was exhausted but little Alister's condition seemed to only worsen despite her administering sweet Cicely and Heartease from their garden to help with his chestiness and persistent cough. After eventually sending for a local doctor from the middle of Wellington, he recommended trying the baby with Dr Browne's Chlorodyne, a batch of which had just arrived from England.

"It's the very latest cure known for coughs and colds, Mr and Mrs Douglas," he said. "Perhaps this will improve the baby's condition."

However, the blocked nose and breathing difficulties had begun to migrate to a nasty chest congestion. With little improvement, Alister offered to set off on his horse to fetch the doctor once more. When the doctor came, he suggested they might also try lots of steam baths, and he prescribed a small dosage of laudanum but apart from these helps, Eliza knew there was little else that she could do apart from giving the young infant careful nursing and fervent prayer. Nursing him and boiling constant kettles took nearly all her time now. It was all she could do to manage to make Alister's lunch and dinner. But she followed the doctor's advice to the letter, sleeping little and nursing baby Alister night and day but his condition seemed to only worsen. One morning, after hours of sponging his little forehead and having just an hour or two's rest herself, little Alister's temperature grew so high that he started to fit.

"Alister, Alister," Eliza cried in fright, "come quickly, the baby seems to be having some sort of fit and I don't know what to do to make it stop."

Alister had been about to leave for work, but Eliza's anxious cry alerted him to the gravity of the situation. He took the baby from her arms and tried in vain to cool him down, even running him outside into the cold air, but all was to no avail. His little face was slowly turning a blue pallor.

"I will ride again for the doctor, dearest," he said, panicking himself. "Keep trying to cool down little Alister, perhaps try a preparation of laudanum if he will take it. I will be as quick as I possibly can."

True to his word Alister was back within the hour and from his heavy breathing Eliza could tell that he had made haste. In his absence, she had tried various procedures to get the baby's temperature down, although he wouldn't take any medication. Before too long, baby Alister's body had grown limp in her arms like a rag doll until she failed to get any response at all. By the time, Alister arrived with the doctor, Eliza was holding the small corpse in her arms and weeping uncontrollably. The doctor immediately confirmed her worst suspicions, little Alister was dead. He suspected pneumonia to be the cause of the high temperatures leading to the convulsions but said that there would have to be a post mortem.

"I could have done more," said Eliza berating herself as Alister looked on embarrassed at her show of emotion and unsure of what to do.

"Unfortunately, I'm sorry to say these things frequently happen to small babies especially in our more basic conditions here but as far as I can see he couldn't have wished for a better nurse. I think the fact that he was small and not a strong baby wouldn't have helped. Mr and Mrs Douglas, I am so sorry for your loss. Perhaps the local minister could come and talk to you?"

"Thank you for your time, Sir but that won't be necessary," said Alister curtly, finding his voice. "As you yourself say, these things happen in life, so we just have to accept them and move on. I dare say we will have other children in time."

Eliza was dumbfounded. This was a side of Alister she hadn't seen before. He sounded so matter-of-fact about the situation. Other children? She couldn't even think of such a thing right now. Baby Alister's body was scarcely cold and he was talking of other children. She couldn't even countenance such an idea. Eliza felt that his death was God's judgement on her, especially if he was the Reverend Reid's child, which she had begun to suspect. But as she grieved for the baby she had loved so completely, she reasoned to herself that her sin was not his fault, he was innocent. She felt it was wrong of God to force such an innocent to suffer on her behalf.

After seeing the doctor out, Alister turned to her and said, "Well, there's nothing more that we can do to help baby Alister now. I might as well go to work."

"I'm sure Joe won't expect you today of all days," she said numbly.

"There's plenty of work to be done and wishing won't bring him back. Better to keep busy and move on quickly."

Eliza was in shock. She knew that Alister was not an effusive man, but he had barely comforted her and now was talking of work. She couldn't imagine getting on with any task with baby Alister lying dead in his cot. Her first-born son dead. The thought started a fresh flow of tears.

"Hush now, Lizzie. Best occupy your mind with some work like me. We'll get over this. Most couples have to expect at least one mortality."

"One mortality? Alister, our little son is much more than just another statistic surely?"

"You know what I mean, Lizzie. It's an unpleasant side of life that must be expected. My parents suffered three fatalities in better circumstances than these. Perhaps we shall have to expect even more than them in these basic pioneering conditions. There will be other children before too long I'm sure of that. We must look to the future now and not dwell on the past."

"I can't even begin to think of a future now without him. You don't seem to feel it like I do. Little Alister was everything to me, a part of me."

"He was a part of me too, wasn't he? He was a part of me too, wasn't he, Lizzie?" Alister reiterated in a slightly raised voice after receiving no reply.

"Yes, no, I don't know."

In her grief, Eliza realised that she had said more than she should have done but now her words were out she knew they would have consequences.

"What are you saying?" Alister shook her in exasperation. "Have you been unfaithful to me?"

He sounded angry, bitter.

"No, of course not Alister. It wasn't my fault, none of this is."

"What?"

There was nothing for it but to tell Alister about the Reverend Reid and his despicable behaviour. Surely Alister was a good man, a kind man, he would understand that none of it was her fault.

But instead of Alister gathering her to himself and weeping with her, he went strangely silent.

After a few agonising moments, Eliza called out his name in a tremulous voice, "Alister, Alister, this changes nothing between us."

"It changes everything," he said clenching his teeth. He had moved right away from her.

"You are not the woman I thought you were, the woman I married. I presumed you to be pure, a virgin, faithful to me, but now I discover you to be dirty, sullied, another man's goods."

"But I was never the Reverend Reid's, he had a wife."

"That makes it even worse. Adultery."

"Alister, he forced himself upon me, we were alone."

"You could have resisted."

"Don't you think I tried? I was all alone, and the Reverend is a large man, I couldn't fight him."

Alister had gone strangely silent again. Eliza had never felt so alone.

Alister made a move to leave.

"If you're going out, please would you ask the Reverend Yate to call?" Eliza said in as steady a voice as she could muster. "I would at least like Baby Alister to be christened and lie in a consecrated grave."

"But he's a bastard."

"Even if you believe that, surely you can see that's not his fault?"

"Aye, well that's true enough," said Alister in a distant, matter-of-fact tone. "I will ride over to his house on my way to work." And then he walked out the door without another word.

Eliza was shocked. Alister had always been kind to her but this hard, unforgiving side of Alister was a part of him she hadn't seen before. It seemed as if she had experienced his kindness when he believed her to be his pure, loyal wife but now when he had discovered her guilty secret, all that kindness had evaporated.

He must have at least contacted the Reverend Yate, as that afternoon there was a gentle knock on the door which announced his arrival.

"Reverend Yate," said Eliza, going to the door. "Please do come in."

"Mrs Douglas," said the Reverend Yate holding out his hands to her in greeting. "I came as soon as I could after your husband called. I'm so sorry for your loss, you must feel devastated." It pained him to see her this way, she looked so young and lost.

At the sight of him, Eliza began to weep again.

"I really am so very sorry," he said once more, looking moved but embarrassed as he studied his feet.

"Forgive me, Reverend Yate," cried Eliza noticing his discomfort, as soon as she had sufficiently composed herself. "I didn't mean to make you feel ill at ease, but I find it hard to cope with my grief at the moment. Baby Alister is . . . " she sucked in a breath, " . . . was my first born, my life."

"Naturally. Any death is hard to bear but the death of a child is one of the hardest griefs we must suffer in this world."

"You have suffered similar yourself, Sir?" asked Eliza hastily drying her eyes and looking at him with renewed curiosity.

"No, simply the grief of not having children. It's a different kind of grief and loss. But enough of me. I have come here to comfort and assist you and instead I find myself confiding in your good nature, deplorable."

"But I can see from your tone that you seem to understand something of what I'm going through. I would like to have baby Alister christened now if that's possible. I cannot bear the extra grief of him lying in an unconsecrated grave. That would break my heart."

"Well, there's no need for that. I saw your husband Alister this morning. Where is he now?"

He seemed surprised when Eliza explained that Alister was at work.

"Well then, I can come over later and perform the service once your husband returns."

"Yes, of course." *How foolish!* Eliza realised that she had been thinking that the Reverend Yate would perform the short service for baby Alister then and there without even a thought of Alister's presence. Even if Alister wasn't little Alister's father, she knew that would look most irregular.

"Will ye no take a cup of tea before you go for your trouble?" she asked wishing to delay his departure.

"Aye, Mrs Douglas that would be fine. Thank you." He sat down as she busied herself filling the kettle, stoking the fire afresh and placing the kettle on the stand above the flames. As she busied herself, she stole a few furtive glances in his direction. His features were more those of an artist or learned man than a rough pioneer. But there was a determinedness in his air that would most probably stand him in good stead in their hard surroundings.

"How are you settling in, you and Mrs Yate?" she asked, handing him a cup of tea. "I don't believe you've been in the parish long yourselves?"

"Just nine months. Yes, well enough. Although it's hard to get to know folks when Mary can't manage to entertain much. She gets so tired you see."

"That must be hard for you both."

He continued, "But I knew in marrying her that we'd have to accept we'd never raise a family."

So, Mrs McMann was right. Mary was barren. Eliza couldn't help but come to her defence.

"But surely, Reverend Yates that is hardly her fault. She is probably as sad as you are about not holding her own bairns in her arms."

"Of course, yes," he said flushing with embarrassment as he said apologetically, "I don't know why I'm rattling on again about myself. You must excuse me, Mrs Douglas."

Perhaps all men were the same, Eliza mused. Blaming their womenfolk for having children out of wedlock from no fault of their own and blaming them when they couldn't have any children.

But all she said out loud was, "Life is often hard on us, Reverend Yate."

"Please let us be friends and not stand on formality, Mrs Douglas. Call me Robert."

"Certainly, it's good to be hospitable," she said not desiring the intimacy and not supplying her own name.

"Have you been long in New Zealand, Mrs Douglas?"

"Just under a year. I was nursemaid to another reverend's children, a Reverend George Reid and his wife Jessie," she said spitting out his name with a sense of disgust. "He was the minister in the Stair Estate Parish where I was brought up."

"Stair Estate Parish, where's that?"

"Ayrshire."

Robert nodded. "I don't know the man though."

Eliza continued with a profound sense of relief, "I lived across the other side of Wellington with them in Karori."

"So how did you meet Mr Douglas if you don't mind me asking?"

He seemed rather forward, but Eliza surmised that he was just making polite conversation.

"We met on the ship on the way over. *The Adventurer.* Alister was travelling alone and he got to know myself and the Reid family."

Eliza felt bolder. If the Reverend Yate could ask her the details of her background perhaps she could also ask something of his. "I can see you're a good, conscientious minister," she began, "but aren't you rather young for such a responsibility?" Then thinking that she had perhaps overstepped the boundaries of civility in this instance with someone she had only just recently met, she blushed and said, "I'm sorry, you must forgive me. What an impertinent question. You don't have to answer."

"I see no problem at all in answering. It's a good question. Yes, I am young, but they have considerable trouble in appointing ministers to these pioneering positions and so they took me fresh from training. They also have trouble in getting them to stay too I understand."

Eliza nodded her head remembering about the Reverend Cleverly in Karori who hadn't been able to take to the situation.

"It can't be the best situation for Mrs Yate though?" Eliza felt emboldened to enquire further. After all it was better to hear the truth from the Reverend Yate than from the lips of the likes of Mrs McMann.

"No, it isn't. Unfortunately, I struggled to find a suitable position back home with Mary being an invalid. It left us with few options."

Eliza nodded again. She felt some sympathy for this young man saddled with an invalid wife at such a young age, but she was also somewhat wary of his role as a man of the cloth.

"Well I must be off now," he said draining his cup and standing up. "I can be back in an hour or two?"

"Alister is normally back around five when the night is drawing in. Or will that be too late for you?" she asked taking his cup from him.

"That will be fine, Mrs Douglas, it's my job."

"Yes of course. We'll see you later then."

She listened out for him mounting his horse then heard him ride off. She felt somewhat comforted by his visit, but her thoughts were still all over the place. She kept being drawn to the little baby lying in his cot and momentarily she would forget and go to pick him up and then feeling his stiff, resistant body, she would remember and then weep for him once again. God seemed cruel and prayer seemed to elude her.

She would write a letter to Kitty before Alister's return and the christening. She needed to talk to someone. There was so much to say.

October 5, 1852

My Dearest Kitty,

I hardly know how to write this, but my heart is broken. The cold and fever baby Alister had suffered from which I mentioned in my last letter has been the death of him. Even now he lies cold in his cot as I write. The doctor suspects pneumonia but there must be a post mortem which of course, delays the funeral. I cannot stop weeping but Alister seems so matter-of-fact about it all. He simply says, "All parents have to expect at least one mortality. We will have other children."

Other children? Honestly Kitty, I cannot even consider the possibility at present. I miss baby Alister so much and although he died only this morning it already seems like an age since I last held him in my arms.

Thankfully the Reverend Yate has been to call to discuss christening little Alister. He is to call back this evening to perform the christening when Alister has returned from work.

Yes, he went to work this morning after Alister died. He said that he felt it would help him to keep busy. I cannot understand him. He gave me so little comfort but perhaps that is his way of dealing with things. It is certainly not mine. I wish you were here with me dearest, you would be such a comfort to me and so understanding.

I will write again when the funeral is over.

Your sad, despairing sister,

Lizzie

Robert was back at the cottage promptly at five. Indeed, he arrived minutes before Alister and again put out his hand to greet Eliza, saying, "How are you faring, Mrs Douglas?" She did not have any desire to trust a man of the cloth but was, nevertheless, grateful for his kindness in asking.

"As well as can be expected, thank you for asking. There just seems a strange unfamiliarity about everything," she said truthfully.

"You're bound to feel like that for a start, but I promise you the pain will ease in time. Not get better but ease."

His words helped to dull the ache inside. *Not get better,* he had said, *only ease.* Baby Alister would never be forgotten or surpassed by future children. He would always hold a special place in her heart despite his origins.

Alister arrived back as they were talking. He shook the hand of the young minister firmly and then said, "I must clean up a minute before the service."

He sounded to Eliza as if he were about to attend evening prayer. Eliza glanced towards Robert to see how he would react. But Robert didn't betray any surprise, he merely smiled and said, "Of course, Mr Douglas. I am a few minutes early."

Eliza held the stiff, cold corpse in her arms. It no longer felt like her baby, her Alister. Robert's voice, as he performed the simple service, was but an echo in the distance to her, her mind being with her little Alister.

The next Sunday at church, Robert made a special point of speaking to her at the church door.

"How are you finding things?" He enquired with a note of care in his voice.

"Difficult, very difficult," she started to say when Alister came up behind her and grabbed her arm.

"Thank you for your kind attention, Reverend Yate. It is good of you. But we are coping fine, thank you very much. Good morning to you." And he marched the shocked Eliza off before she could say anymore.

"Alister," she said a little sharply, "Reverend Yate was simply being kind, doing his job of caring for the flock. You were a little short with him."

"There are some situations that should be shared only between a man and his wife," said Alister after a pause, "we must comfort each other at this time and not seek outside interference, even from a minister."

Eliza was silent. That comfort had never seemed further away.

Chapter Six

A COLD, ICY WIND BLEW on the day of the funeral. It felt as cold as Eliza's heart. All that occupied her mind was the fact they were burying her firstborn son.

As Eliza and Alister took their places at the front of the church, Eliza noticed that it was full. She tried with difficulty to acknowledge the settlers' kindness in turning out for her and Alister. Alister chose to avert his face from the church folk looking straight ahead of him during the service and as they followed the little coffin out to its place of rest. Eliza stood stock still as Robert chanted the familiar words "ashes to ashes, dust to dust," and wished that she could take the place of little Alister.

After the service, there was tea and light refreshments for folks in the small hall beside the church. Eliza didn't wish to go, but Alister told her it was her duty to thank folk for their kind support. She gratefully took a dish of tea from one of the ladies but found herself unable to partake of any of the home-made goods baked for the occasion, unable to contemplate eating the sweet treats even though she knew they were well meant. She did, however, have the presence of mind to shake Robert's hand and thank him for the simple service.

"You're very welcome," had been his reply, "but it's one duty I would rather not have performed. The Lord knows life doesn't always turn out as we would wish it." Eliza smiled gratefully, knowing Robert's circumstances weren't easy either and she felt a certain painful connection with him.

In the following days, it was as if she and Alister led separate lives. She continued to pack his lunch for him each morning but on his departure found herself unable to apply herself to her usual tasks or to prayer. Alister seemed to carry on going to work as if nothing had happened of any real significance, although it was hard to tell what he was thinking. They hardly spoke except to exchange pleasantries. It was only with Kitty she felt able to share her deepest thoughts and feelings.

November 2, 1852

My dearest Kitty,

Now that the funeral of little Alister is over I find myself unable to get back to any semblance of normality. Alister appears on the outside, at least, to have adjusted back to life before little Alister, almost as if he never existed. But I cannot so easily forget him.

What a cold, hard day it was on the day we buried him. I had no real appetite to go to the funeral but Alister insisted I should go if only for propriety's sake and to thank our neighbours and friends for their help and support at such a difficult time. I managed to get through the service and burial by imagining that I was playing a part in another's drama. I found however that when I got home I had to take to my bed. The exhaustion of pretence had fair worn me out.

Alister shows very little affection to me at present. But I do not wish to mar your own joy at the birth of your dear little Charlie by speaking any further of our troubles. How I should love to see your Charlie and hold him and so be comforted for the loss of little Alister.

Your grieving sister,

Lizzie

Although Alister had rebutted most of Robert's attempts to speak to them as a couple, he did seem to recognise Eliza's need of the young minister's pastoral services. At least, he appeared to have no objection to Robert visiting her regularly to sit and take tea in the afternoons. Eliza was glad to have someone to share her grief with in the young minister and looked forward to his visits as an oasis in her day. He did indeed seem to have some understanding of her feelings, at least more than Alister but then he did not know the whole story. *Would he still sympathise with her if he knew her true nature?*

"Could we not invite the Reverend Yate and Mary to dinner sometime, Alister?" she asked after nearly a month had gone by since the funeral. "He has been kind and supportive to me at this difficult time."

"It's his job," said Alister gruffly. "And he might not be so understanding if he knew your nature."

So, he was still dwelling on her shocking revelation. "Besides," Alister continued, "we see him often enough at church. Why should we want to spend even more time in his company?" Eliza noted a tinge of jealousy in his voice and felt slightly irritated. *How could he blame the young minister for being her confidant when he had rejected the role?*

Soon after this something happened to unsettle Eliza further. The summer gave way to a wet autumn and an even wetter winter. The series of rains seemed to go on for weeks. All the rivers and lakes nearby had become swollen and Alister had to devise new routes to work to avoid the worst of the excesses.

Eliza worried about Alister setting off to work each morning at the sawmill, but there was so little communication between them she was almost afraid to express her concerns.

One day she felt especially uneasy in her spirit, although she could not explain why. The weeks of continuous rains were building up floods which even the dense bush could not hold back.

"The weather isn't improving, Alister," she said nervously. "Why don't you tell Joe that the way is too dangerous for you to travel? The rivers are becoming more and more swollen and impassable."

"Dinna, you fret yourself, Lizzie. I've been trekking through the mire and finding me all sorts of other routes to go through these past few weeks and have been managing just fine. I've no doubt I'll be able to continue till the rains abate. I canna afford not to turn up. If I lose my wages how will we manage?" he asked setting his mouth in a determined line.

Eliza knew when he did that there was no persuading him. But she had to acknowledge the truth of his words. Rain or no rain, wages were essential. She could still pray for his safe return and God's mercy towards him, even though she could not pray for herself.

Alister had been gone for only around an hour and Eliza was busy getting on with sweeping the cottage and preparing their evening meal when she heard urgent battering at the door. Alarmed she ran to the door to see Robert and another man half carrying and half dragging Alister and all the men were wet through.

Robert seemed exhausted and was breathing heavily. "I found your husband and his horse floundering in the lake near our house Mrs Douglas," he said at last. "I'm afraid the horse is drowned but myself and this good man, John, managed to pull your husband to safety."

"Oh mercy. Thank the good Lord then that you and John were passing," said Eliza alarmed. "Come in, come in. I feared something like this could happen, the rains have been that fierce and persistent. You must dry yourselves by the fire."

After they helped to drag the inert figure of Alister near to the fire, John seemed to decide his services were no longer required and he doffed his cap to Eliza and Robert saying that he would be on his way.

"Thank you so much for helping to rescue my husband, John," said Eliza. "Are you sure you won't stay to take a dish of tea with us?"

But John shook his head. "No, thanks all the same Missus but I have work to do."

"Of course."

Robert was silent as he helped Eliza to remove the wet shirt of Alister. "I should be going too," he said uncertainly. Then, suddenly he said, "I did it for you, you know Eliza," and her heart practically stopped.

"What?" she said. She hadn't yet given him permission to use her first name, even though they had shared so many confidences. He was still a minister and as such she didn't want their relationship to take on a more intimate nature.

"I saved your husband for your sake. I didn't want you to be husbandless as well as childless."

Eliza felt that she deserved all this and more but said, "How kind of you. I guess it is your job to take care of the flock."

"No, Eliza," he said reddening slightly, his next words seeming to fall over themselves as if in a rush to get out in case the inert figure of the man lying in front of the fire should rise up and challenge him. "I thought only of you, Eliza."

Eliza was at a loss to know what to say. *What did he mean? He was the minister, how on earth was she to respond?* She grew fearful as she considered the consequences of his words. She couldn't face another minister forcing himself upon her.

"Please go," she said, and her voice trembled.

"I'm sorry I didn't mean to alarm you. It's just that I've begun to grow fond of you over these last few weeks as we've met together."

"Fond, fond. Oh, yes, I know fond," she replied angrily. "As you know I'm a married woman. You men of the cloth, you're all the same."

Eliza saw the Reverend Yate visibly pale.

"Mrs Douglas, I'm so sorry I meant you no harm at all."

And as he moved away from her, Eliza breathed out heavily in relief. It was only then she realised that she had been holding her breath for very fear. She didn't know what to think but her words suddenly seemed to be on an unstoppable course as they poured out of her.

"The Reverend Reid wasn't as particular as you, Sir. He didn't even say he was fond of me, he just forced himself upon me. And like you he was a married man."

"What are you saying?" The Reverend Yate looked as pale and shaken as she felt.

"I, Sir, am a scarlet woman whom my husband despises. Baby Alister wasn't his but the Reverend Reid's bastard child."

And she began to weep.

"I am so sorry. My feelings for you are genuine but you are right, I will do my best not to mention them again. You, Mrs Douglas have been greatly wronged by one who should have known better. One who should have respected and cared for you as a member of his flock and household. You are no scarlet woman—you are a wronged woman and I apologise wholeheartedly for all men of the cloth. It was a shameful act done to a defenceless woman."

Eliza was surprised. His defence of her had been vehement and sounded, by all accounts, genuine. But still she trembled.

"Please, I beg you don't mention this to anyone, Robert" she said fearfully. It seemed only right to use his first name now that he knew her deepest secret.

"Not a word of it will ever pass my lips, you can be assured of that my poor, dear, Eliza."

"Please, not even Mary."

"Not even her. You have my word before God." And looking at his face, Eliza realised that here, at last, was a man she could trust.

At that moment, Alister began to stir. Eliza stooped down to him, "Alister," she called quietly in his ear. "You have had an accident and the Reverend Yate here and a man called John rescued you and have brought you home."

Alister began to slowly raise himself off the hearth. As he did so he clasped his head. "My head," he moaned, "it hurts."

"I will ride for the doctor at once," said Robert struggling to compose himself after the shock of all he had heard.

"But you're wet too. We don't want you to catch cold," Eliza said in concern.

"I will dry out as I ride," he said. "For it's not raining at present. Don't worry. I'll be home in no time."

It took Alister a few days of rest and recuperation before he was fit enough to return to work. Robert looked in on Alister once over the next few days and even stayed for a cup of tea, but he seemed more distant than before, not someone who she could confide in. It was like the awkward moment that had passed between himself and Eliza had changed everything. Eliza began to imagine that telling him her guilty secret had been a mistake.

August 18, 1853

My Dearest Kitty,

Where do I start to tell you what has taken place?

Robert, our minister and a local man, John, saved Alister from drowning just a few days ago—we've had that much rain and many swollen rivers. I had thought at the time that I would be husbandless as well as childless if they had not acted so quickly to save Alister. But, thank God, Alister is safe now and has recovered and returned to work. We all hope that the rains will cease soon.

I send a kiss for you and little Charlie.

Your loving sister,

Lizzie

Eliza could not tell Kitty of all that had passed between her and the young minister, but she was thankful that Alister's life had been saved. She tended to him most carefully and in response, in his gratitude, he deigned to lie with her again. Soon after his return to work Eliza discovered she was pregnant again. At least now she knew that Alister was the baby's father. However, Eliza still expected divine retribution to visit her and her thoughts turned to anxiety for the baby she was carrying. She was anxious that the baby might die in birth or if it was born it might die within months like little Alister. Her thoughts were all over the place and she began to lose weight and grow pale. Robert appeared to notice immediately.

Drawing her aside at the end of church one Sunday, he said in a quiet, urgent tone, "Eliza, Lizzie, I am concerned for you. You look pale and I'm sure grow thinner. This is no way to progress for someone in your condition."

"I'm frightened for the baby, Robert," she breathed. "I worry that the pregnancy and birth won't go well and then I worry that if the baby is born it will die again like little Alister."

"But, there's no need to imagine things will turn out the way they did before. We must trust God and pray it will be different this time. I will pray for you and the baby." And Eliza felt comforted by his concern.

"What did the Reverend Yate have to say to you this morning?" asked Alister curiously as they began the short walk home.

"He thought I looked a little pale and was anxious for one in my condition," said Eliza.

"He should see to his own Mrs and not concern himself with others' wives," Alister said forthrightly. "Doesn't he think I take enough care of you myself?"

Eliza thought perhaps that may have been in Robert's mind, but said, "He meant no harm, Alister. Surely it's his role to take care of his flock and their well-being."

However, Eliza kept well this time and the labour wasn't as long as that of baby Alister. Alister and Eliza were delivered of a healthy little girl. Eliza decided she should be called Charlotte after Alister's mother, partly to assuage her guilt because of little Alister. Eliza also noted that Alister seemed anxious to take a more active part in her care than he had in the case of baby Alister and she rejoiced in this. After all, she mused, he knew that Charlotte was his.

May 8, 1854

My Dearest Kitty,

Just imagine, Alister and I are parents again. I thought I might never have the joy of holding a little life in my arms once more until Charlotte made her entrance into the world. I will never forget little Alister or love him any the less, but Charlotte's birth has comforted me somewhat for the loss of him. I think it has seemed to comfort Alister as well, especially perhaps because we named her after his mother. Certainly, he is much more attentive than he was with baby Alister, although of course he says, "it's a shame she wasn't a boy." But maybe it's because she is a girl that he can play the doting father. You know what they say about fathers and daughters!

I only wish you could be a godmother to young Charlotte and that you would be able to join us here for her christening. Maybe you could be an absentee one? We are planning her christening at the moment which, I hope, will be a more joyous occasion than the emergency one of poor baby Alister. I also wish you hearty congratulations on your forthcoming birth, which I understand is imminent. I pray you may be delivered safely, my dearest Kitty and have the joy I now have with little Charlotte.

Your, loving Lizzie

The christening was indeed a joyous occasion. The church was full again but not for a sad occasion like little Alister's funeral. This time Eliza could enjoy parading Charlotte in the church.

Kitty had agreed to be Charlotte's godmother and to be attentive to all her spiritual and physical needs and sent out a small Bible inscribed with Charlotte's name along with the very latest book, *Mrs Beeton's Book of Household Management* for Eliza. She had inscribed Eliza's book with the message—"for Lizzie so that you won't have to worry about the health and well-being of Charlotte as you did about little Alister's."

Mrs Moffat, the church warden's wife, had agreed to stand in for Kitty, and Mary and Robert were to be the other godparents. Robert had accepted the role wholeheartedly on their behalf, Mary seemed a little reluctant but complied nonetheless. At least Alister didn't think it strange to have the minister and his wife as Charlotte's godparents especially when Eliza persuaded him of how attentive Robert had been to them during little Alister's death.

She was impressed by the gentle way Robert held Charlotte over the small font as he drew the watery cross on her forehead. The baby's eyes followed his movements with interest and confidence, sensing, it would seem, that she was safe in his arms.

After the short afternoon service, tea and cakes were served in the small hall attached to the church and this time Eliza could enjoy the refreshments and the fuss people were making of the baby. She felt proud to show her off and her feelings of anxiety for Charlotte were diminishing as she saw how well she thrived. Baby Alister had always struggled to hold his weight and seemed weak and prone to sicknesses but Charlotte was quite the opposite, a bonny, healthy child.

Mary congratulated her on little Charlotte's christening but when Eliza offered her a hold of the small baby she declined as if she had been offered something distasteful merely sniffing and saying, "thank you, no. I'm not a great lover of young babies although I guess she looks a fairly bonnie one."

Eliza, who wasn't quite sure what she meant by these words, smiled politely. Mary's reluctance seemed to be tempered with a kind of fear, natural perhaps from someone who had no experience of children. But maybe, Eliza surmised, this was Mary's way of dealing with her childlessness.

Robert rejoiced with her and Alister. He had been especially moved to be asked, along with Mary to be a godparent.

"It will be an enormous honour, Eliza, Lizzie," he had said. "It's the closest I, we, can get to caring for children ourselves and, for me personally, there's no one's child I would be more honoured to care for than yours."

He hadn't mentioned Alister's part in the parenting of Charlotte and had hardly mentioned Mary's role in their joint one, but, surprised, Eliza chose not to comment.

Chapter Seven

WHEN CHARLOTTE WAS JUST OVER a year old, Alister heard word that good grazing land had become available in the north of the South Island, in an area known as Golden Bay just outside Gibbstown.

"I know that it necessitates us crossing over to the South Island by ship, Lizzie," Alister explained, "but it's not as if we'll be crossing the seas again, only an expanse of water between the islands. The climate of Golden Bay is known to be kind and even if the land is a bit rocky according to some reports, I've a mind to go and see for myself, so I'm going to put in a bid for a plot of land there, if you're in agreement?"

Eliza shuddered at the very thought of another sea journey, even if it was, as Alister suggested just a crossing between the two islands.

"The thought of travelling on a ship again after the last time isn't something I'd relish or wish to subject my children too either," said Eliza, although she knew Alister was determined to go and that if he was successful in his bid, she wouldn't have much choice except to follow.

Alister, noticing the anxiety in his wife's voice said, "Well, I'm only going to put in a bid as yet, nothing is settled." Eliza had to agree.

"If I find the land is workable and a good price, I'm minded to employ a local Maori, who is familiar with the land, to clear it of native bush for me and plant some seed. At least I'll have made a start then and not have to take months off work which might make Joe suspicious. As it is, I fear that I will be away for a few weeks and must take unpaid leave."

"Maybe Robert could call on me in your absence," Eliza suggested cautiously, turning away to pick up Charlotte as she did, aware that she was blushing at the mere thought of Robert visiting and not wishing her husband to notice.

"Yes, I suppose that's a good idea if you wish it," Alister replied casually as if the idea was of little consequence.

Eliza realised that Robert's visits and their regularity were becoming something she valued and the proposed move to the South Island began to fill her with dread because then Alister and herself would lose touch with the Yates.

Alister was gone for several weeks but returned with enthusiasm. She hadn't seen him so elated since the birth of little Charlotte.

"It seems good land and a nice climate, Lizzie. Much better than anything around here and the swampy Hutt Valley. The land may be a bit stony and it needs a fair amount of clearing from bracken, large tree ferns and native bush, but it shows promise. I'll warrant the crossing is difficult and cumbersome, but we'll manage."

"It will be a long journey for us all though, Alister, and not just Charlotte."

"I thought you'd rejoice with your husband though despite your anxieties for the journey or is there another reason for your reluctance?"

Eliza blushed. "No, of course not," she said quickly. In truth, she was thinking of Robert but couldn't admit her feelings even to herself. After all, she couldn't be sure of them, much less the feelings of the young minister, whatever he'd tried to tell her once before. He'd certainly been more than willing to resume their regular afternoon meetings, but no word of feelings had passed between them since her shocking revelation after the rescue of Alister.

Alister nodded. "Of course, it's natural that the practicalities of the journey might cause you some concern. But I'm sure there will be others going that way who might be willing to lend us a hand."

Others, yes but not the one *other* who alone made her life just a little brighter. They had shared so much of themselves over the daily visits that leaving him behind suddenly seemed very difficult.

"Anyway," Alister said breaking into her thoughts, "It will be a while before we have to think of leaving. There is even a chance things won't work out for us, although I hope that won't be the case but I'm not about to tell Joe Byatt, at the sawmill, of any plans of ours to move yet or anyone else for that matter."

But Robert knew. She didn't have to hide the truth from him. Alister had told him of their plans when asking him to keep an eye on Eliza and the baby but he seemed non-committal about it. Eliza couldn't tell if he was sad or glad, his expression gave nothing away of his feelings which were quite guarded these days. Whatever he had said about her being blameless, perhaps he didn't believe in her innocence anymore than Alister.

A few weeks later Alister told Eliza of his plans to return to their land and see the progress made. This time he would be away only around a week—he couldn't risk Joe becoming suspicious. He would have to purchase a herd of cattle from Wellington and ship them over to the land. If all went well, he would be able to return, and they could make plans for the move.

She explained all this to Robert who stared at her afterwards for a good few minutes before speaking.

"Maybe it won't happen," he said.

"No, maybe it won't," responded Eliza not sure what to make of this curt, bald statement.

He looked embarrassed as he shuffled about nervously before he added, "In truth I would rather it didn't, Lizzie. I've got so used to our taking tea together, sharing little confidences, it gives me the strength to go on when life sometimes seems so hard and joyless."

"We must all face our own battles," she said, not sure of what response he expected from her. "God gives us the courage to live through the tough times as well as the good."

"God knows I should know that more than most," he responded. "Life is tough here in this new country, tough for us all, I know that, and I'm sure that my problems are no worse than many, probably better than most. I'm just ashamed to say that my feelings for Mary aren't as strong as they should be and it's not because of her handicap. It's true that we had been promised to one another it seemed forever, but I was just considering asking her if she still wanted our agreement to stand when she became ill. When Mary become an invalid, it was clear to me that she would never find another to marry and I felt I owed it to her to keep to our agreement. Perhaps Mary saw some of my doubts in my face because she asked me if I was certain I wanted to marry her. I said I was as certain of anything as I could be, my fondness for her was still strong and blended now with a sense of duty. I really believed I did love her which is why I married her but since I've met you . . . " He broke off suddenly, flushing and a look of bashful uncertainty lined his face.

"I'm not so sure now, Lizzie, my lovely Lizzie."

He seemed suddenly overcome by the strength of his feelings and put his face into his hands.

"I'm sorry if I've shocked you. Since my first outburst after trying to save your husband from drowning I've tried so hard to keep a lid on my feelings, but it's no good. I can't deny that what I feel for you is more than a minister should feel for one of his flock, more indeed than the feelings of a friend. Perhaps you'll think me a bad man, Lizzie, for sharing my guilty secret. I wonder if you can respect me now. But perhaps I've said too much as a minister, a man of God. Maybe it's God's will we should be parted. My feelings for you I know are out of order. I—"

He got up quickly and turned his back on her ready to make a quick exit, but Eliza was up in a minute and by his side.

"I now realise that I feel the same, Robert. I wasn't sure I loved Alister when I married him but circumstances, which you very well know, made it difficult for me to refuse his offer. I believed I would learn to love him. Now I'm not so sure, especially as his love has waned since he discovered my past. He wasn't as ready to forgive and forget as you."

"My poor dear, Lizzie, life hasn't been kind to you either has it?"

Eliza reached out her hand to touch his. "We're both trapped in our circumstances."

"You're very forgiving after the Reverend Reid's behaviour towards you," he said looking into her eyes tenderly. "It still makes me angry to even think of it."

"May God, bless you for your belief in me. It warms my heart. I have felt so powerless, so deserving of God's judgment."

"The only one deserving that is the Reverend Reid," Robert said angrily balling his fists. "You have nothing to chastise yourself with, my love, nothing at all."

"You reassure me that Alister's offer was my best option. And of course," she finished, looking up at Robert shyly, "if I hadn't taken that course of action I wouldn't have met you."

"Oh Lizzie," he breathed unclenching his fists and taking her small hand in his, "how you haunt me." Turning back to face her, he let his lips touch hers gently for just a moment.

"I must go, I need to go," he said quickly, his face reddening. "I hope and pray with all my heart that you'll stay even though I know I should pray you'll go for both our sakes."

Then he was gone. Eliza touched her lips where his had so recently pressed and she knew in her heart that she had never been kissed or received a man's kisses with such enthusiasm or joy before. She ought to pray that they would move and quickly too for propriety's sake, for his career, but even so, she couldn't help but pray in her heart they wouldn't move. Alister was first and foremost a farmer and she knew it was his dream to have his own land. She wanted that for him too, just not yet. Robert had told her that he was obliged to stay in the living for a minimum of three years, and he and Mary had only just passed their second year in the parish.

When Alister returned a few days later, he was disappointed and despondent.

"The Maori chap I left in charge has disappeared," he said. "What's more he never sowed any of the seed but sold it to make himself a small profit. I was forced to sell the cattle I took with me to another settler there. At this rate, I'll never get my own land."

Eliza knew he had set his heart on the land on the South Island and this was a blow to him and his pride. Even though she was relieved in her heart that they would not be moving at present, she could not voice these feelings to her husband.

"Alister, my dear," she said reaching out her hands to him. "Perhaps it's just not the right time yet. Maybe if we wait you will come by more land, better land."

"I do hope so, Lizzie," he said sadly. "I do hope so."

May 3, 1855

Dearest Kitty,

I thought I would be writing to you to give you our new address on New Zealand's South Island. Alister has been look-ing at land there in the northern corner of the island, just outside of Gibbstown in an area known as Golden Bay. He had managed to purchase a small piece of land, buy some seed and after setting a local Maori in charge, he had to return to work at the sawmill, not wishing Joe to think he had taken more than a short break. Full of optimism, Alister returned a few weeks later with a small herd of cattle only to find the seed sold and the man gone. Needless to say, the small piece of deserted land was then of little use, so he sold it again, along with the cattle to a local man and made his way home. You can imagine how despondent he is. He likes building but farming is his passion and now he has little heart for the sawmill. Naturally I am truly sorry for him, although I must admit I write with some sense of relief. I hadn't wished to make that arduous crossing over the waters with our Charlotte still less than two. I still haven't got over the last crossing. Maybe Alister can try again later?

Do write soon and let us know of your safe delivery. I am sure you must have given birth by now. What a frustration our distance apart is when we must wait so long for such news!

Your loving sister,

Lizzie

Eliza could feel the disappointment of her husband even though he was a man of few words and had largely ceased to share his feelings with her. His attitude towards his work at the sawmill seemed to have changed. He still went early each morning and returned around five each evening, but his heart no longer seemed in the work and Eliza knew that after his recent brush with farming and owning his own plot of land, the dream had been re-ignited in his heart. She felt she could not deny him her duty as a wife as a form of comfort even though Robert was still in her thoughts even as they lay down together.

Charlotte was just under two years old when Eliza found she was expecting again. The pregnancy didn't hold as much fear for her as the last time now that Charlotte continued to thrive and seemed in good health. Her first joyous thought was to tell Robert but on consideration telling him first seemed inappropriate and so she decided to put pen to paper and write to Kitty instead.

January 6, 1856

My Dearest Kitty,

Thank you for your letter which at last contained the good news I had been waiting for! Congratulations on the birth of your Jack. Two fine bonny sons, Charles must be over the moon for joy. You are the first to share our good news too that I am expecting again. This time I don't have as many fears or anxieties about it as I did about Charlotte. She continues to thrive and do well and I see no reason why this little one should not do the same.

I continue to feel relief that we did not move a few months ago, although I suppose it may have been easier to have attempted the hazardous journey with one rather than two or more young children. Still, it may be for the best. I so love it here in Taita and I love my regular meetings with Robert, our minister and now my dear friend. I would have struggled to make another move so soon. Still, perhaps another chance will come up for Alister before too long. I hope this finds you and the family well.

Yours,

Lizzie

Eliza gave birth to a second daughter whom they named Annie, after Alister's sister. Again, Alister seemed to take an interest in the young baby and Eliza let him, thinking that it might help with the disappointment of the lost plot of land. Eliza and Robert were careful to treat each other in the casual way that a minister would treat any member of his congregation in public but even so Eliza felt the growing hostilities of the parishioners and wondered if this hadn't something to do with Mary, who might have guessed a growing attachment. Certainly, Mrs McMann would have something to do with the gossip, Eliza was sure of that. Many of the women in the church would pretend not to hear her greetings and turn their backs on her at church or if they met her in town. This was a constant source of grief and upset to Eliza who, despite her feelings for Robert, knew she had done nothing wrong in the sight of God. Even Mrs Moffat who had been so helpful in standing in for Kitty at Charlotte's christening was now giving her the cold shoulder. When she had greeted her in church in recent weeks it was all she could do to acknowledge Eliza's greeting with a reluctant, "Good morning to you, Mrs Douglas," and not the friendly "Eliza" she had called her previously.

"What is it, Mrs Moffat?" Eliza had asked her. "Why the formality when we were on first name terms until recently?"

But Mrs Moffat simply put her nose slightly up in the air and repeated the, "Good morning, Mrs Douglas" and walked off. Tears pricked Eliza eyes. She had truly liked Mrs Moffat and she was sorry to lose her friendship because of the likes of a gossip like Mrs McMann.

What was on their minds for goodness' sake? Did they really imagine that Annie was Robert's bastard? Was this the rumour that Mrs McMann was circulating?

Robert and herself had kissed only the once and their friendship had never trespassed beyond those boundaries. It was unimaginable that it could. They had thought they had been careful enough not to behave in any way to arouse suspicions. His position as a minister and man of the cloth wouldn't allow such assignations. But had they been at all indiscreet in the sharing of an odd glance or two? Perhaps it was better that they left the parish after all? Maybe Alister should try for land again in Gibbstown?

It was a while after this when rumours of the Reverend Yate and his wife Mary leaving the parish reached her ears. Eliza felt certain that these were just rumours and idle tittle tattle. But with feelings growing against her in the parish she didn't feel able to test the truth in these rumours by asking anyone. It might show too much of a personal interest on her behalf. Surely Robert himself would have told her if he and Mary had plans to leave? After all, he was a regular visitor to the little cottage and they had shared a certain amount of intimacy over the past year, telling each other everything. Why wouldn't Robert have told her first of their plans? Although it was true she had kept her distance from him a little of late. However, he soon confirmed the truth of the rumours himself with another visit to her cottage.

He cleared his throat as he watched Eliza manage to skilfully sip her tea and rock the baby on her knee. "Eliza, Lizzie, there's something I need to tell you. The rumours you might have heard circulating around the church are true, even though I swear to you I never said anything to anyone and nor did Mary, I know. I expect a certain Mrs McMann might have caught wind of something and spread the rumours," he gave a wan smile at this point but when Eliza failed to share it, he continued. "Mary and I have served this parish of Taita nearly five years now, and I have been offered a new parish to the east of here, in a town called Frampton. We leave in just a few months' time."

Eliza was devastated, so much so she couldn't trust herself not to drop the baby in her distress and she placed her cup down on the cottage floor before putting the baby slowly back in the cot. She felt betrayed by Robert. She knew Mrs McMann's reputation for sure but surely as a confidant of hers, Robert could have confirmed the truth of such rumours, which, in her complete trust of Robert, she had laughed away. In her anger, she turned her back on him tucking the baby into her cot and fussing over her.

"I know that this probably comes as a shock to you hearing it from me at this late stage and I'm sorry for that, I really am. It's just that we've only recently had it confirmed, so I couldn't let anyone know the truth of the rumours before the invitation was confirmed, even you."

He seemed to wait anxiously for Eliza to turn around and when she finally did, she vented her anger and distress at him.

"Did it not occur to you once, Robert, to share your news with me as I had shared our possible move with you? I thought we were friends, nay, more than that and that we would share all our feelings, our news with one another whatever you had to keep from the world in general. Obviously, I was wrong, I seem to have expected too much of our friendship. I'm sorry."

"Eliza," Robert stood up slowly making his way towards her holding out his hands, but she turned away again. "There was another reason I kept it from you, I didn't want to raise your hopes or those of Alister after he lost that land in Gibbstown, I know how disappointed he was at not being able to farm as he wished. But I have heard reports of the land near the Waihaha River to the east of here as being some of the best in the whole of New Zealand. Of course, the area can be accessed only by a few days' journey over the Tararua range of mountains but at least you wouldn't have to cross water this time if you came with us."

"Oh, you think it's that easy to move a baby and a toddler over such a known mountainous area as the Tararua Range? I've heard that the track over those hills is not only narrow and difficult but also dangerous," she said. "Who knows how many Maori warriors might be hiding in the hills waiting to pick on us?" and she shuddered at the thought. "Charlotte's not yet three, how can we subject her to such danger?"

"I only know I couldn't even think of moving without you. You are so much a part of my life and my thoughts that I couldn't even countenance the idea of a life without you."

"So how does that work then? You simply tell the parish of Frampton, 'I'm sorry I now find my wife and myself can't take up the offer of a living as my mistress is unable to come with me?'"

"Lizzie, it isn't like that. I want you with me, I want . . . "

Before Eliza had time to respond to Robert's impassioned speech, Charlotte woke from her afternoon nap and started crying lustily, which then awoke the baby. For once, Eliza was grateful to her children whose interruptions gave her time to consider Robert's words and behaviour.

Preoccupied as she was, Robert could see this wasn't the time to argue his case. Eliza was busy attending to the two children when he rose, taking up his hat, his passing words being, "Please tell Alister, Lizzie, I'm happy to make the first journey over the mountains with him to stake out the land ahead of our journey and hopefully, I can help him put in a bid so that you can come with us."

That night Eliza considered Robert's words as she lay in bed. She still felt so bitterly hurt by Robert and such a fool for thinking their friendship was intimate enough for him to share his plans with her. What a fool she had been. She had clearly mistaken his feelings for her, and she felt bad that as yet she hadn't told Alister of the new possibilities for him in Frampton. As she lay awake with Alister snoring beside her she knew that she owed it to him to give him the chance to fulfil his dreams. Just because she was upset with Robert, she mustn't let her personal feelings stand in the way of her husband's dreams. She resolved she would tell him the following evening on his return from work when he would have occasion to take in her words.

As she expected Alister was excited by the plan.

"This is what I have prayed for, Lizzie," he said his face at once animated. "You know how I have been struggling at the mill for some time now. The joy I once used to feel in construction has all but deserted me. I wonder if Joe has noticed because at times I have seen him looking at me long and hard, but he's not said anything. I like to make things with my hands, but farming is different, it's in my blood and getting so near to having my own plot and then having to relinquish it again was a bitter blow to me, Lizzie."

She nodded sympathetically. This was the most her husband had said about the lost plot. Mostly he had clammed up about it, like little Alister's death. It seemed his way of dealing with difficulties.

"I'm going to take up young Robert on his offer," he said. "It may be on the other side of the Tararua Range but if the land is as good as reported, surely it'll be worth it and only consider, once we have negotiated that difficult crossing through the hills we've only the Waihaha river to cross before we reach Frampton. At least if we travel with the Yates we can help one another to share the load."

Elizabeth thought of Mary and considered that she might be assisting Mary more than receiving any help from her.

Alister continued his positive view of the journey. "Even though Robert knows little or nothing about farming, just to have another there for a second opinion might be helpful. I won't need to place anyone else in charge of my land this time either. Robert and I will make an initial visit to stake out the available land then I can go in person, purchase and run it myself. And just think, Lizzie, if the Reverend Yate and his wife go with us, at least we'll know the local vicar on arrival which doesn't happen very often." And he chuckled at the thought.

Eliza smiled with him, but her heart felt empty. *Did she even want to have Robert and Mary's company over the next few years,* she asked herself. *Oh, yes, Robert was helping her husband to fulfil his dreams but what about hers?* All she asked for was someone who she could trust implicitly with her secrets as they would with her, but it seemed this was not to be.

She wrote to Kitty of the proposed move but didn't feel she could be entirely honest, even with her about what had ensued between her and Robert.

February 16, 1857

My Dearest Kitty,

Although Robert and I have become firm friends and I had imagined we had no secrets between us, it seems that he has kept much from me. I had dismissed the rumours of the Yates moving to the small town of Frampton, to the east of here, as idle tittle tattle convinced that if it was true Robert would have told me himself. He was here just yesterday and yes, he did tell me himself then that it was true, but only when it seemed that everyone else in the parish knew first. He explained his keeping it from me was just a formality until it had been confirmed by the inviting parish, but this was hardly a valid explanation to me. He could have let me know of the possibility of the move surely, or didn't he trust me to keep a secret? This is how I feel. Then he expects me to be understanding towards him.

What is more, he wants Alister and me to accompany them saying that he will help Alister to look out good land there. I know this is what Alister wants too; indeed, he is excited by the prospect, especially after his last hopes were so cruelly dashed, so I suppose we must go. It will be a hazardous journey for us all, but at least I suppose this new parish of Frampton isn't quite such a long journey for us all as crossing between the islands, but it still necessitates crossing the treacherous Tararua range of mountains which doesn't make me feel easy either for my youngsters or myself.

Your loving sister,

Lizzie

Robert made several more afternoon visits to her after Alister had met with him to enthusiastically endorse his plans, trying to persuade her of his devotion to them as a couple and especially of his care for her, again declaring that the secret of their move wasn't his to share. Eliza, however, maintained a distant front to him.

Alister was able, with Robert's help, to put a bid in for 50 acres of land just outside of Frampton but hoped to purchase more on arrival.

In early April, just before they were to set off on their journey, Robert preached one of his last sermons at the Knox Chapel and one that had Eliza sitting up in her seat.

"I'm going to talk to you all today about forgiveness," Robert began. "We've probably all been in the position of hurting the ones we are closest to by angry words or simply by acting unwisely and misjudging a situation. I am guilty of this. I fear I may never regain the trust of one of my dearest friends because of a misjudgment and there is no one sorrier than I am at this prospect." Eliza noticed a muscle twitching in his cheek as he struggled to control his emotions, her own heart was beating quickly too as she tried to keep a lid on hers.

"My heart feels bruised and broken to think I could have hurt such a dear friend. But friends all we can do is pray for forgiveness and pray that maybe in time the one we have hurt might be able to forgive us too."

As he reached the end of his sermon, Robert seemed quite overcome and the church warden, Bill Moffat, had to step in and announce the next hymn. Eliza also struggled to sing, her attention caught by Robert, who had seemed close to tears at the end of his sermon. *Could it be that his words had been directed towards herself?* She felt almost sure of it. She had refused to listen to his arguments in private and so he had taken the huge risk of publicly asking for her forgiveness from the pulpit. It was not a risk he had taken lightly, some of the gossips might have guessed that the words were meant for her especially as he had glanced her way on more than a few occasions. Or maybe her fast beating heart and flushed cheeks had betrayed her? Supposing Mary or Alister suspected? She dare not look to the faces of the other folk either but kept her head bowed down low in the pew.

Robert had called her "a dear friend." Was he truly sorry for not confiding in her sooner and sharing his plans for the move?

Alister's face seemed to betray no understanding of anything personally meant though. Instead he clasped Eliza's hand under his as they left the church. She had hoped to have a word with Robert at the door but Alister marched her off, clearly having something on his mind.

As soon as they were alone he said, "Eliza, Lizzie that talk moved me greatly. I feel I need to ask your forgiveness. I know I've been difficult to live with over the last few months since the land in Gibbstown fell through. I don't find it easy to express myself at times like these. I know I should share my feelings with you and not block you out, so I am truly sorry. It is good that we live in peace with one another."

Eliza noticed that his forgiveness stretched far enough to ask for her understanding concerning his inability to share but not far enough to forgive his hard attitude towards her rape. But even acknowledging that, Eliza felt lighter of heart than she had done for many weeks. At least Alister had acknowledged that he should share more with her and she felt able to squeeze his arm affectionately as they walked. He was a good man, which she was sure was much more than she deserved.

That afternoon, when the children were both asleep they made love with lighter hearts and more genuine affection than they had for some time.

She wrote again to Kitty the very next day.

April 3, 1857

My Dearest Kitty,

I have forgiven Robert. Because I hadn't been able to forgive him in private although he had begged me on several occasions, he took the enormous risk yesterday of publicly asking for my forgiveness. Yes, he preached a sermon on forgiveness saying that he wanted the forgiveness of a dear friend who had misunderstood him. I was all a flutter while he spoke. As he glanced at me once or twice I was quite sure that he was speaking to me and I felt that everyone's eyes would be upon me, especially those of Mary and Alister.

Of course, I was keen to speak with him at the end of the service to find out his meaning, but it was not to be. Alister marched us off home in great haste making a big speech about how difficult he can be to live with, so reticent with his own feelings that the talk had spurred him on to ask for my forgiveness. Isn't life strange? So, it seems we are to move to Frampton with the Yates after all.

Kiss your dear boys from me.

Yours,

Lizzie

Chapter Eight

FRAMPTON

IT WAS BUT A FEW weeks later that the two couples and the children were ready to tackle the treacherous pass before the onset of winter. Eliza would have preferred more time to pack, but it was already late autumn and it wasn't wise to cross the difficult pass in the winter months especially with young children and so there was little choice. She had hastily dug up a few precious cuttings from the herbs they had cultivated to bring along with them. They had been invaluable over the last few years as simple remedies for them all and it would take a while to grow mature plants once again. The most important thing for them all was to try and remain cheerful and determined for the long, laborious journey ahead of them. Eliza was at least relieved that she was leaving behind the clacking, gossiping tongues, as she imagined Robert was.

Although they had all heard tales about how treacherous the trek could be, nothing could quite prepare them for the narrow, rutted pathway that twisted its way upwards towards the summit and at times seemed an indeterminate step away. The horse Alister had purchased recently, following the death of the other, was younger and stronger than the last, but even he struggled at times to negotiate the steep track with a full cart load of possessions.

Charlotte and Annie were remarkably patient with the proceedings, even though their progress was slow. Eliza carried Annie in her arms for a portion of the time while Charlotte occupied a small seat beside her father on the front of the cart. But after a time, Elizabeth found the weight of the toddler overwhelming, and Robert, quick to notice, immediately said, "Eliza, you're fair flagging there. You look done in, let Mary have the child for a bit while you climb up beside Alister and young Charlotte."

Gratefully Eliza handed over little Annie to Mary who reluctantly took the small bundle from her. Eliza could almost sense the fearfulness in her eyes. Her own eyes met those of Robert briefly in the exchange. Then Alister lifted Eliza up on to the front of the cart beside him and Charlotte.

Mary had been riding alongside Robert the entire journey, not having the strength to negotiate the steep track at all. She looked done in as well although she had hardly ventured a step.

In the gathering gloom, spying a small shack just ahead of them, Eliza quickly realised how tired she must be from the relief she felt at seeing it.

"Isn't that a small shack up ahead?" she asked.

Alister could just make out the shape of a small dwelling. They could see that it was none too large but would suffice if there was just enough room for the women and children to take shelter rather than sleeping out in the bush where they would be bothered by the hundreds of mosquitoes beginning to make their presence felt in the early evening light. The two men went on ahead to seek out the house owner. It wasn't very long before they returned with grim faces.

"Miserable old skinflint," said Alister with feeling. "I explained to him that we have travelled a fair way over the treacherous Tararua mountains with one invalid woman and another expectant mother with two young children needing shelter, but he was having none of it. 'I've not been in the habit of taking in lodgers afore and I'm not going to start now,' says he and without letting us entreat him any further he shut the door in our faces, saying he had work to do and that his stock wouldn't feed themselves while he stopped to chat."

"Never mind, dear," said Eliza trying to be optimistic despite her heart sinking within her. She touched Alister's arm sympathetically, saying, "We're all pretty used to roughing it by now. I dare say we will manage once again."

"Well we can't go on now anyway," Alister argued, "mosquitoes or no mosquitoes. If we continue the light will only grow dimmer which can be a potential hazard with such unfamiliar country and a river to cross before us. I suspect we're all too tired to go any further."

Eliza nodded as she heard Robert agree with Alister. And as she glanced across at Mary's pale demeanour she realised that she wouldn't be able to stand much more of being thrown around in the cart especially in the dark.

Eliza managed to get a good fire going with a couple of stones and some plentiful wood from the nearby bush while the men unpacked the two tents at the top of each of the carts and managed to erect them. Eliza then tried to prepare a simple meal for them all of fresh bread that she had baked just before their departure, along with cheese and eggs from their faithful hens. This took her longer than she would have liked in the difficult conditions, especially as she had to go into one of the tents to feed Annie as soon as it was erected. As she fed the hungry baby, she felt nervous as she listened to the strange sounds of the unfamiliar bird calls and detected a rustling in the native bushes all around them. *Could it be Maori warriors moving in to find out their business?* She shivered with apprehension.

At last, after the simple meal had been cooked on the fire and eaten, Eliza's heart began to grow steadier with her full stomach and the comfort of the man she loved by her side. She knew there was little opportunity for Robert and their shared friendship with Alister and Mary looking on, but took comfort in the few shared glances they were able to pass between them.

Despite her worries about strange noises, Eliza found, as soon as she had settled the children, her exhaustion from the full day of packing and travelling caused her to fall asleep almost immediately. She awoke as soon as it grew light to a strange bell-like sound. Half-awake she dreamt she was on the boat again and it was the ship's bell portending some storm or disaster and she cried out, "mercy, we'll all be drowned in our beds."

"Wake up, Lizzie," said Alister shaking her gently and placing a warming cup of tea into her hands. "I think you must have been dreaming. We're on a mountain top and the Waihaha River lies well below us, there's no water here."

"But I'm sure I heard a bell, Alister." Alister chuckled.

"I think you heard the native bell bird of the bush, Lizzie. He likes to make his presence felt in the early morning. A type of New Zealand cockerel I suppose you could call him. There are other calls too. I haven't learnt the names of all these birds yet but if you listen carefully I think you might hear the sound of a Parakeet and the mischievous Kea bird."

Eliza smiled. How unfamiliar this place still seemed to her. None of the familiar song birds she was used to at home like the robins, blackbirds and tits. These birds were as different as the land they now inhabited.

Alister interrupted her thoughts. "Even though it's early we'll need to be on the road soon if we're going to reach Frampton before nightfall. Don't forget, Lizzie, we still have a river to cross."

Eliza nodded. She was only too aware of the crossing that still lay ahead of them. She knew that Mary and her own youngsters would struggle to spend another night in the bush, never mind the rest of them. Finishing her cup of tea, she stumbled sleepily out of the tent and made her way carefully into the bush for the necessary and then down to the river for a quick wash. After making her rudimentary toilet, Eliza was on her way back to their tent when she spotted another bird pecking up grubs just outside Robert and Mary's tent. She laughed as she watched his precise little movements. The bird lifted his head curiously at the sound of her laughter and regarded her carefully for a moment before carrying on with his task. He seemed to have little fear of her presence. Robert, hearing her laughter, came out of his tent to see what was happening. Even his closeness to the bird didn't seem to worry it unduly.

"He's a brave little bird that Huia," Robert observed.

"Aye, that he is," agreed Eliza. "He looks a little like a blackbird but bigger and more spectacular with that striking flash of orange on his head and those pretty white tail feathers. What a funny long hooked beak he has too."

"She has," corrected Robert. "I believe it's only the female of the species that have the hooked beak—probably because they do most of the hunting for food."

"Always mindful of their young, a little like us women I suppose," mused Eliza reminded of the tasks awaiting her. "I should be preparing our breakfast rather than chatting to you, but I must say, watching the little Huia bird makes me wish I were as brave as her."

"Maybe you are, Lizzie and you just don't realise it," said Robert with feeling.

Eliza unsure as to his meaning, didn't like to ask, not sure whether his statement alluded to her rape, or his feelings for her. As she pondered these thoughts, Mary emerged from the tent and acknowledged Eliza with a brusque nod of her head.

"Good morning Mary," Eliza said hurriedly, feeling like a naughty child caught for some misdemeanour. "I was just leaving. A little Huia bird outside your tent distracted me for a moment, but I can't stand here talking when there's work to be done and children to be fed. I'll see you at breakfast," and she dashed away blushing, hoping that Mary hadn't heard her talking to Robert or misunderstood it if she had.

The poor hens had suffered a battered journey in their coop but nevertheless, still managed to produce a few more eggs for their breakfasts, almost against the odds and along with the last of the bread, the four of them and the children were able to enjoy a warm breakfast cooked over the fire that Alister had re-lit and fuelled first thing. The food was very welcome, giving them strength for the tough journey ahead.

Following a few more miles of rough travelling, the families reached the Waihaha River. Despite observing its fast-flowing current which gave it the name of the noisy river, the two men managed to push first one and then the other loaded cart across the shallowest part of the river. Mary and Eliza carrying baby Annie, were to follow, on a simple punt fashioned from a few logs Alister had bound roughly together. Charlotte had been able to stay on the cart, thankfully.

"You really expect me to cross on that construction with my poorly leg?" Mary asked Eliza tersely.

"I'm sorry, Mary," said Eliza patiently, "but we must all play our part. There is no way that the cart could bear any more weight than that of one young child and our meagre possessions. We're all tired."

"But not all of you suffer like me," Mary complained. Eliza, although sorry for Mary's condition felt a little exasperated with her. She had been able to travel in relative comfort until now and even though she was an invalid, at least she had only her own needs to consider. Eliza was exhausted both from having to care for the two youngsters with her and from the weight of a new baby inside her, which chose to make its presence felt from time to time.

It was growing dark again as they made out the simple wooden sign in the dusk welcoming them into the small township of Frampton. The small town seemed to boast just one very small inn, a couple of churches, a basic store which Eliza assumed to be like the one in Karori, selling anything and everything, and a few scattered houses. Fortunately, the inn had a couple of rooms to spare, which they were very grateful to find after their night in the open. Then after a simple meal and a drink, they all fell into their beds.

Robert and Mary were to live in the Manse beside the small wooden church they had caught a glimpse of the previous evening. The Manse wasn't very large, just one main room and a bedroom but Robert insisted that it was to be Eliza and Alister's home also whilst Alister constructed a new home for Eliza and the children.

"I'll not see you, Eliza and the children living in some inn here whilst we have accommodation to offer," Robert said.

Eliza felt uncomfortable as she considered the inevitable arrangement and she noticed that Robert's offer wasn't endorsed by Mary, which made it seem even more awkward. Although she did feel some sympathy for Mary with her need for rest and quiet, she wished in her heart that Mary had at least supported Robert in his offer. After all, what alternative did she, Alister and their family have? They couldn't afford to stay at the inn until Alister had built them a home and there was nowhere else for them to go. The Manse was certainly a very small space to be shared by so many and Eliza hoped and prayed that they would not have to impose on the Yate's hospitality for too long.

The living arrangement with the Yates' was to be like that Eliza had experienced with the Reids, one sleeping area divided in two by a simple calico curtain. Eliza's heart sank as she saw the close proximity of their bed to that of Robert and Mary's. He was becoming her life even though Robert was a man of the cloth and married to Mary and she wasn't free herself. Yet she knew she had no right to make any emotional demands of Robert. His reputation would be damaged forever and having seen how the gossips had behaved in Taita, it seemed unwise to repeat their folly in this new place. Yet, sometimes at night, unable to sleep because of his closeness, she longed for him with every bone and sinew in her body. Longed for his touch, for his lips to capture hers, to make love to him. She blushed at the very realisation of her passion. It was impossible. Far better not to entertain such thoughts at all. She must pray harder to take each thought captive to Christ as the Bible instructed. "God help me," she mouthed. Would her faith be strong enough to keep her from her wandering thoughts? Suddenly the words of the Lord's Prayer had never seemed more relevant or poignant—"Lead us not into temptation and deliver us from evil." *God help me. God help us all,* she said to herself. Robert looked a little pale too and she wondered if he might be having similar thoughts and then she chided herself for her stupidity, in her large, pregnant state he was probably unlikely to accommodate such notions.

It was obvious that Mary was struggling with their living arrangements from very early on. "Can't you stop those children making so much noise?" she asked after just a day. "Their noise hurts my poor head. It is rather delicate you know. I'm used to resting especially in the middle of the day. I rely upon it. Children should be seen and not heard anyway. That's what I was always taught."

"I'm sorry," said Eliza trying to be patient, "I will try to keep them quiet but they're only babies and the living arrangements for us all are rather cramped. We do hope to be able to leave you in peace as soon as we can." She felt a little peeved by Mary's reaction. *What did she expect of such young children? The sooner Alister could finish their new home the better.*

"Well I hope you'll not be here for too long," said Mary, making her own feelings about their living arrangements very clear.

Alister was keen to make further land purchases now that they had arrived and bought another 104 acres just outside the small town to add to the acreage he had already secured on his recent trip with Robert. Using his carpentry skills, he set about building a house for himself and Eliza on the new land as both he and Eliza weren't keen to impose upon the hospitality of the Yates for any longer than was necessary, especially with Mary's continual complaints which were wearing them both down. Not having much opportunity to speak to Robert, who was busy establishing himself at St Andrew's, or to speak to Alister, who was building all day and half the night, Eliza had never felt so alone. She longed for someone to pour out her loneliness and frustrations to and turned at once to write to her beloved sister.

May 30, 1857

Dearest Kitty,

We survived the crossing over the Tararua Mountains and the Waihaha River and believe me, the mountain range was every bit as treacherous as the reports suggested. Not only is the track steep rutted and dropping away in parts to absolutely nothing, but we also feared the sudden onslaught of Maori warriors all the time. At least I did, although the Maoris here are reputed to be the friendliest of the two islands. We shall see. After all, I suppose we are taking their land so why should they be friendly to us?

At the moment, we are having to share with Robert and Mary at the Manse while Alister builds us a new house. This isn't easy. Mary is always complaining that the children make too much noise for her delicate head and then there is the problem of sharing the bedroom area with just a thin calico curtain to separate us from them, which isn't easy in my pregnant state. Washing is likewise difficult, a strip wash being just about possible for me and I certainly do not intend to take advantage of the metal bath tub we have brought with us, not while we continue to live here with Robert and Mary. Of course, many of our possessions have had to stay stored on the cart we came on, for there is no room for both the Yates' furniture and ours in such a small space. We have only been able to put our hens out the back of the Manse where they must remain in their coop. Hopefully Alister will have finished our house soon. He is such a skilful builder and has employed some local help, so that I have every faith in him.

Congratulations on your new little daughter, Emily. I am sure that Charles will dote on his first daughter. Alister certainly does take more interest in the girls than he ever did with my poor, dear baby Alister, may God rest his soul.

Your loving sister,

Eliza

Alister had purchased a few sheets of strong corrugated iron for the roof and sides of the building along with some local wood. He set himself tirelessly to the task of building day and night with the help of a few of the local builders and some Maoris. The locals also advised him to fit the window frames with sheets of perforated zinc to keep out the mosquitoes. He guessed there were so many here due to all the surrounding bush, which was still thick and swampy in places. Finally, the house was ready to move into after three months of hard work, which was very timely with winter now upon them.

As with the previous house, Eliza was impressed by Alister's skilled workmanship and although it was a little way from the town and slightly isolated, at least it meant that they would have their own house at last and not have to share with the Yates. Having Robert so near had been a torment to her. Although she had tried to convince herself that thoughts of him were pure foolishness, she was surprised at how often those thoughts had turned to him and his closeness hadn't helped. Being heavily pregnant hadn't helped with her sleep patterns either and the extra space that the new house afforded was especially welcome to her. It was a comfort too to finally have their own possessions around them and temptations kept at bay. There was a sense though in which she missed Robert's nearness and she was ashamed to admit to herself that seeing him every day had certainly intensified her own desires.

Soon after they moved into the new house which they duly named the "New Place" in order to distinguish it from their first home together, Eliza was delivered of another daughter whom they named Margaret after Eliza's oldest sister.

Alister set about acquiring another strong horse from the local Maoris and some basic machinery and began to cultivate and prepare the soil for planting crops. Eliza managed to clear enough land around their new cottage to plant out her cuttings, still in their pots until now.

"Alister, do you not think it would be prudent to invest in some good dairy cows for the land is a trifle hilly for cultivating?" she asked. "Although it's hilly it appears to be good, rich grazing land and should produce a good milk yield." She saw the hesitation written clearly on her husband's face and knew that too many early mornings milking as a young lad had taken their toll on Alister. He had often told her that he was happy raising beef cattle but not dairying.

"Aye, I suppose it would, but who would look after them? It would mean employing a good cowman and I'm not sure we could afford that at the moment. I certainly don't want to get involved myself, if I can help it."

"Well, we might need to get a cowman at first," she acceded, "but I could help a bit too, especially as Margaret gets bigger and Charlotte and Annie need me a little less."

Alister nodded. She could see that he agreed it would make sense to buy in some dairy cattle. Hopefully they might have just enough to stretch to a man's wages.

"It will mean me negotiating the mountain pass again to visit the local cattle market in Wellington," Alister explained. "I'm afraid it will probably mean that I'll be gone for a few days."

"Well," she said, thinking out loud, "it would be a timely trip. Charlotte has all but grown out of her clothes and although Annie and Margaret can make do with hand-me-downs for the most part, some of these are getting more than a little threadbare by the time they reach Margaret."

Alister nodded again. "Aye, that's true. I know that you do your best to keep our clothes stitched up, getting as much life from them as you can, but there is a limit. Some of your own dresses are beginning to look a little worn too and we must keep up appearances here. You could do with a new dress or two."

Eliza noticed that Alister's statement about her need for new dresses wasn't so much because he wanted her to have some, but more because he felt they should keep up appearances with the locals. She felt suddenly self-conscious. *Were her clothes really looking that worn and patched up? Alister wasn't particularly observant but if he had noticed others must have noticed too. Robert must have noticed.* Then she chided herself. *Why was she so concerned about what Robert thought?* She longed for some new clothes for herself, never mind others, but to go and choose her own frocks wasn't practical. She couldn't haul three young-sters through that dangerous pass again. It was bad enough with just two and Annie was older that last time than Margaret was now. It was out of the question.

"Just chose me some suitable material for a couple of dresses," she said, "and some woollen material for undergarments too." She blushed, she still wasn't used to talking about such matters with her husband when they shared so little intimacy, but she knew she would need a new corset before long and the woollen material would be warm and serviceable.

"I'll do my best," said Alister tersely, noticing his wife blush.

Eliza nodded her assent and swallowed her disappointment, certain that Alister's choice of materials probably wouldn't be hers.

"I'll take a couple of good Maori men with me. They are sure footed on the paths and know the best routes. Then I'll get Robert to look in on you whilst I'm away, like before."

"I'm sure there'll be clothes and provisions that he and Mary will need too," said Eliza, trying to keep her mind from the thought of Robert's visits.

"Yes, I was minded that I should ask them before setting off," he said as if he'd thought of that all along, but Eliza felt it was she alone who had placed the idea in his mind. "I'll go tomorrow."

Alister was gone for nearly a week and although Robert did drop in to see her every day, Eliza felt more nervous at Alister's absence than she had been in Taita. There were rumours circulating that the local Maoris were growing restless incited by the other more aggressive tribes. In different parts of New Zealand, especially further north, the Maoris had killed the white pakehas, as they called the new settlers, and the folk in Frampton and its surrounding areas were worried that their local Maoris might follow suit.

Alister returned with half a dozen good milking heifers and hired one of the local Maoris, Anaru, who had accompanied him on the journey and seemed, by all accounts, to have a good eye for cattle. Eliza began to help a little with the afternoon milking. Annie and Margaret had their afternoon sleep around this time and little Charlotte, who was now walking quite steadily, was happy to accompany her mother and try to get involved. Although she was somewhat of a hindrance to Eliza, Eliza was pleased by how enthusiastic the youngster seemed. *Maybe she would be milking herself in a few years' time?*

Margaret continued to thrive until she began to teethe. With the advent of teething she caught a nasty cold that went to her chest. Eliza began to relive those fearful days with baby Alister as she nursed the baby day and night. After dosing the baby with Heartsease to relieve the symptoms, which seemed to have little effect, as with baby Alister, the local doctor was called. He agreed that it was surprising for a baby to take so badly to teething, but fully expected her to pull through.

"After all," he reasoned, "you've seen your other two daughters through teething happily enough haven't you, Mrs Douglas?"

Eliza agreed but looking at the hot, flushed face of little Margaret, the image of baby Alister kept coming back into her mind. Alister had said that every couple could expect to lose one child but two? Eliza couldn't face going through that again and she became pale, weak and fretful, losing her appetite and being unable to concentrate on much else.

"Lizzie, Charlotte and Annie still need you too," Alister reminded Eliza with some irritation when he saw her sitting over Margaret's cot when he awoke and when he went to bed. "All this sitting up day and night you'll be too tired to see to their needs and anyway, the doctor said she would make it through teething the same as Charlotte and Annie."

Eliza remembered the doctor's words more clearly than Alister appeared to, only suggesting that Margaret would pull through and having a more resigned view of things she said, "But Alister, supposing Margaret should die. I had thought that now we'd got her to nearly a year we could breathe easier, but it seems not."

A few days later, even Alister could see Margaret's condition wasn't improving and the doctor was called once more. This time he prescribed a little laudanum to keep her temperature down, which had kept consistently high and suggested giving her cool baths and trying to gently tap her chest to remove the stubborn mucus. But all was to no avail. One night when Eliza was sitting by the cot and had fallen asleep from sheer exhaustion, Margaret seemed abnormally quiet when she awoke. They had all grown so used to her crackly breathing of late that it took Eliza a moment or two before she realised what was wrong. Stooping over the baby she lifted her out of the cot. Her body was already stiff and cold. She must have died while they all slept.

Eliza beside herself with grief woke Alister. "Alister, Alister," she cried softly for fear of waking the other children as she shook him awake.

"Wwwhat . . ."

"Margaret has died whilst we were all asleep. She must have died alone. I'll never forgive myself."

"There's no need to be dramatic, Lizzie," said Alister tersely. "Perhaps you're wrong and she is on the road to recovery in her stillness." But as he took the small body from his wife's arms he too recognised the signs of death. "You are right. The Lord giveth and the Lord taketh away. We must be grateful for the time He saw fit to loan her to us," he said as he placed the stiff little body back into the cot. "We've done all we can for her. Whether you slept or were awake, I fancy that Margaret wouldn't have known. She's been far too ill of late to know any of us."

Eliza knew this, but her husband's stern factual assessment wasn't what she needed to hear at that moment. She felt guilty, as if she alone were responsible for Margaret's death.

"God was with her," repeated Alister. "I don't think she wouldn't have suffered much at the end." Eliza recognised that this was Alister's way of trying to comfort her. "Sit down and I'll make you a cup of tea."

Eliza watched as Alister stoked up the fire again. They hadn't let it go out in the weeks that Margaret had been ill, but it had died down now. Alister was kind in making her a cup of tea but that wasn't what she wanted. A hand of comfort would have sustained her more. At least he was less full of hypotheses about infant death this time and she was grateful at least for that. There was no need for them to call the doctor until the morning. They had logged her approximate hour of death and there would probably have to be a post mortem as with little Alister. As Eliza looked over at her two other children still asleep, she thanked God for them and prayed that they would be spared their lives.

They told Charlotte and Annie the next day but unlike their parents, they seemed largely unaffected by the little drama that had unfolded in their midst. In the way of youngsters, full of life and energy, they quickly moved on to the next thing to take their attention.

Eliza had decided that Margaret should be buried within sight of the house so that she would always be with them.

"I can't bear the thought of her lying in some churchyard miles from us all like little Alister whom we left in Taita," Eliza said in a fresh burst of tears. "This is our home now, where we all live, and I want Margaret to be among us, watching us, looking on day by day."

"That seems a little irregular, Eliza. Surely she should be buried at the church?"

"No, I want her here, as I said. She should be a part of us, of the farm."

Alister shook his head. It seemed he thought her ridiculous and dramatic, but he didn't seem to understand how she was feeling. She had lost a son and now a daughter. Of course, she knew that was normal to lose children in infancy, especially here, but it didn't make it any easier. At least Alister conceded to dig the hole as Robert carried out the christening followed by the burial. Eliza hardly dared look at Robert as she knew her heart would break if she caught a look of shared sympathy and understanding from him, when Alister seemed so remote and distant. There was little opportunity for much more to pass between them anyway, as Mary had accompanied her husband in order to help make the simple tea for those folks who had come to support the young couple in laying their child to rest.

As Robert said the familiar words "ashes to ashes, dust to dust," a tear slowly made its way down Alister's cheek. Almost afraid at being seen as less than a man, he brushed it away quickly, but Eliza who had seen this first visible sign of grief respected her husband just a little more at that moment.

Chapter Nine

AT ONCE, ELIZA SET ABOUT writing to Kitty.

January 10, 1858

My Dearest Kitty,

What I dreaded has happened. We have lost a second child. Dearest Margaret breathed her last just a few days ago and was buried yesterday. Even Alister now thinks we have had more than our fair share of grief and he no longer speaks of figures and expectations of bereavement. Poor Margaret, it still makes me weep to think that she died alone. If only I hadn't been so tired, if only I could have stayed awake to see out her last few precious hours on this earth, but I am probably being foolish. At the end, she hardly knew any of us and was so delirious with the fever that she wouldn't have known whether I sat with her or not. Alister believes, as I do, that God Himself was with her and carried her gently up into His arms. He has her company now in heaven but we on earth feel bereft.

Robert came and took the little service and a few of our new neighbours came to support us. Even Mary came and helped me out with a few refreshments.

My only comfort is that Margaret is buried just near the house, so near to us it is almost as if she were still with us, at least I console myself with this. Poor little Alister is miles away in a lonely graveyard in Taita. At least the same fate will not now be Margaret's. I know I'm talking like a mad woman, as in truth Margaret's soul is no longer with us, but I know that you will humour your poor dear sister at this sad time. Even Alister shed a surreptitious tear at the funeral when he thought no one was looking. Poor Alister, this has been hard on him too, on all of us. The girls don't quite understand, although in their own way I know they miss Margaret too.

I must stop here though. I don't want to make you feel too depressed. I only hope things are somewhat better and more cheerful at home. Please write and let me have all your news and I know I will be comforted.

Your,

Grieving Lizzie

Although still grieving for Margaret, the Douglas family had much reason to be grateful to God that they had chosen to farm in Frampton and not in Gibbstown on the South Island. Reports began to circulate in early 1859 of the entire town having been razed to the ground.

"I now thank God for sending that Maori to sell Alister's seed," wrote Eliza to her sister, "for if we had moved there, none of us might have survived, nevermind just Margaret."

Life settled down to a normal rhythm as once more Eliza found herself with child. In the spring of 1860 another daughter was born to them and they named her Isabella after Alister's oldest sister.

Eliza tried not to worry that Isabella (affectionately known by the family as "Belle") seemed slightly smaller and less robust as a baby than either Charlotte or Annie, but they soon discovered that Belle possessed a wiry and determined streak despite her size. This encouraged Eliza to believe that the child might thrive after all.

There may have been no problems with Belle but there were plenty of problems on the farm. In the summer after Belle's birth, the Maori worker, Anaru, who had been such a help with the dairy cattle, decided to leave, having secured a better offer on another farm with more dairy cattle. Alister, who had supplemented their income with a bit of contract work on other farms up until this point, was then forced to come home and get involved in looking after his own dairy cattle which had now increased to a dozen in number. Eliza found herself unable to offer much assistance either, with two youngsters and a new baby to look after.

"Why don't you write to your brother Alexander in Scotland," she suggested. "New Zealand is still seen by many as the land of opportunity, and I'm sure if you were able to offer a fare out here or perhaps even a part fare, you would have men queuing up to come."

"Aye, that's not a bad idea, lassie," said Alister. "It may not be an immediate solution to our problem but may prove a more secure and lasting one in the long run. These Maori workers are for the most part a restless breed, they soon tire of one opportunity and look to moving on to another, though we've been more fortunate than most in Anaru, who's been with us for a good few years. I doubt we'll replace him quickly and certainly not for a similar length of time."

Alister wrote immediately to his brother, Alexander, desiring a dairyman for himself and a foreman for his neighbour and the reply came back within weeks. Eliza smiled as she read the letter along with Alister. It was clear from the letter that Alexander hadn't had the same educational advantages as herself or Kitty.

October 16, 1860

Dear Alister,

I have lost as little time as I could in fulfilling your contrack for the men you wish out. I have got two engaged and half of ther passage money which you sent to me paid. They are to sail from London to Wellington direck on 28 November, the name of the vessel is the Weymouth. The one designed for your dairy cattle is well schooled in dairying and very quiet and willing to oblige. The one for your neighbour, George Smythe, he has been a forman to Mrs Cosine, whom you may remember. I understood from your letter that you was to give each of them £40 in the year and pay there passage money also and give them £5 of a present if they give satisfaction so I have engaged them on these terms.

Hoping this finds you, Eliza and the bairns in good health.

Alexander

The two men did indeed arrive in the March of the following year, but only after the vessel they had travelled in, *The Weymouth*, had suffered considerable damage from the furious gales around the Cape of Good Hope. Like Eliza, the two men vowed they would never travel anywhere by boat again. At least Eliza felt, Albert Tinsley, the new dairyman, would be more likely to stay with them in the long term than Anaru. Eliza was also in a position herself to go back to helping with the afternoon milking, although she felt more than a little encumbered now with two inquisitive toddlers following her around anxious to help. At least little Belle was still taking her afternoon nap. Alister continued once again to do long hours contracting on the surrounding farms to make some extra money for the family. Eliza didn't mind too much as Robert would often find some excuse or other to drop by most days to see them, often towards the end of the afternoon's milking. Eliza looked forward to those visits more than she let herself believe. She often walked across the yard with her two youngsters to see Robert standing there waiting for her at the door to the house. Sometimes, if he heard Belle awaken, he'd carry her out in his arms, nursing her so tenderly that Eliza's heart melted. Her heart always fluttered at the sight of him and his curls blowing gently in the breeze with or without the baby. Although his visits were the highlight of her day, she still found the excuses he made for them mildly amusing.

"I've the church newsletters to distribute and I thought you'd like yours before Sunday." Or, "I thought it was my duty to tell you the news about George Smythe," or "did you not hear the news about this or that person," even, "I was just riding past, so I thought I should call in and see how you were doing." Eliza hardly dared say that it had only been a day or so since his last visit and nothing much had changed in the interim. But he would declare he was concerned for her wellbeing as a nursing mother and being newly pregnant again, especially with her continuing to help in the milking parlour.

Unfortunately, it seemed some of the parishioners at St Andrews in Frampton had noticed the Reverend Yate's preference for visiting Mrs Douglas and Eliza began to face the same hostilities as at Knox Chapel.

"I don't know why the Reverend Yate seems to see the need to deliver the church newsletter in person to you, Mrs Douglas," said a certain Mrs Jones to her one day at church. "The rest of us seem to have to make do with collecting ours at church on a Sunday."

"Well, we are a little out of town, perhaps that's what he was thinking," Eliza said, although her excuse sounded pathetic even to her with many of the other residents' properties being slightly out of the town too.

His regular visits did look rather suspicious Eliza realised, more than the usual care of a Reverend for one of his flock. She couldn't blame the folk for their suspicions. She knew she was wrong in encouraging the regular visits, but she looked forward to them as much as Robert did. But it certainly wasn't helping Robert's reputation in the new parish.

Eliza was delivered of a fourth baby girl in May 1861. They called her Jean after Eliza's sister. Eliza continued to feel sad that no son had been forthcoming since the death of little Alister and she considered herself entirely responsible. When she raised the subject of their lack of a son with Alister, however, he simply said "We must be grateful, Lizzie, that you're just safely delivered in this rough climate," but she felt in her heart he was disappointed. Perhaps God was punishing her that her only son had been a bastard and for not loving her husband as she should. At least she mused she wasn't barren as she certainly deserved to be.

God, she prayed. *Please don't punish Alister by not giving him a son. Baby Alister's parentage was none of his doing and it's not Alister's fault either that I can't love him. All these things are my fault. Surely as he doesn't have my love he warrants the love of a son?* This was the prayer frequently on her lips and in her heart. Then just nine months later, early in 1862, God seemed to hear her prayer and delivered her safely of another son. They named him Russell, not because it was a family name this time but simply because it was a name that Alister liked and Eliza in her guilt was keen to humour him.

"Perhaps he'll be able to take over the farm from you one day, Alister?" Eliza said. "He might even like dairying better than you, dear."

"Aye, that he might, I pray God." Then on a more serious note he said, "If not, I don't know what will become of the farm after I'm gone."

"Let's not dwell on such gloomy thoughts, Alister," said Eliza quickly. "I've suffered enough deaths since our coming here that I don't wish to dwell on the subject further," and she shivered as she remembered little Alister and Margaret.

The summer of 1862 threw up fresh problems in Frampton which caused Eliza to fear for the lives of her four daughters and their only precious son.

Governor Grant, the chief land purchase commissioner, had bribed the individual Maori chiefs to sell their lands to the Crown on behalf of their tribes, promising them peace, prosperity and a decent price. When it was clear that these things weren't going to materialise, some of the tribes had refused the sale of their lands, blaming the cheating Pakehas for the reason.

Even though she was afraid, especially for her children and their farm, Eliza couldn't help but feel that the dissatisfied Maori tribes were right to feel so angry with the cheating Governor Grant.

"Perhaps we should cut our losses and leave this place, head back to the Hutt Valley," said Eliza thoughtfully to Alister. "I was down at the local store today and heard that Tawhao is going to send for the warlike tribe of the Haus-Haus to help him and the Muapoko tribe in their fight against us and you know the rumours we have heard about the ruthlessness of the Haus-Haus, killing and abusing people in Hawkes Bay and Napier and other areas to the north of us. Those places feel a little too close for comfort and I'd rather our family's scalps weren't among the ones we've heard the Haus-Haus collect."

"Don't worry, Lizzie," said Alister reassuringly. "At the moment, as far as we know, these are just rumours. Everything may yet be well. I will keep a loaded pistol in the house if it helps to reassure you. I would never compromise the safety of the girls, Russell, or you, you know that."

Eliza did know that, but she was still worried. At night, she lay awake listening to the rustling of the flax leaves in the breeze, imagining that she could hear the marauding Haus-Haus tribe arriving in their valley. After a few sleepless nights, she shared her concerns with Alister.

"Alister, I'm not happy about staying here and waiting for the Haus-Haus to pounce. Everyone we know is packing up and leaving to go back to Wellington or the Hutt Valley. We should do the same. Robert says he has a duty to remain, but he is concerned for Mary's safety and recommends that she leave with the rest and they don't even have young children to consider like us."

Alister regarded her for a moment seeming to assess the situation.

"Perhaps you are right, Lizzie. I can sense your restless spirit and I don't want the children to become anxious as well. But I must stay to guard our land, you do understand that, don't you?"

Eliza nodded. She had never felt so anxious or alone, but she knew that Alister was immoveable on this. He had waited so long to possess his land he would stake his life on defending it.

With a heavy heart, she began to pack up a few items for the journey. Robert was going to accompany her, Mary and the children, and Eliza wondered how this would work out. She had already sensed a growing tension between herself and Mary, as if Mary had guessed that there was something going on between her and Robert.

The crossing of the Waihaha River took longer this time with the five youngsters, even though they had only one cart and few belongings to weigh them down. Alister had suggested that they make their way towards the safety of a communal Blockhouse in the Hutt Valley. Robert, then, despite his duties at home, had to join the local militia with Alister and the other men of the area. Governor Grant felt that their presence, as local inhabitants, would help to reinforce his presence as he met with the tribal chiefs in Wellington along with his ally, Chief Ngatuere of the Rangitira tribe.

The communal living they had to endure didn't suit Mary, who complained of the noise which was now much greater than when their Manse had just been shared with the Douglas', but Eliza's thoughts were so taken up with Robert that even the continual complaining of Mary hardly touched her. She knew Alister was strong and well able to fight but Robert was more sensitive and not so cut out for hard fighting as her husband. She was worried that he wouldn't be able to cope. She didn't even know if he had ever shot a pistol before or was adapt at wielding a bayonet.

Governor Grant, it was reported, was intending to force the warring tribes to pledge their loyalty once more to the Queen of England and her subjects. Despite the infighting among the tribes, it seemed that the Governor's message convinced the Haus-Haus and the Muapoko tribes to withdraw without a fight. Therefore, the residents of Frampton and its surrounding areas were able to return to their homes and land once more, grateful that a catastrophe had been diverted. Eliza was relieved that no real fighting had taken place and both Alister and Robert were safe.

Alister was full of admiration for Governor Grant on his return home. "Those savages knew that they had met with an immoveable force in Governor Grant. He was so authoritarian, so powerful that I believe he won them over. Especially with Chief Ngatuere and his tribe backing him up."

Eliza said, "I'm sure you did a very good job, dear." Although she wasn't fully convinced that the strength of the Governor's message would have been sufficient to avoid an onslaught.

She later shared her feelings with Robert who gave a very different story to that of Alister.

"I felt such a sympathy with the Haus-Haus and the Muapoko tribe," he said. "I'm so glad we didn't have to fight them. The Governor had cheated them and his message about loyalty to the Queen didn't quite stick with me. No, I'm convinced that it wasn't his presence or his message that caused them to withdraw but rather the sight of the soldiers' colourful uniforms, badges and bayonets that cowed them into submission rather than anything else." And Eliza agreed.

Chapter Ten

WAIREKA

ELIZA WAS STRUGGLING TO HELP Albert now that she had three youngsters under the age of five with Charlotte and Annie not much older. Her time seemed to be carved up into minute portions caring for each of their needs. Even when Robert visited her, her attention was divided, and they couldn't talk to each other in any real depth having to survive on quick snatched kisses when the children were otherwise occupied.

Albert was struggling to handle all the milking alone with more than a dozen cows to be milked by hand, it almost seemed like he had hardly finished the morning milking before it was time for the afternoon shift. Alister worried that Albert would wear himself out with the tiring milking schedules combined with the deliveries they were now making to many of the farms in the surrounding area.

"It's costing us time and money we can ill afford," he said to Eliza. "Without you being able to help, I can see the work becoming too cumbersome for Albert, and I can't see a way to replace him easily. Besides we aren't making enough money for our milk to justify the time Albert's putting in. I was thinking that maybe we should try our hand at butter-making as there's more money in that than just the milk alone. What do you think?"

"I think that if Albert is struggling to cover the work he has now that we cannot put an extra burden on his shoulders," said Eliza practically. "How do you think we're going to add butter-making to his work load when he can barely cope with just the milk production?"

"Share milking, in one simple word. It's one of the very latest ideas in farming."

"What on earth is that?"

"It means we pool our resources, cows, men etc. with other dairy farmers in the area. It would give us better resources for running our own factory to produce milk and butter. If successful, who knows we could transport our goods across both islands."

"But do any of the settlers agree with you or want a share in this?"

"Young Peter Jepson who farms in nearby Mangapai is all for the scheme. In fact, he suggested it to me."

"I've never heard you speak of him before, dear."

"Oh, maybe I forgot to mention him. I met him recently at the local cattle market in Wellington. It was then he mentioned share milking to me. He is so much of a mind as me, hates milking too. We got on so well from the start. He's come from a place near me too, Spean Bridge. Farming here in the region from the start."

"Oh, I see." Eliza was glad that Alister seemed to have found a kindred spirit in this man, even though she worried about the scheme. Alister was such a solitary man it would be good for him to have someone to share his heart with. She felt she had failed him in this respect.

She was still lost in her thoughts as Alister continued, "We just have to convince a few more farmers in the area."

She had to think for a minute before she could remember what they'd been discussing. Getting back to the subject in hand she said, "And could that be a problem?"

"It could but nothing ventured nothing gained, as they say. I've a mind to read up all I can about share milking. I could certainly build us a factory."

Eliza had no doubt about Alister's building skills and could see that he was really enthused by the scheme, but the idea of the share milking scheme filled her with foreboding as she explained to Robert the next time she saw him.

"I worry about the scheme, Robert. The settlers can be quite stubborn people, frightened to take chances. We all have so little money to venture and I can't see them being favourable to buying into any co-operative scheme, but Alister seems so determined to give it a try."

"Dinna fret yoursel', Lizzie, love," said Robert gently placing an arm around her shoulders. "Surely it is right for Alister to go ahead with a scheme he believes in that might help with your practical needs? If he doesn't give it a try he will always wish he had. A bit like his first try to move here. Mind you, I thank God every day that he spared you all from that horrible situation in Gibbstown," and he visibly shuddered.

Eliza nodded. Robert always seemed to have a knack of silencing her doubts and worries.

"Let's pray about this share milking and put the situation into God's hands letting Him do the worrying," Robert suggested.

So, they knelt on the cold stone floor with hands linked and gave the whole situation up to God.

Alister, despite Eliza's concerns, continued to read up about the subject of co-operative share farming with enthusiasm as well as that of butter-making. First with some books that Peter Jepson had lent him and then after he'd read those he sent to his brother Alexander for some books on butter-making from England. He was full of excitement when they arrived.

"At last, the books from Alexander and he includes a short letter too," said Alister reading it out to Eliza.

August 14, 1863

My Dear Brother,

I am glad to inform you that I have received both your letters and we ar all glad to hear of the men being satisfactory for you all. We were surprised to lern of your plans to make buter, but I have found some books that I hope will help you in your plans. We are within two days of being done with our harvest. It has not been so heavy to go through this year owing to the dry summer the corn is light and everything els is an average crope with us.

By the way, you did not say if the men had wrote there folks, I intend to write them and let them know our brothers are all well as far as I know. I am glad to say my Mrs and family are all in good health, hoping this find you enjoying the same blessing. The male leaves tomorrow so I must close and go to bed. Be sure to send us your photographs, with love to you all. I remain your loving brother,

Alex B Douglas

"Not a great harvest for them by all accounts," said Alister, looking up from perusing the letter.

"He seems to be surprised by your plans to do butter making too, dearest," Eliza remarked, her attention distracted by the baby at her breast.

"Ah, but if he were here he would understand and come around to my way of thinking, I'm assured of that," said Alister confidently.

Eliza said nothing but prayed in her heart that God might bless her husband's plans. Soon after this, Alister and Peter held a series of meetings amongst the local farmers to try and get them on board; however, none of them, save Peter and Alister, had any enthusiasm for the scheme.

Disappointed but undaunted, Alister returned with an account for Eliza.

"Stubborn, short-sighted settlers," he grumbled. "Can't grasp the vision or see when Peter and I are on to a good money-making scheme."

Eliza thanked God for His resolution to the situation. However, what her husband said next rocked her to the very core.

"I'll not give up on this though, Lizzie," he said, the strong determined set of his jaw filling her with foreboding.

"If they haven't the vision to see this through, we'll go ahead anyway and build us a factory."

"But there isn't the room here dearest," persisted Eliza.

"No, not here there isn't but I've a mind to purchase some more land further into Frampton for my project. Then we could move to that land and that's where I'll build the factory. That way you won't be quite as isolated as we are here. The land I've a mind to buy adjoins that of the Manse, so that will please you, dearest . . . "

"You have to obtain the land first," said Eliza, ever the pragmatist. "And sell this," she added.

"No, I'll not be parting with this land. We might need all the land we can get for grazing, especially if we increase the herd. There's little work for me in contracting at present so I can devote my time to building the factory, equipping it and making plans for our new adventure. You will prefer to be in the centre of Frampton, surely Lizzie, and next door to the Yates?"

"And where are we going to get the money from, Alister?"

"We'll manage. Find a way," he said with a determined glance at his wife.

Eliza could hardly admit to Alister just how much this part of his scheme appealed. She would be as close to Robert physically as was practically possible, that had to be a blessing. However, she was still concerned for her husband's scheme. She feared it could bankrupt them. She couldn't devote much time at present to helping Albert and if they had a larger herd to milk and were making butter at the same time as delivering the milk, how on earth was Albert going to cope? In her concern, she dashed a letter off to Kitty.

September 5, 1863

My Dearest Kitty,

How surprised and delighted we were to receive your letter and learn of the birth of the twins, John and Josephine. Thank the Lord you are well and safely delivered now although I hear it was a difficult and long labour and I should have worried excessively about you if I had been there. Perhaps it is best that I wasn't. Anyway, warm congratulations! I only wish, of course, that I had been there to help you through your ordeal. I understand now, from your letter that the doctor has ruled out any more children for you. Well, five is a fine number and I am heartily glad you haven't had to suffer loss like Alister and I have. I am sure Charles will be a great comfort to you now and be just as devoted to you as he ever was.

I find I can't help Albert, our dairyman, very much with the milking these days. Five young children with three under the age of five takes all my time and energy, as I'm sure you know. Alister has time on his hands with the contracting work having a lull and you know what they say about time hanging heavy on people's hands to make mischief? It has made plenty with Alister. Albert is already overworked with over a dozen cows to milk twice a day and then the milk to deliver to our neighbours around a large area. The poor man never stops. He will be wishing he'd stayed put in Scotland, even with no work! But now Alister has thought up a scheme to build us a factory and get us into butter-making too. Imagine!! Initially he did think of going into a co-operative milking scheme known here as "share milking" whereby several farmers get together and share cows, resources and profits. But he couldn't convince any of the settlers here to join the scheme apart from a Mr Peter Jepson from the nearby town of Mangapai. I think that most have such few resources and with money being tight they are frightened to take such a huge risk. And now, would you believe it? Alister has decided to go ahead anyway and build us a factory on new land he hopes to acquire and to make butter here regardless. How this is supposed to work out I shudder to think, especially how Albert can take on anymore work at present! My heart is fearful at the mere thought of it and where we will find the money but Alister is so determined that I see he will not be stopped. My dear Robert says we must just pray and God will take care of things. I only hope he is right. The best thing about Alister's new scheme is that the new land he has acquired for the scheme adjoins that of the Manse and so we will be Robert and Mary's next-door neighbours. My heart soars at the very thought of living next door to my dear friend, Robert.

I am your devoted sister,

Lizzie

Alister set about building the factory first rather than the homestead, as it was the priority in his mind.

"It'll be the first of its kind in the area, Lizzie," Alister said with conviction. "Peter Jepson's has caught hold of the vision too and is keen to put money into the scheme."

Eliza meeting Peter for the first time, a tall, red haired individual, stoutly built like her husband and of the same gruff, no nonsense kind of nature, was relieved to hear from him of his financial involvement in the scheme. It seemed vast, so vast in fact, that Alister had to hire other builders to help him in erecting the dairy sheds. He showed Eliza his plans for a two-storey building with a steeply pitched roof. His intention was that the second floor be used as a loft for storing the hay and animal fodder and in addition, two single storey lean-to buildings behind the main building in order to house the calves and a piggery—the pigs and calves would be fed on the waste whey, he explained. The plans also included a ninety-gallon separator machine for separating the milk and enough stalls to house around two hundred milking cows at one time as well as three stalls for housing the three extra horses needed to help in the distribution.

"Two hundred cows," remarked Eliza in horror. "How's that going to work? Albert struggles to milk those we have and distribute the milk. And three Clydesdale horses? I know they're a good hardy breed, but have you thought that if we are to have three more horses in addition to our two, we would also need the additional carts for them to pull if they are to be at all useful?"

"Yes, my dear, all in good time," said Alister with determination. He seemed to her like a man on a mission that nothing was going to deter. "We will of course need to find additional labour and of course, milk by machine rather than by hand. The machinery will then necessitate an engineer to service the machinery and keep it running smoothly and we'll need to buy more horses and carts, etc. This factory is going to be the first of its kind in the new land. We must think big to be successful."

Eliza felt baffled by all the extra resources her husband had in mind for the new factory. This would take their farm on to a whole new level and she wasn't sure if she had the vision at present to keep up with all his plans for the farm, with almost all her energy being taken up by the children.

The work continued to progress well, until the rains started in the winter of 1863 and continued into the spring of 1864. It was then that Eliza discovered that the New Place could take only so much rain before its defences gave up. Water had started to seep through the walls and under the door until she was desperately afraid for the health of her children.

"Alister, if these rains continue we can't stay here," said Eliza anxiously. "We've already lost two children. These damp conditions aren't good for their health and I worry about them."

Alister nodded. "Maybe I should call a halt on the factory and start on the accommodation for ourselves instead. Would you like that, Lizzie?"

"I think that might be wise. Apart from the damp which means buckets everywhere and parts of the house that are out of bounds to the children, we seem to be struggling with space now, Alister."

"I was thinking of building us a two-storey house. What do you think, Lizzie?"

"I think it might well suit our present needs better than the New Place," she said. "But what would you do with this place then?"

"It would make good accommodation for one of the workers we need," was Alister's answer. "By the way, the new land is good and the grazing sweet because of the stream running through it. Peter and I were minded calling the new farm "Waireka." What do you think?"

"I don't know," said Eliza puzzled. "What does the name mean?"

"It's the Maori word for "sweet waters," and as the stream from the Waihaha River flows through our land, making the pastures rich and green, it seemed appropriate."

"Well then," said Eliza practically, "Waireka it is. A good name for well-watered land for sure and a Maori name seems appropriate too in this land which once was theirs."

It was just over two months later that Eliza and family were to move into the new two-storey house. The move couldn't have come any sooner as far as she was concerned as she was tired of living with buckets everywhere and was struggling once again in the early stages of pregnancy. The children had seemed to go from one cold to the next, but Eliza was grateful that they all hadn't suffered from anything worse, and she had prayed daily for their protection in fear and trembling.

Robert came to help with the move along with a few other neighbours including Peter and his wife, Sue. Eliza was so busy shepherding the children from here to there and assisting in the packing and unpacking of the boxes she had little time to talk to Robert. But she was very grateful for his help and the help of others, especially in her condition.

"Lizzie, you must sit a while," Robert said as the morning slowly drifted into the early afternoon. "With all this exertion, you could easily lose the baby."

Eliza acknowledged the wisdom of his words. She felt worn out and supposing the child in her womb was a second son and she lost the child through her own carelessness? After a short while, Alister, noticing her sitting, came across to her.

"Lizzie you're not to do anymore unpacking," he scolded. "You'll make yourself ill in your condition. Our bed has just been carried in and you're to go in and rest on it at once."

"How can I Alister. Who will look after the children?"

"Sue Jepson has offered to take them for a couple of hours."

"How kind of her."

"Yes, the Jepsons are good sorts," Alister said with conviction and almost as an afterthought he added, "I'll get Robert to bring you up a cup of tea."

Eliza smiled to herself. Her husband was probably thinking that a minister was a safe option for the task, hardly realising that Robert was not in the least safe.

As she sat resting, Eliza noticed her husband talking to a stout, blonde-haired lady who looked of a very practical nature. She straightaway came across to Eliza and made her acquaintance. Wiping her hands on her apron she put out a hand to Eliza.

"Hello, I'm Sue Jepson, Peter's wife. I understand you're Eliza. You poor wee thing, you look fair done in with all the unpacking. I'll be only too glad to look after your brood for a wee while. It'll be a change for me from unpacking too. No trouble at all. I've raised six of my own, so I know what to do."

Eliza had no doubt about that. She was a plain woman but looked very capable of anything she set her mind to.

"It's so kind of you, Sue, I'm most grateful."

"Now don't you fret yourself. It's nay bother."

"How are you faring, Lizzie love?" Robert asked as he brought her the tea. "You look very pale."

"But all the bonnier for seeing you, Robert," she answered, the colour coming back into her cheeks at the very thought of seeing the man she loved in such an intimate setting.

"I know I shouldn't really be here," he said taking her hand and kissing it, his eyes fixed on her face. "But I canna help myself sometimes, despite my resolve. You look lovely, my darling."

"Robert, I'm three months pregnant."

"I know my love and never looked better or lovelier. Sometimes I wish with all my heart it was my children you were bearing."

"Robert, don't," Eliza said turning her face to the wall.

"I'm sorry my darling, I truly am. It's just that my feelings sometimes get the better of me and my flesh speaks out of a full heart, rather than the resolve of a holy, God fearing man."

"I know Robert. It's hard for me too, but we have to be strong for the children, for Alister's sake . . . and your Mary's," she finished with a catch in her voice.

"Oh, my darling, I don't wish to distress you," said Robert leaning down and placing a gentle kiss on her lips before leaving.

As soon as he had gone, Eliza put her fingers to her lips to touch the spot where his lips had been and feeling both its gentleness and strength, she drifted into a deep contented sleep. Later she penned a letter to Kitty.

December 10, 1864

My Dearest Kitty,

At last we are moved into the new place, which we have called, along with our land, *Waireka* (Maori for "sweet waters," as a tribulatory from the Waihaha River flows through our land making it rich and sweet) and I am free of leaks and buckets, thank the Lord. We are still a bit chaotic, but anything is better than the floods. However, with the new little one's advent just a few months away, we must get a space ready for him. But I cannot see space being a problem here. We have two storeys at this house, just imagine! I feel a bit like a princess in my castle.

Do you remember how we used to play princes and castles? Well now I have both, just not in the way in which I imagined. I have my castle, but my prince, who is Robert, I must now confess my dearest, lives next door and will never be mine. Sometimes I quite fill up when I think of it. So, close yet so far. But enough of this.

How are things with you and Charles? I hope your little tribe of five aren't running you both ragged. I am so glad he is proving your very prince and that you are both so deliriously happy. You deserve to be my dearest.

Please write soon. Hopefully when I next write to you I will be able to tell you of the birth of another wonderful son, I do pray so, for Alister's sake.

Your,

Loving Lizzie

It was six months to the day when Eliza gave birth to her second son. They named this son David, after Alister's brother, who had recently succumbed to a fever and died, but like David in the Bible, this David was a little man after Eliza's own heart.

The factory was beginning to take shape when Eliza received her next letter from Kitty.

June 20, 1865

My Dearest Lizzie,

What are we to do now? We were, as you said in one of your recent letters, so deliriously happy my Charles and me but perhaps we were too happy as everything has now changed for us. I weep as I think of it. Poor Charles has lost his job. The farmer, Jeff Black, who employed him, says that Charles is a good worker, but he cannot afford to keep him. The farm isn't doing well, and he can only afford to keep and pay two workers and at least our Jack is one of them, so we are thankful for that. As Charles was Jeff Black's manager and more expensive to employ he is forced to lose him, and he such a good cowman. He wouldn't think of Charles taking a salary cut either. Mind you, I don't think we could manage on any less than we now have with five mouths to feed. What is to be done? I guess we must up and look for more work elsewhere as there is certainly none to be found in these parts. Charles is naturally heartbroken. I know that he is trying to put on a good front for me but when I am not looking I have seen him put his head in his hands for very sorrow and shame. Shame that he is unable to keep me and the children as he would have wished to. Soon we will lose our little cottage too, as it is attached to the land. Thankfully, Mr Black has given us a few months extra to stay on, to help Charles find another job. This is more than generous but he says it is because Charles is such a valuable worker and he wants him to have sufficient time to seek another position.

I am your sorrowful sister,

Kitty

Eliza cried as she read the letter and fed her son. She was heartbroken for Kitty and her family and knew that Kitty would be suffering for Charles too. Then as she finished feeding David, an idea began to form in her mind. At once she took baby David with her, wrapped in a shawl, and left the other children playing in the yard in front of the house. She ran outside to Alister carrying Kitty's letter in her eager hands.

"Alister, Alister," she called out to him as he was working alongside the other builders in the factory. "I have a letter from Kitty here, can you stop work for a moment?"

Alister stopped and came across to where she was standing. "But you get lots of letters from Kitty," he said, smiling and wiping the sweat from his forehead.

"Yes, I know I do, but this one's different. Charles has lost his job at Black's farm and they must vacate their cottage."

"Oh, I am sorry my dear. This is heavy news indeed." He did look genuinely sorry too.

"Yes, it is but I was thinking that we might perhaps be able to help them," said Eliza enthusiastically

"What send them money?" Alister looked slightly worried by the thought. "I'm not sure I have that much to spare at present with all the expenses of the new homestead and factory to bear, much as I'd like to help them."

"No, not money, Alister, don't you see? You will have need of workers in the factory before too long and Kitty says that Charles is a very good cow man, a manager. I was thinking . . . "

Alister's brow cleared as he appeared to follow his wife's train of thought. "Ah, now I see. Well, there's no problem with the scheme in theory. I don't think we could help fund their travel, but he sounds like a good worker from what you have told me in Kitty's letter and we could do with someone of his calibre and experience. I know too how much it would please you to have your dear sister here with you, and we now have enough room in our two-storey house. By all means ask them if you wish."

Eliza was so delighted by her husband's generosity and thoughtfulness that she reached up and kissed him on the cheek.

"Well, lass," Alister said, "nice though that felt I can't spend all my time making love to my wife whilst others do all the hard work, I best get on. Go and write to your sister, we can only make the offer but don't raise your hopes too high." He added as a last-minute warning, "Charles may well have found another job before your letter arrives. Perhaps," he said as an afterthought, "I might write to Alex too and see if he can send me a couple more workers. Three good men, at least to start with, might stand us in very good stead with the factory."

Eliza never ceased to be amazed by her husband's generosity to her when she deserved it so little. She rushed inside at once to start a letter to Kitty.

September 20, 1865

My dearest Kitty,

My heart is full as I write to you and I can scarcely manage to put pen to paper for very elation.

You said in your last letter that Charles has lost his job. Naturally I am heartbroken for you both and wept copiously as I read your letter. But now I am filled with joy as I think that we, here at Frampton may be the answer to your problem. How do you and Charles fancy coming out to New Zealand to start a new life here with us? I know that you will be excited by the scheme just like me. I have always wanted you here with me and yet could not until now devise any scheme to bring you here. Of course, practically speaking I know that there is the problem of your passage. Unfortunately, most of our funds are currently sunk into the factory and homestead and getting this scheme off the ground so I do not think we would be able to help you in this department. It grieves me that we cannot. But is it at all possible that Mama or Papa might help you and Charles? I believe, in addition, there is some scheme run by the New Zealand Company to provide subsidies for those whose services are deemed necessary in the new country. I can write on your behalf and say how necessary Charles' dairying experience will be to us here at Waireka, just say the word. I am also sure that our parents will see that this scheme is a great one for you both. How I long that you may say "yes" dearest, only consider, it has been so long, what is it, more than ten years since we last parted? The time seems like an eternity to me, dearest, and I am wild to see you. Please think it over, we could be together again within a year. My heart skips for very joy at the thought.

I am your dearest sister,

Lizzie

Eliza sealed the letter and walked into the town's store, keen to get it to the mail as soon as she could. She could hardly wait to tell Robert when he visited the next day.

"Imagine, dearest, my own dear Kitty here with me. I am wild for very joy at the scheme."

Robert, on seeing his beloved's face so animated with joy, hesitated before replying. "Lizzie dearest," he said worriedly, "don't set your heart on this, for pity's sake. If you do and they can't come for money reasons or because he has found other employment before they receive your letter, I know that you will be bitterly disappointed, and I do not think I could bear to see you so undone."

Eliza knew in her heart that Robert was right, but she couldn't help hoping above all hopes that Kitty would be in her arms and in her life within the next year.

Chapter Eleven

ACCORDING TO KITTY WHEN SHE next wrote, the very day Eliza's letter arrived Charles had been on the brink of accepting an offer of work.

December 14, 1865

My dearest Lizzie,

Only imagine, the very day your letter arrived, Charles had been about to accept a position as cowman on the Scottish/English borders. Neither of us was very keen on the prospect, it being so far away from both our families and friends and a demotion for him. Coming out to you may indeed be further than the border farm in miles but at least it will be nearer to you my dearest and Charles can continue as a manager. There is, in coming out to you, of course, the problem of the children and their passage. I think we may have to consider leaving our oldest two boys, Charlie and Jack behind. Ballymore will have need of a new gamekeeper soon, Father is on the brink of retiring, being not as quick and able as he once was, which means that John could then train Charlie in the job. I'm sure Charlie could then live with Mother and Father. Jack, as you know is in the employ of Jeff Black and he seems to like the work as far as we can see. We are loath to unsettle him during his first year of employment anyway.

On seeing my joy at the prospect of possibly joining you, Charles set off straight away to talk to our parents and then to talk to his own. He was away a few days in all and I could hardly wait for his answer. You see, as you suggested, we approached them both regarding funds for our journey not having sufficient money ourselves even for a second-class passage. I cannot abide the thought of steerage, the only option of a subsidised passage. Imagine my delight when both sets of parents agreed and said it would be a good prospect for Charles.

I wish you could have heard Mama's views on the subject, though I dare say that they would not surprise you greatly.

She said, "I can't imagine why first Eliza and now you, could even contemplate such a hazardous and unpleasant journey but I know that you have been desperate to follow your sister ever since she left and so we won't try to stop you. As I said to Eliza all those years ago, 'on your own head be it!'"

I think Mama thinks us as foolish as one another. Anyway, it turns out, this is a timely moment for them to fund us, with some investments Papa had made around a decade ago coming to maturity. Imagine that! Charles' parents can't afford as much as ours but have sold one or two personal items to support our passage. I feel quite touched and tearful when I consider the sacrifice Charles' parents are making in sparing him, for they know that in doing so they are in effect losing Charles and most of their grandchildren forever, whereas Mama and Papa are used to such a prospect. Therefore, we won't need to apply for the subsidy you mention which, as I explained earlier in my letter, means a steerage passage. Besides, I have heard the application takes considerable time to process, time, which we don't really have. Of course, leaving my two oldest boys behind is a sore trial to me but I know this is best for them both at present and who knows that they might not join us eventually when the time is right. We will still be a family of five though, with Charles and my dearest

Emily, who will be a great help and support to me with the twins who are still a bit of a handful.

Therefore, my dearest, it is with great joy and excitement that I must tell you that our passage is booked on the Aurora which sails out of Glasgow in just eight weeks' time. There is so much to be arranged and organised before then that I am dizzy with the very thought of it. But just think, dearest, at least I know this time about the clogs for walking the decks and the nailed down furniture!!

In haste. Your dearest sister,

Kitty

Eliza picked up the letter and danced around the room with it. "Imagine, children," she said, "your Aunty Kitty and Uncle Charles and family will be joining us here in a matter of weeks. What a family we shall be, shall we not with your Scottish cousins?" And the children, even though these people were just names to them, felt their mother's joy and excitement and danced and 'whooped' with joy too. Indeed, so much so that Alister, coming in from a hard day's labour, looked at them all in amazement.

"I must be the only one not party to such antics. Tell me, Eliza, what is the meaning of all this?"

Then spying the crumpled letter in her hands, he began to nod his head and smile.

"I'm guessing that Kitty, Charles and family are coming out then?" he asked, as he went across to the stone sink to wash his hands.

"Yes dear, isn't it wonderful," said Eliza, her whole body glowing and joy smiling out of her eyes. "Although sadly they must leave their oldest two boys, Charlie and Jack, as they have employment back home. It's a shame not to be able to meet them but Kitty has to be practical, I guess."

Alister nodded, taking the letter from his breathless wife who had stopped spinning round by then and was instead trying to calm down their over-excited children.

Perusing it quickly, he said, "Well, I'm right glad for you, Lizzie. I know how much this means to you." Then after a moment he asked, "When will they be here, any idea?"

Eliza, feeling a little self-conscious at her high feelings beside Alister's calm acceptance of their changing circumstances, coloured and said, "Kitty says in her letter that their passage was booked by then with just eight weeks before sailing, so my estimation is that they will be almost, if not already, afloat by now."

Alister nodded again.

"Well this is grand news. I am looking forward to making Charles' acquaintance and taking stock of his skills. I'm thinking too that Alex's men might even be on the same vessel, wouldn't that be a strange thing if it were so?"

"Yes, indeed it would," said Eliza all smiles.

Robert shared her excitement when she told him.

"Why this is great news," he said smiling. "Mind you, I do feel a little jealous, I must say, for now, I'll not only have to share you with Alister but come a very poor second to a beloved sister."

Eliza gave him a playful look. "Oh Robert, how can you think of saying such a thing," she said pretending to be outraged. "You know that you will always have first place in my heart don't you?" and just to prove the point she reached up and planted a passionate kiss on his lips.

Robert grabbed her waist. "Oh Lizzie, my Lizzie, sometimes I find it hard to keep my feelings under check," he said responding to the kiss with an equal passion before withdrawing quickly as if burnt. Eliza could feel his physical arousal and had no doubt of the sincerity or depth of his feelings. Her own breath was also coming in short, sharp bursts which made her feel quite weak at their intensity. Before she realised quite what was happening they had caught hold of one another's hands and were heading upstairs to the bed she shared with Alister. Alister was busy working at the town's survey offices, having been asked to give his opinion on some of their building plans for the town and Sue Jepson and Charlotte had offered to look after the children for a few hours, while Eliza rested with the baby.

"We shouldn't Robert," she breathed striving to gain control of the situation.

"Oh Lizzie, I have wanted you desperately for so long."

"And I you," she breathed.

Then she was reaching up, undoing his necktie and pulling the shirt from his back. Before long he had pulled off his trousers and undone the buttons on her dress. Her various layers were soon divested, it seemed with much more haste and less decorum than when she was with Alister.

His lovemaking was all she anticipated it would be. Tender and gentle although demanding. Unlike Alister, he was quick to please her and enquire as to what she wanted, making her feel special and loved. Eliza all but lost sight of the time, as they enjoyed one another to the full. This was the love she had always dreamed of, being lifted on to a higher plain, an ecstasy she had never expected to feel. He was magnificent.

It was Robert who finally broke himself away. "Oh, my darling, Lizzie. I'm sorry, I shouldn't have taken advantage of you. May God forgive me, but it's hard to see you day after day, especially when I haven't lain with a woman for many years."

"Mary?" she asked breathlessly.

Robert gave a short mirthless laugh. "At first when we married we did comfort one another but soon after I met you she never seemed to be in the mood and I didn't care to push it, only thinking of you when Mary and I came together."

"As I do with Alister," said Eliza blushing. "But how can it be wrong, Robert, when we love one another?"

"Oh Lizzie, I wish I could be yours, you know I do. But unless circumstances change that will never be."

Eliza's eyes filled with tears, "I wish . . . "

"Don't Lizzie," Robert said swallowing hard. "Or I'll not be able to hold back my own tears, which, God knows I'm struggling to do."

Realising the time, Eliza gently but reluctantly released herself from Robert's grasp. "It must be late, the children . . . " she said panicking. "What will Sue Jepson and Charlotte be thinking? It seems like hours ago, when I left them in their charge. I must go. It's a mercy that Charlotte or Sue hasn't come to look for me before now."

"Aye, and I must be about my work," Robert said, struggling into his trousers in haste.

Eliza knew she could never share this moment with Kitty but still she longed to talk to her, to be able to share with her at least some of her feelings for Robert. Although, having a close relationship with Kitty, she guessed Kitty had probably already understood what was going on and chosen not to comment.

Over the next few weeks, Eliza's feelings were all over the place. Sometimes she would feel a joy almost akin to ecstasy in the thought that she and Robert had lain together and then she would think of his position as a minister and her own state before God and she would be consumed with guilt. The Bible clearly taught that adultery was sin, so the moments of joy she and Robert had experienced were sinful moments. She may not have been guilty of the rape, but this was different. She had been a willing partner. *Could God forgive her, forgive Robert?*

She shared her feelings with Robert who completely understood.

"I have tried to repent," he said, "but when I think of the sheer joy of the moment, I cannot be sorry for my sin. I wonder if there's any hope for me as a minister of God."

"But surely God cannot be so hard," Eliza reasoned. "We understand Him to be a loving, compassionate God. Surely He will understand and deal with our sins but lightly." Yet despite saying this, still she felt she had wronged her husband and wronged Mary and cried bitter tears of repentance when she thought of the hurt she had caused others. She only hoped she and Robert would somehow be able to conceal their sin from others if not from God.

In her guilt, Eliza found herself being much more considerate of her husband's needs. Making his favourite dishes to eat and asking most particularly over the progress of the work at the factory. She caught Alister looking at her intently once or twice before he said, "Is there something amiss, lassie?"

"Only my worry over Kitty and Charles and their journey here," she answered quickly. "It can be so hazardous, as you will remember."

"Aye, but I'm sure they'll enjoy the journey too, seeing all those strange, unfamiliar lands. I know I did," he answered trying to calm her fears, which made her feel even guiltier.

Eliza nodded. But in truth she hadn't told a lie. She was very anxious over her sister's journey and the gap of time between her last letter and Kitty's arrival seemed immense. Of course, once they met the necessity for letters would soon be forgotten, but in between the silence felt interminable, as it was on her arrival in New Zealand all those years ago.

Within months, word began to reach them of treacherous conditions in the Tasman Sea and Eliza began to pray fervently for her beloved Kitty's safety. "Please don't punish me by harming, Kitty," she prayed. But then she reasoned that perhaps Kitty and Charles hadn't reached the Tasman Sea yet. Both Robert and Alister were quick to reassure her of this. Eliza also found herself pregnant again which was another source of anxiety to her, fearing the baby's parentage.

One day, towards the end of February, as Alister and the team were working hard on the new dairy, they were stopped in their tracks by the sight of two men dragging themselves into the yard, bare footed and with clothes half torn, looking as if they hadn't eaten in some long time. They dragged themselves into the yard before both collapsing in a heap. Alister and his team ran over to the men to take stock of the situation, Alister immediately began hollering for Eliza.

"Lizzie, Lizzie, come quickly," he shouted, "and bring some water with you."

Eliza knew something serious must be afoot. She gave strict instructions to the children to remain where they were, not knowing what she was likely to encounter, and dashed outside with a jug of water.

Gently they lifted the heads of the men who were, by all accounts, slightly delirious. Slowly they managed to pour some of the liquid into the men's mouths and their eyes fluttered open in gratitude.

Before long the biggest and strongest of the men, blurted out a few incoherent sentences.

"Big winds, storm, ship sank, only survivors."

Eliza's blood ran cold, and her heart began pumping wildly within her. *Kitty's ship?* Surely it didn't have to be. Many ships crossed between Britain and New Zealand all the time, this incidence might bear little or no relation to Kitty's crossing.

Alister glancing up and seeing the horror-stricken look on his wife's face reached out and gently took hold of her hand and reiterated the thoughts running through her own head.

"Many ships cross between Britain and New Zealand all the time, Lizzie, we have no evidence that these men were travelling on the same ship as Kitty and Charles. Quite likely they weren't. We don't even know who they are and why they have come here."

Eliza's mind reasoned all these thoughts to her too and she nodded in agreement, but a cold sense of foreboding had already gripped her. She found shelter for the men on rudimentary mattresses she had rigged up on the floor of Waireka, but it was to be several weeks before they discovered who the men were and where they had come from.

One day, a few weeks later, Eliza turned to see the eyes of the larger of the two men open as they followed her about the room. Tremulously she addressed him, "Who are you and where are you heading?"

"To Waireka, the dairy farm near the Waihaha River," said the man, who said his name was Murray. "We rather thought we might have found it too, before we both lost consciousness. Our enquiries had certainly led us here."

"Yes, you are right. This is Waireka," said Eliza realisation dawning on her of who the men must be. "You must be the men that my husband, Alister, is expecting from Scotland. Who sent you?"

"Alexander Beattie. I'm from Tulliallan itself, whilst Henry here is from the nearby village of Longannat, both of us out of work cowmen seeking employment."

Eliza nodded. "Well then, Murray, you are very welcome here. We were expecting a third, but I know that my husband, Alister will be grateful for any extra pairs of hands. There is much to be done." Eliza smiled slightly, but the sense of dread within her intensified.

"There was a third, a fellow by the name of Jake but he didn't make it, like many."

"I'm so sorry," she said looking away, uncertain of what she might hear next.

"We hardly knew him, he was from further away."

"Oh. I don't suppose you were on the ship *Aurora* and knew anything of a couple from nearby in Scotland did you, a couple with three young children with them. Their name would be McKenzie, a Charles and Kitty McKenzie?" Eliza said tremblingly.

The man thought for a moment and then seemed to recall something.

"*Aurora*, aye that was the name of our boat. And now you mention it, I do recall a couple with two very young children and an older girl. The Scottish lady was fair, much like yourself and her husband had brown wavy hair. I recall that I heard their name was McKenzie. He was a cowman like Henry and I but a manager, so we didn't have much to do with him and his family."

"Was?" said Eliza swallowing hard.

"Aye, I last saw them before the ship went down. The man said he was a fair swimmer and we tried encouraging him to join us and to swim to freedom. It's my opinion he might have made it too but for his wife and the bairns. He said he couldn't leave them and they couldn't swim. He was hoping for a rescue boat to find them. That's the last we saw of them. Did you know them?"

The man had hardly finished his question when an unearthly howl broke from Eliza's lips. It was the only sound she uttered before fainting in a heap on the floor.

Alister, on hearing the sound and fearing that one of the men must have taken bad, dashed into the house and found his wife lying outstretched on the floor.

Eliza next remembered waking up in bed with her husband gazing anxiously down at her.

"Wwwhat happened. Oh no, Kitty," she sobbed, the whole ghastly truth coming back to her.

"Hush, Lizzie," he whispered gently. "You mustn't upset yourself or you'll lose the baby."

"I care nothing for the baby or anything else now," she said listlessly, turning her face to the wall. "Nothing matters now that my Kitty is gone."

"Yes, Murray told me what he had said to you. Of course, he had no idea of the impact such news would have on you or who Kitty was. He's truly sorry for any distress he's caused you."

"That's kind of him. But that won't bring my beloved Kitty back, will it? Nothing will bring her back," and she burst into a fresh bout of sobbing. Then she stopped all at once, the realisation dawning on her, "my Kitty will never come to me now and I can't even read her dear letters. It would be better if she'd never attempted the crossing. At least then I would still have her letters." And she broke into sobs again, big sobs that seemed to rack her whole body.

"Aye, it's heavy news indeed," said Alister, stroking her hand gently. "I was looking forward to meeting her and profiting from Charles' expertise but we must comfort each other now, my Lizzie and move on. I'm sure that's what Kitty would want you to do. The children have been so worried for you, as I have, and you must think of the baby."

Eliza knew Alister was doing his best to comfort her, but she found his philosophising again irritating and unnecessary. He seemed more concerned about the baby than her or her heartbreak at losing her beloved Kitty. Kitty, who was irreplaceable.

Instead of getting up and making the best of things as Alister had hoped, Eliza's fright caused her to go into premature labour. The baby was born small and weak, and Eliza took bad with childbed fever. Drifting in and out of consciousness she was aware from time to time of one or another of her daughters Charlotte or Annie sitting by her, also in the evenings after work, of Alister himself, but she cared little for anything and had no appetite. She just wanted to die to be with her beloved Kitty. She was also aware of the doctor visiting from time to time and whispered voices and being bled. She cared little if all the blood seeped from her veins.

But as she lay there, one day, she knew not when, as each day seemed to drift into another, her eyes hardly able to adjust to the light, she perceived she heard a man crying. She remembered her husband's gentle imploring words for her to get better, but it was unlike him to show his feelings quite so openly. As she slowly managed to focus she saw it was Robert, her own dear Robert, who wept so piteously. If Alister had called for him things must have gone on apace. Robert could only be here to administer the last rites to her. If that were his present mission, then she would see her dear Kitty again very soon.

"Is that you, Robert, and are you crying?" she asked in a small, rasping voice.

"I can only weep my love at the thought of having to administer the last rites to you," he said in a heartbroken voice. "How shall I manage without you?"

"You have Mary."

"You know that it's you that fills my thoughts every waking hour of the day and my dreams at night. How should I go on without you? It's like cutting myself in two."

"But maybe it's better this way if we can never have each other. We will not be able to so forget ourselves again."

"Just seeing you is my food and drink. I don't think I could exist without at least knowing we occupy the same space."

How different this man was from Alister, thought Eliza. She was sure Alister was fond of her but equally sure that if she were to die he would manage well enough without her before long, just as he had without little Alister. Always looking towards the next thing, the eternal pragmatist.

But this man, she realised, really needed her. Loved her passionately. If she had ever doubted his love before, now she was wholly persuaded of it.

"Then I will rally, my dearest, for your sake," she whispered.

"And the baby's," he responded. Although in his books the baby seemed to come very much second to her. Alister had never said as much.

"The baby?" she questioned.

"Like you, my dearest, she is clinging on to life. I don't wish to give either of you the last rites."

"Then don't," she said weakly grasping his hand. "I have lost my dearest, loveliest sister but I'm not going to quit this world and lose the one who is first in my heart. Kitty, my Kitty has her beloved Charles beside her now but how should I enter eternity without my beloved? It may be that God will still have mercy on me, on us."

Her tears began to flow and as he reached across and kissed her gently on the lips, their tears mingled together as one.

Within days Eliza's health slowly began to improve. But both she and the baby were weak, and everyone was still unsure as to whether they would finally pull through, although all rejoiced when they did, no one more than Robert.

Eliza named the small baby, Kitty, no other name would do. Kitty herself, had been named after their mother, Catherine, but the derivation of Kitty had seemed more fitting for her, and had helped to distinguish her from their mother. Similarly, the name seemed right for the young baby.

Little Kitty was small and weak and Eliza worried that her weakness might cause her to succumb to the fever like little Alister had but fortunately, like Belle, she appeared to have the same tenacious will to live. However, as the days progressed she saw more of the likeness of Robert in her than Alister, and she feared that Alister would also notice. He might wash his hands of her entirely then, thinking that she had participated in illicit sexual relations not once but twice and each time with a minister.

Eventually after nearly a month in bed, Eliza could get up for a few hours each day. She still missed Kitty every single day, often forgetting she had been lost at sea. She would think of little things that the children had done or that Robert had said to her and then she would think "I must tell Kitty that when I next write to her" and then she would remember.

Of course, she had to write to Mama and Papa once more but this time to tell them what had happened. It was one of the hardest letters she had ever had to write. True to form, Mama had said by way of reply, "I always told you those sea journeys would do you no good. It's a mercy that you survived one, I suppose I should have guessed that two daughters surviving such a hazardous journey would be impossible."

Then Eliza had to write to Charles' family which was even more difficult considering that she had never met them. But through all this, Robert sustained her, reminding her daily of his love for her. Alister seemed too preoccupied with building the dairy sheds to find time for much else.

As Kitty grew, Eliza had seen Alister gazing intently at the child more than once with her dark hair and dark eyes, but he said nothing to her, although she noticed that he had become more distant. Robert loved all of Eliza's children, but she noticed a certain predilection in him to spoil Kitty over and above the others and questioned him over it. "I fancy the wee lassie has more than a look of me about her," he said, "is she?" His words came out tremulously and Eliza sensed his desires fighting against his sense of propriety and the respectability of his role.

"I think you know, Robert," was all she said.

"Oh Lizzie, the knowledge fills me with both a sense of joy and a sense of foreboding. What will my parishioners think now if they suspect the likeness of the child to me? They are already suspicious that you are dearer to me than you should be. This could finish me as a minister. And what if Mary suspects? I sense she is hostile enough to you already. Or Alister? He might throw you out of his house."

Eliza paled. "Yes, I had thought of that, Robert. But what can I do? What is done is done and I must be wicked indeed to say that I don't regret a single moment of it. Nor shall I ever."

"Oh, my darling, be assured that I don't regret it either. I only wish—" Eliza laid a finger on his lips. "Hush my dearest, don't say it. I can't bear for you to say it."

Robert nodded. His eyes glazed over with emotion. Neither of them could speak. Finally, with a quick kiss on the cheek he turned and left her.

When little Kitty was about to celebrate her first year, the first shed was nearing completion along with the ninety-gallon milk separator. Alister had made some enquiries regarding suitable machinery locally, but this was limited. Much of what they needed had to be shipped in from Scotland with Alexander's help.

Pete and Sue Jepson had incorporated their own land into the Waireka plot by this time, helping Alister to run the farms together. With the increasing size of the herd, it was decided that the Jepsons should move out of their own house to a cottage on Waireka and that Pete would be the manager of Alister's herd along with his own, in the absence of Charles' arrival. The cottage for Pete and Sue Jepson was soon built and ready for them to move into. Eliza was glad of this as Kitty was a bit of a handful now that she was walking, and she herself wasn't getting any younger. Charlotte and Annie had always helped her with the other children, but in recent years, Charlotte had taken to walking out with the Jepson's oldest lad, Adam, and seemed to have little time for much else. At least with Sue's cottage being on their land, Eliza would at last have some female company. Although Mary was next door she kept herself very much to herself and Eliza saw little of her. But she felt the censure of Mary grow yet more severe. She would nod if she met Eliza at church or in town simply to acknowledge her existence for propriety's sake, but it was all she could do to pass a greeting or a comment about the weather. When she did, it was always with animosity, blaming Eliza, it seemed, for taking her husband's attention from her and perhaps, she suspected, bearing him the child she couldn't.

The dairy at present wasn't large enough to run as a business. But Alister and his team of men continued the building expansion programme, increasing the herd as their resources allowed. Indeed, they could still only make the new butter supplies stretch to their own family, the Jepsons, and the Yates. Although this meant the families were largely self-sufficient for dairy produce, it wasn't enough to pay the bills or to make a profit. In addition, Alister and the other dairy workers were still forced to take on contracting work.

With the deepening friendship of Charlotte and Adam, now seemed a good time for them to marry and make good use of the new shed before it was filled with cows. Robert was happy to marry them, and a date was set for a December wedding when the Pohutakawa trees would be in full blossom as wedding confetti.

The day for the wedding began with a glorious blue, cloudless sky which bode well for the young couple. Eliza felt quite emotional as she saw her beautiful daughter escorted up the aisle on the arm of Alister to an expectant Adam. It seemed like yesterday when she had held the tiny Charlotte in her arms at the christening, just over seventeen years ago, thanking God that this child had thrived unlike little Alister.

She then thought back to her own wedding to Alister and prayed that her Charlotte might find true love, like her Aunt Kitty, not just a marriage of convenience as hers had been. As she heard her dear Robert's voice ringing out she caught a glance from him and smiled, although her heart ached. Mary caught the glance between them and glared at Eliza. How different her life would have been if this man had been her husband and not Alister. She mentally shook herself out of the reverie. How selfish she was, this was Charlotte's day not hers. She should be thinking today of the happy couple, rejoicing with them. After all, it wasn't so much as if she was losing a daughter but more like she was gaining a son as Charlotte and Adam were to live nearby at the New Place, which had been altered and made water tight for them. Adam, like his father, Pete, was to work at Waireka.

The empty shed made a great place for the meal and party afterwards and Eliza could enjoy a couple of Scottish reels with Robert before he had to leave the dance early as Mary was tired or at least she made out she was. Eliza suspected that if Mary couldn't dance herself, the last person she wished to see dance with her husband was Eliza.

A few months after the wedding party, in the spring of 1872, Eliza discovered to her surprise that she was pregnant again. She and Alister hardly had conjugal relations these days since her confinement with Kitty, although she remembered back to the occasion of Charlotte and Adam's wedding which seemed to have awakened a latent desire in him for something similar and guessed that Alexander's conception was the consequence. She had imagined her child-bearing years were drawing to a close and wondered if she would be able to cope with yet another baby with Kitty just five and David six. At least Russell, Jean and Belle were a bit older with Russell and Jean both ten and Belle eleven and Annie a very capable sixteen. Charlotte would be on hand to help too, although she imagined that she might soon be supporting Charlotte in a similar role.

Alexander, named after Alister's favourite brother, was born in the summer of 1872 and thankfully in the year following Alexander's birth, Mrs Blake started a school in her own home and Eliza went to enroll Russell, David, Jean and Belle straight away. She knew how capable Ertha Blake was from the Sunday school at St Andrews where she had served so faithfully for the last twenty years. The children, especially the older ones, all knew and loved her, but Eliza also knew that Mrs Blake was a very capable teacher who didn't stand any nonsense.

"I'm afraid I can only manage three mornings a week to start with, Mrs Douglas," Mrs Blake announced forthrightly when Eliza came to enroll her youngsters.

"Oh, but that will be such a help with two youngsters still at home, and I will be glad to see the children get some sort of education. Teaching them all has been so time consuming for me over the years with my other duties at the dairy."

"I expect you will be able to find the time for all those other duties, now, though," said Mrs Blake slightly caustically.

Eliza blushed. She knew Mrs Blake was referring to her relationship with Robert which was a subject of gossip amongst the parishioners, especially since Kitty's birth and she felt the disapproval in Mrs Blake's tone. Before she could think of a suitable response, Mrs Blake continued, "I felt it was important for me to open a school for our young," she explained. "I was thinking we couldn't have a town like Frampton with a public house and no school. What sort of example does that set the young people of our town? And we must set them a good example, mustn't we, Mrs Douglas?"

Again, Eliza noted her personal censure and flushed. If only these narrow-minded parishioners knew her situation and how Robert brought her so much hope and joy. *Mind you*, she surmised, *if they knew all her situation, the disapproval might be even stronger.* She was determined not to rise to the bait. She responded simply by saying, "You are certainly setting them a good example, Mrs Blake, by showing our youngsters just how important education is." Then with a slight smile and nod of her head she turned around and made her way back home.

"I shouldn't worry about her narrow-minded opinions," Robert reassured her when she told him what had happened. "None of my parishioners has had to face the trying circumstances you have had to. If they had, they might be more understanding. At least she'll make a good school teacher, I'm sure of that. Her skills will be missed at the church, even if not her opinions, and I think time has hung rather heavy on her hands since the death of her Harold just over a year ago. Being busy will help her to fill her time so that she doesn't engage in idle tittle tattle and will help you find more quality time with your two youngest."

Eliza nodded. "I only wish Charlotte and Annie had been afforded the same opportunities to learn as the others, my tuition has been rather limited, although they can at least read and write passably well. At least four of my six will benefit straightaway, and Kitty and Alexander in time, so I'm grateful to Mrs Blake for that."

"Charlotte will probably have other duties and opportunities to engage her soon anyway," said Robert smiling. Eliza smiled too. They had both been delighted at the news of Charlotte's impending birth, as was Alister.

"I dare say she will," agreed Eliza, "for I feel my child bearing years are over now, after birthing ten, two in the grave and eight surviving. That's surely enough for any woman, especially one of my age."

"But one who seems just as young and beautiful to me as the day I met her," said Robert drawing her to himself and planting a kiss on her cheek.

"You flatterer," said a smiling, delighted Eliza. Robert still had the ability to cause her heart to race even after all this time.

Chapter Twelve

THE FACTORY HAD BEEN DUE to open within months when Alister received a letter from his father, Adam. This was an unusual occurrence, with the last time he'd received a letter from him being just before the birth of young David announcing the death of his brother, David. This time the letter shook Alister far more, telling him of his favourite brother, Alexander's, untimely death.

March 6, 1873

Dear Alister,

I am sorry to have to writ this leter just a few years after the death of your brother David but now I writ this leter to lern you of the death of Alex, taken befor his time. He was killed by a Fresian Bull we had just bought. I wish now with all my hert we hadn't thought to have bought him, such a tempr you never did see on a Bull befor. Pore Alex was injured badly but didn't live more than a moment or too after.

I no what a help he had ben to you out their at the farm and how he wed wish you to keep going and set up your dairy now. Your Mither and I send our best for the dairy and to the pimple out there, including your waif and bairns.

Your Father,

Adam

Eliza found her husband sitting quietly with the letter laid out before him and staring into the distance at a space ahead of him. Silently she took hold of the letter learning, like him, of the tragic death of Alex.

190

"Oh, Alister, dearest," she said with feeling. She knew that Alister had been fond of Alexander, who had been so much help to him in the setting up of Waireka and in the sending out of suitable staff. "This will put a blight on the proceedings we had arranged for the opening in just a few weeks time. Do you want to delay it now?"

Alister looked towards her, taking in what she had said before letting out a long sigh. "No, everything is now in place and the local dignitaries booked, we can't delay. I'm certain that wouldn't be what Alex would want either. He had helped us so much over the years we can't let him down now."

"I wasn't suggesting letting him down, dearest, merely changing the date by a few months or so."

"No," said Alister abruptly. "I've told you my reasons. We'll stick to our plan, which we need to anyway, to make the official opening before the winter sets in."

Eliza nodded. She could see the wisdom of this. A delay would bring the proceedings closer to winter.

Alister got up and went to the door. Eliza again saw his reluctance to share anything. He had changed the subject so abruptly as if the last few moments hadn't happened. "There's a lot of work to be done if we're going to open in the autumn. Must keep busy." And he was gone. His way of dealing with grief seemed to block it out in the everyday routine of work. It had been that way with little Alister and Margaret and his own brothers, first David and now, Alex.

Eliza told Robert of Alex's death a few days later.

"Alister has never talked about it again since that day," she said. "In fact, he crumpled up the letter and threw it away. If it had been about one of my family, such as Jean or Margaret I would have kept the letter, read and re-read it and grieved but Alister never shows any emotion."

"But he must feel it deeply, my love," said Robert. "This seems to be his way of dealing with things."

"It's as if he doesn't need me though," said Eliza. "I would at least like to feel I could give him the dutiful comfort of a wife in such sore circumstances, even if we're no longer close."

"You can give me all the love and comfort you have to give now and always, my dearest," said Robert catching Eliza round the waist and drawing her to himself before kissing her lips.

"I know that of course, my love," she said returning his kiss and the subject was closed.

The day marked for the official opening of the dairy in May 1873 dawned fair, and a large crowd gathered. Alister had asked all the chief representatives of Frampton to the opening. There was William Hill, the publican from the Feathers Public House, the school mistress Ertha Blake—all the children were grateful for a day's holiday—John Woods from the survey office and Samuel Jenkins from the local store. Robert, as the minister of St Andrews, was to proclaim the place open for business at last. It looked splendid decked out with the bunting saved from Charlotte's wedding a couple of years previously.

"I declare the Waireka Butter factory open," announced Robert with a quick glance at Eliza as if to win her approval. He did. She returned his smile, her heart full of joy for the future that lay ahead for their family. She was proud of Alister's hard work in building the factory and establishing the business. The factory, although relatively small yet and milking only around fifty cows, would soon grow. It would certainly be the first in New Zealand to use the combined churn and butter worker, advanced machinery which would help to increase the rate of butter making from the simple hand labour of the past. She felt in her heart this was just the beginning of something much bigger, although she knew they would all have to work hard to grow the business and increase the cows to the projected two hundred they envisaged. Along with Murray, Henry, Peter and Adam, Sue, Annie, herself and the children would all have play their part in the success of the company. They would have to learn to operate the new equipment and become proficient in butter making if Alister's plan to export the butter across New Zealand was going to work.

Despite his seeming delight at the opening, Alister began to spend more and more time in the survey office soon afterwards. Eliza surmised that it might help him get over the death of his brother for a while, but it soon became a more permanent arrangement than she had at first realised.

"John Woods needs more help at the survey office," Alister said after a few months had passed. "Not only are they experiencing an increase in land purchase, but he thinks we could do with more structure in the town and perhaps a few central buildings such as a town hall. After that initial consultation recently, he respects my opinions, knowing that I have building expertise."

"We all know that," said Eliza in exasperation, "but there is plenty of work still to be done here. More buildings if we are going to expand the business. As it is I don't have enough hours in the day what with helping with the milking and butter making, and with Charlotte and her children, not to mention our own family. Most of them may be at school now but children still need feeding and looking after."

"I know that, Lizzie, but I have an interest in helping the local community too. We have profited so much from our time here that I think we owe the community something in return. Perhaps now that we cannot receive any more men from Alex we should think of our employment options here in New Zealand. There might be some men who came over here earlier still looking for work. New Zealand's a growing economy with folks emigrating all the time."

Eliza didn't see any point in arguing with her husband. If he was determined about something there was no stopping him. She had seen that before when his share milking scheme had failed but he went ahead regardless and built the factory and business. She had noticed too his slight allusion to his brother, but he'd glossed over the mention very quickly and she didn't think she could broach the subject with him again.

The answer for their need of increased manpower, especially builders, happened in a most surprising way. Eliza received a letter from her nephew Jack.

September 8, 1874

Dearest Aunt Eliza,

I know that you don't know me in person, although you will know a lot about me from my dear departed mother, Kitty, God rest her soul. From her, you will know that I was in the employ of one Jeff Black, my father's old employer, on the farm. I enjoyed the work there too for a few years but still felt a sense of being unsettled. Unlike my father, I knew that dairy farming wasn't quite what I had in my heart to do. I might never have discovered what that thing was either if Jeff hadn't needed an extra barn built. At once, with little experience of building, I asked him if I could lend a hand and fortunately he agreed. I took to it immediately. Jeff declared that although I was a passing good cowman I was a much better builder. Of course, he hadn't sufficient building work to keep me busy for long but knew a man who was looking for a young apprentice in the building trade. I have been apprenticed these three years but unfortunately the work has now all but dried up. I know that Uncle Alister is still in the process of building up his milk factory and I wondered if he could do with an extra pair of hands to build? I would work hard, not expect much pay as family and have nearly enough saved to pay my own fare out to New Zealand—I'm minded applying for a subsidy to the New Zealand Company to make up the shortfall—so I don't need to worry you on these particulars. What do you think? I know I would be leaving Charlie my eldest and only brother in Scotland, but he has recently wed a local lass by the name of Kate Hamilton and I see little of them.

Please write as soon as you can so that I can book a passage if I am needed.

Kindest regards, your nephew,

Jack

Eliza showed the letter at once to Alister.

"What do you think, dear?" she asked. "You are increasingly busy at the survey office and the men here are struggling to keep up with our building plans."

"I hope you're not asking simply because he's Kitty's boy," said Alister tersely. "You can never replace her, you know."

"I know that full well," replied Eliza curtly. She was shocked that Alister could be so callous.

"But he is Kitty's son and family. Surely, we owe them something. They lost their lives in coming out to our employ."

"Well yes, we could certainly do with his skills, by all means let him come."

"I'm sure Alister doesn't mean to be brutal," said Robert as Eliza later related the incident to him. "He's probably still suffering himself from the death of his brother and the reminder of Kitty brings it all back to him. And it will be a comfort to you having Kitty's son here with you, not to mention a real help."

Eliza smiled and nodded. How understanding Robert was.

"I must write to him at once and tell him how welcome he is here," she said.

June 26, 1874

My Dear Jack,

We were both surprised and delighted to receive your letter. Of course, you will be welcome here. You would be welcome even if there was little work to do because you're family, but I can assure you there is more than enough work to keep you busy. Please book your passage, I will apply for a subsidy to the New Zealand Company on your behalf, assuring them of your usefulness to us here at Waireka. You must let us know, as far as you are able, when we might expect you. We wish you a pleasant and most of all a safe journey, indeed, we pray God's protection over you.

Your,

Aunt Eliza

The next few months passed so quickly that it hardly seemed any time at all before the young man made his way to Waireka in the early summer of 1875.

With his light brown wavy hair, Eliza imagined he took his appearance from his father Charles rather than her beloved Kitty. But he wasn't long at the farm before she noticed that he possessed some of her sister's little mannerisms, so much so that at times she could almost feel Kitty standing beside her.

True to his word, Jack was a hard worker, and even Alister admitted he was skilled at building with his skills soon separating him out as the natural leader of the work and Alister felt more able to leave the building to him. Eliza also noticed that a change had come over her Annie since his arrival. She seemed keener to help with the baking and to take out the regular refreshments for the men. When Eliza challenged her about this, Annie flushed.

"Jack is our cousin and family, surely it is only right we treat him well."

"Well, naturally, but I wondered if I didn't detect a certain partiality," said Eliza questioningly.

"Oh mother," was all she got by way of a response.

But Eliza noticed how Annie became very quiet at evening meal times and appeared to blush furiously if addressed by Jack. She also noticed the young man glancing admiringly at her daughter when he thought Annie wasn't looking.

"We'll be having to arrange another wedding before too long," Eliza said to Alister when Jack had been with them just over a month.

"Oh, whose," he said absentmindedly.

"Our Annie's. Have you not seen the way she and Jack gaze at one another?"

"No, I can't say I have, but you women know more about these matters than we do."

And Eliza reflected sadly at how true this was in the case of her husband.

Annie and Jack's wedding was arranged for the following spring in 1876. With two daughters now married and the dairy business growing more profitable by the year, Eliza had never felt happier. As well as Jack, they had employed a couple of other cowmen and now had three new sheds operating and two four hundred-gallon separators, a testing machine and a rudimentary sterilizer, much of which Jack had helped to build. He had also helped to install the very latest herringbone cow stalls to make the milking easier as well as a new barn which now housed the horses instead of them being squashed into a corner of the main barn. This made it possible to acquire five new ponies to pull the carts—Possum, Dobbin, Ginger, Zakky and Tom (all named by the children) and three extra carts.

Belle seemed to take special delight in looking after the horses and was a natural horsewoman, riding out whenever she could and often transporting some of the milk to the surrounding farms. But as the work increased, the horses began to demand more time than Belle alone could give to them and it became necessary for them to seek the services of a skilled horseman. A new local young man called Montgomery King, fondly known as "Monty" joined them. He seemed to have a real feel for the horses and they seemed to respond well to his handling, as did Belle, who now seemed to spend more time with him and the horses than at the milking. This shared interest seemed to bring the two of them together and at the end of a day's work Eliza often saw them going off for a ride.

It was in the autumn of 1878, when everything seemed to be going well, when the flu epidemic struck.

Many were laid low by the epidemic which seemed to largely pass by Eliza and her family, although she had to support Charlotte and Adam in the death of their youngest child, Martha. This was hard, both for them and Eliza, bringing back to her the loss of little Alister and Margaret with frightening clarity. But then Mary Yate was similarly struck down.

In her already-weakened state the flu didn't bode well for Mary and many didn't expect her to survive it. Eliza saw little of Robert in the ensuing weeks and at first feared much more for Robert's health, with his being in constant contact with Mary, than in praying for Mary's health. She soon had to repent of her sinful attitude. She reasoned with herself that even if Mary died, she wouldn't be free to marry Robert. This might make the temptation of seeing one another daily even worse for them both. Realising this she began to pray fervently for Mary's recovery. After a month passed it seemed as if her prayers had been answered and Mary rallied. Eliza's spirits also rallied. Everything could go on just as before, couldn't it?

But soon after, Robert came to her cap in hand looking sad and withdrawn. She knew at once from his gait that something was wrong.

"Mary's not gone into decline again has she Robert?" she asked at once.

"No," he said immediately, "but we must go away, leave this place."

Eliza paled. "Leave? Whatever do you mean?" she said grasping his hands. She feared him continuing but knew she must hear the worst.

Robert had also turned pale as he struggled to get his words out. "Mary's health is so delicate now that the doctor says the windy climate here no longer suits her. He suggests a sunnier climate, somewhere more central like Palmerston North or perhaps Hastings on the coast." He finished speaking as if he had dispensed a huge burden.

"But that's miles from here and we have the business . . . I don't see how we could move at the moment," said Eliza thinking out loud.

Robert looked sorrowful but resigned. "My love, you cannot move, I know that. But we must. There is nothing else to be done."

"What am I to do without you?" said Eliza panic stricken as his words sank in.

"I suppose we will have to make the best of things," said Robert sighing heavily. "It's not what I want either but what can I do? I'm duty bound to care for Mary, she's my wife, whatever my true feelings dictate. I'd be a monster indeed, if I sacrificed her health for my own desires."

"St Andrews and your living—what will you do about that?" asked Eliza vaguely like one in a dream.

"They will have to be told but I wanted you to be the first to know. This time I know that you must hear first being the first in my heart."

The merest trace of a smile crossed Eliza's lips as she remembered the previous time when Robert had accepted the living here in Frampton making all the arrangements with the church before thinking to tell her. He was a different man these days. Her man. Her heart ached at the thought of the impending separation, indeed, she thought it might break.

"Besides," Robert continued still thinking of his parishioners. "Since Kitty's birth, I have noticed a certain hostility in the church, a distinct lack of support for me and my ministry."

"Well, more fool them then," Eliza said with feeling. "They're losing a first-class minister who really cares for the word of God."

"I doubt they'd see it that way," said Robert sadly.

It was just a few months later, in the early spring of 1879, that the Yates were to leave Frampton. The speed at which everything took place was frightening. As it turned out, a Reverend James Patterson, newly arrived from Scotland, was looking for a living and was happy to move into the Manse of the Yates and take over the running of St Andrews almost immediately. He had a young wife, Fanny, and two young children and declared that the living would, "suit them all perfectly although they would need to extend the Manse in time." Everyone seemed happy with the arrangement except Eliza. Even Alister considered him a sound choice.

The dreaded departure time remained etched forever in Eliza's memory. Robert had managed to slip away quietly the night before and met Eliza in the town.

"I dinna want our private farewells to be mixed in with the general ones, lassie," he said sadly.

"But it needn't be a final farewell surely?" said Eliza, anxiously clutching at straws. "M . . . Maybe in time we could come and visit you?"

"Ah lass, maybe," he replied sighing heavily. "Although I'm not sure what Mary would have to say about that."

Eliza sadly acknowledged the truth of his words. Mary would probably be relieved, even glad to leave them, leave *her* behind.

"Until that day, my dearest love," Robert continued slowly each word being laboured over. "I will keep you always in my heart and write to you often if you wish."

"Indeed, you'd better," she answered fiercely, "for your letters will be my very life's blood."

"Aye, and mine too," he replied brusquely.

Then words were done. He clasped her tightly to himself and gazing up into his eyes she could feel his heart reflected in them before his lips claimed hers in the most passionate kiss she had ever experienced that seemed to go on forever. He only stopped when there was practically no more breath left in either of them.

"I'll no say goodbye to you, lassie," he said after a few minutes when they had both regained their breath, "for that word and you can never go together. Instead, I'll leave you with a 'see you again soon'. Look after yourself and our little Kitty."

Eliza nodded. She couldn't trust herself to speak at that moment without breaking down and wailing so hard she imagined everyone would hear her. Instead she clung to him fiercely once more before turning around sharply and walking in the opposite direction. She didn't dare look back for her tears were flowing so hard and fast down her face it was all she could do to make her way home. But somehow, she knew if she had caught a last glimpse of him at that time he would be battling similarly with his emotions.

The next day Alister went over to lend a hand with the packing and to say a last farewell and was surprised when he couldn't persuade Eliza to go with him.

"I made my farewells of him and Mary yesterday," was all she said. "No need to make them again." It took Eliza all her strength and resolve not to go again with Alister to catch just another glimpse of Robert and to feel his arms around her once again. But she knew it was impossible. She could not be intimate again with him in the company of Robert's wife and her husband and it would be sheer agony to see him there and not be intimate. It was a pain she couldn't bear to put him through, nevermind herself.

As for Mary, she had seen Mary briefly nearly a week ago and wished her well, and Mary had seemed pleased with the idea of the move, even though she was still pale and weak. She had told Eliza how much she was looking forward to the new sunnier climate of central New Zealand, exchanging more words with Eliza than she had in some long time. She even appeared to Eliza to bid her farewell with a certain amount of satisfaction.

Eliza managed to catch a last glimpse of their cart as it wended its way down the road and past her driveway in the late morning. She was hanging out the washing and for a moment time itself seemed to stand still for her. She wondered how her life was going to go on without him as a part of it, but she only knew it would.

Chapter Thirteen

LIFE WENT ON MUCH AS before for Eliza even though it felt as if her world had ended with the departure of Robert. At least she could now live for his letters, but it was a few weeks before she received the first. She knew at once it was from him because was addressed just to her—

Mrs Eliza Douglas

Alister had shown some surprise when he first saw the letter. He turned it over in his hands, a puzzled expression on his face.

"Who on earth would be writing just to you, Eliza, and not me too? I know that your sister Kitty would do so, but I cannot think who else might. Should I open it I wonder?"

"No, no, it's fine," said Eliza quickly, reaching out to take the letter from him. She was sure her face must betray her guilt. "Margaret has told me Mama's health is failing," she said blushing at the lie she had to tell which implicated her family. "She has told me she will send me regular updates." Eliza felt this at least would help to explain the frequency of the correspondence between her and Robert. "I told her to address them to me rather than both of us because I know you are busy and wouldn't want to be worried by such particulars when I can easily share her news with you."

"Ah, I see," said Alister but Eliza wasn't sure he was completely convinced and blushed again at her boldness.

"Well how is she faring?"

"Margaret says she has taken to her bed but is receiving a little gruel which has strengthened her somewhat."

Eliza sent up a silent prayer begging for God's forgiveness in using her mother as a pawn to hide the illicit correspondence between Robert and herself.

"That's good then. I'll leave you to read it. I'll be at the survey office today if you need me." And whether or not he was convinced at her audacious story, he turned towards the door to leave.

"Right you are, Alister," Eliza said, trying to sound relaxed and feeling anything but.

At least she could rejoice for once in her husband's local government concerns. His absence would allow her the privacy to indulge herself in Robert's letter once the children were away at school at Ertha Blake's.

After dropping them off she came back to the house, made herself a cup of tea and sat down to read Robert's letter.

October 6, 1879

My darling Lizzie,

Every day of the last three weeks I have thought of you constantly. Once or twice I have even woken up calling out your name in my sleep. Thankfully Mary has not heard me as we are now in separate rooms. Mary has preferred her own room since suffering the flu so badly and I thank God for that.

The living here is tolerable and the people friendly and welcoming (of course they have no reason to indulge themselves in gossip!) and Mary has even invited some of the ladies of the parish to take tea with her. I do believe Mary's colour is improving daily and her health is becoming more robust which allows her to take on more such duties, but I, personally would give anything to be back at St Andrews with you. I am sure you are very busy with the milking and butter making and perhaps this keeps your mind from straying on to thoughts of me. I pray so. I send a kiss to all of your children but especially to my dearest Kitty. Do let me know how she fares. Never forget the depth of my love for her and you.

I am,

Yours Devotedly,

Robert

After reading through the letter a few times and imagining Robert writing to her, Eliza hastened to write her reply so that she could post her letter at the local store when walking down to collect the children.

October 16, 1879

My dearest Robert,

How lovely to hear from you. I am writing a reply back straightaway in order to help speed another of your letters to me! How can you even imagine that I should forget you for a moment or be able to so bury myself in my work as to have no thought of you? I think of you as I milk and as I make butter, as I see to the children and even, I am ashamed to say, when very occasionally love making with Alister. It is always you I have in my arms, not him. May God forgive me. You haunt my sleep too.

I was surprised to read about Mary's new lease of life but maybe the climate is indeed more suitable for her or maybe just being away from me and having you all to herself suits her better.

You ask of the children, especially Kitty. They are all doing very well. Kitty loves to come and help me with the milking and butter making. I only wish she would attend to her lessons with the same passion!

Never doubt my love for you, my darling. Having you away
from me does not suit me at all however it agrees with Mary!

I am and always will be,

Your own,

Lizzie

As Eliza shared the day to day concerns of the business at Waireka
with him, it was almost like having Kitty back as a correspondent, although it could never be quite the same as their passions were poured
out upon the pages. She missed Robert in every way, in both his
personal and official duties and was also finding the prospect of the
Reverend Patterson being the minister officiating at the forthcoming
wedding of Belle and Monty difficult to contemplate. They were to be
married in the summer of 1879, just months after the Yates had left.
Belle insisted on the horses taking a huge part in the proceedings and
after marrying in front of the house the young couple departed on a
cart decked out with flowers by Eliza and the children and pulled by
Possum and Tom. Eliza wondered how they should manage the milk
deliveries without the two horses, but Belle assured her that they were
going only to Grantley to stay with some cousins of Monty's for the
weekend and would have the horses back for duty on Monday morning.

It was the following year, in the spring of 1880, when the school,
run so efficiently by Ertha Blake in just an old shed, burnt down. Eliza
wrote an account of it to Robert.

October 11, 1880

My dearest Robert,

You would not know our community now. The old shed
where Ertha Blake her school these past few years, is no
more! Yes, indeed, it has burnt down! You should have
seen the commotion it stirred up in our small community
that evening last Wednesday when the Reverend Patterson

discovered it. It was the early evening around half past seven, when he was taking his constitutional, as he calls it, when he saw a bright glare coming from the school room window. On opening the door, he was met by such a roomful of smoke and such a strong smell of burning he said his eyes started to sting and he began to choke. He then saw flames licking out from schoolroom and the intensity of the heat coming at him was so great that he was forced to beat a hasty retreat. "Fire, fire," he yelled so loudly we all came running to see. As you can imagine, within a very short time, nearly all our small community was gathered around near to the school, so near in fact, that Bob Bunting and his fire crew had to shout at us to move back so that they might get through to tackle the blaze. Unfortunately, it was probably too late even by the time the Reverend Patterson discovered the fire and the shed couldn't be saved. It's now thought that it might have started before seven just after Mrs Blake locked up. The loose screw in the door of the wood burner seems to have finally worked itself loose enough to allow a smouldering log to drop out on to the floor. Of course, Mrs Blake, in her own words, blames herself for not "having seen to it earlier" but no one else blames her. Luckily the Reverend Patterson has loaned Ertha a room in the Manse for the continuation of lessons—of course with the new extensions our Jack had built for him, they now have two more rooms than ever you or Mary did. The school was therefore up and running again within a few days. This was to the disgust and dismay of some of the pupils, including our Kitty, I'm afraid, who cannot see the point of book learning when there's work to be done on the farm! Jack has already drawn up plans to build us a new school and will start on the work very soon.

So, you see everything is changing here, your house included. I'm thinking you would hardly know the place if you were to return, which I know is not possible even though it is my dearest wish.

I send you my deepest love.

Your,

Lizzie

The school continued to meet at the Manse until the summer of 1881, when Jack finally finished building it on the site of the old one. It took him longer than he wanted or indeed, Mrs Blake wished, but Jack had also been kept very busy with even more extensions to the Manse. It grieved Eliza to look at the new Manse which had changed almost out of recognition. It felt to her as if Robert had been written out of the town, although everyone else, including Alister, considered the changes for the better.

Then in 1885 when life had settled back to some sort of normality Eliza feared she had nearly lost Alister a second time only this time there was no Robert to rescue him. Alister had gone into Wellington for a few provisions, a trip he had made hundreds of times before. Monty had gone with him, they had taken a cart and a couple of horses and gone off for a few days. Belle had begged to go with them but as she was now suffering from morning sickness and an almost certain pregnancy, this was considered unwise by both Alister and Monty.

The two men had gone off just before Christmas of that year and were expected back before the family celebrations. But within two days, reports came back of a huge fire at Wellington's Lambton Quay where Eliza feared the two men had gone. She didn't tell Belle for fear that the shock could cause a miscarriage, but she told Kitty, along with Charlotte and Adam, Susan Jepson and the Reverend Patterson, who vowed to send up prayers for the two men's safe delivery. Kitty, in particular, was a real strength to her during those worrying few days.

To Eliza's relief they finally returned on Christmas Eve looking battle weary and with few provisions.

"Thank God you're both safe my dear," she said going to Alister and giving him a kiss on the cheek. "We all feared for the safety of you and Monty with the reports we have heard of the Wellington fire and have said prayers for you every day, as the Reverend Patterson has. We didn't breathe a word of it to Belle though for fear she might lose the baby."

"Very wise," said Alister patting her arm gently. "Fortunately, Monty and I weren't staying at the Branch Hotel or the Occidental which were chiefly affected and where we often stay. They were both completely full for the holiday period. We were at the Queen's and although it seems none of the guests at the two aforementioned hotels were injured, they did lose all their possessions and the hotels were badly burnt. I have a copy of the *Evening Post* if you wish to read about it. It seems that they apportion blame to a Mr Myers at the picture framing shop. According to the paper, he had been melting glue in the grate of the room behind his shop and what started as a little fire the previous evening was raging by dawn the next day."

"All I can say is thank the Lord no one was killed or injured," said Eliza with feeling.

"Amen to that," said Alister. "It also seems that Whiteford's fire team have been blamed for the fire spreading so quickly. They didn't assess the situation quickly enough and the water pressure was so low that it didn't tackle the blaze as well as it might. With the high winds of Wellington, the sparks from the fire spread very quickly leading to widespread damage."

"Will Mr Myers be prosecuted for his part in starting the fire?" asked Eliza.

"I don't know if they'll be able to prove anything and I think it sounds as if the fire team are equally to blame for the extent of the damage," said Alister, "but I'm afraid we didn't get the meat we wanted.

Wellington's Meat Company was for the most part saved but a rascal went off with their cash register and they couldn't sell any meat after the fire. It will necessitate a further trip early in the new year in a few weeks' time."

"We're just grateful to have you both back safe and sound," said Eliza. "And as to provisions, we'll manage, we always have."

By 1886 the milking and dairy operations were well established. Each cow was milked and then the milk taken to a cooling room where it was weighed. Alister had finally succeeded in persuading the other farmers to come on board his share milking scheme and could now boast a share in four dairies on four different farms. Each dairy had its own brake or cart now to transport the milk and could carry forty cans on each. The business was finally expanding in the way he had envisaged.

All the milk from the dairies was delivered to the Waireka factory and then entered into a 400-gallon separator where the waste whey was skimmed off for the calves and pigs. There was a constant supply of cream run off into a chilling tank which was chilled overnight before it was churned into butter.

The problems for Alister and Eliza didn't occur in the manufacture of the butter but in its transportation.

"We've received yet another letter from a dissatisfied customer Alister," said Eliza. "He says the butter was bad yet again and smelling distinctly rancid on arrival with him, and he's not paying the bill. If he and other customers continue to complain and the problem can't be resolved, we'll be bankrupt before long."

"Did you pack the butter with lots of salt, Eliza, to preserve it?"

"Of course, we did," she replied annoyed that he should doubt the girls and her efficiency.

"Just checking," he said defensively. "But we can't go on losing money this way, that's for sure. There must be a solution to this problem—if only we could find it."

"Giving up long distance transportation I suppose," said Eliza despondently.

"No, we can't afford to do that. There aren't enough local customers to keep the factory viable. Leave it with me, I'll come up with something," he said leaving her as if mulling over the options in his mind.

Alister really was the eternal optimist thought Eliza, though perhaps it was a good thing in this new country where everyone was struggling to start up new businesses and compete with one another.

Alister soon decided it wasn't that the salt wasn't the fault for the butter not being preserved properly but the huge glass containers the butter was transported in, they weren't providing enough insulation.

"What we need, Eliza, is tins."

"Tins. And where do you imagine we're going to obtain enough tins for the job?" she asked unconvinced. "They're a fairly new product and expensive to buy."

"I know. That's why I thought Cyril and I might manage to build us a tin-making machine fit for purpose."

"Cyril's an engineer, dear, not an inventor," said Eliza in exasperation.

"Just you wait and see. We'll have her up and running in no time," Alister said optimistically, off to share his plans with Cyril.

"Don't worry, Mama," Kitty had said, "we will find a way to solve this problem one way or another."

In her frustration, Eliza wrote to Robert—

September 12, 1886

My dearest Robert,

You know how stubborn Alister is once he takes a scheme into his mind? Well his latest idea is to build a tin-making machine. Just imagine! Poor Cyril is an engineer not an inventor, as I told Alister. I know we do need to find a way to stop the butter going rancid in transportation, but I cannot see how either Alister or Cyril have sufficient knowledge or experience to succeed in making a machine that will turn out tins. Alister often thinks I am woefully lacking in faith but I believe I sometimes have a more practical eye than him. Thank goodness, I have dear Kitty, who consoles me that Alister will find a way sooner or later. She has more faith in him than I do. However, I am certainly not lacking in faith as far as our love is concerned. I believe in the veracity and long-lasting nature of your love for me and you can have no doubt that I will love you forever and a day. Please write soon and let me have your news.

Your,

Lizzie

Eliza was right about the tin-making machine. This scheme of Alister was a step too far for the skills of either Cyril or himself and they finally had to admit defeat.

Soon after this though Alister read in the local paper that the first refrigerated ship had transported a consignment of butter from Dunedin in the South all the way to England without the butter going bad.

"This is the answer we've been looking for, Lizzie," he said excitedly running out of the house with the paper in his hand and pointing to the article as Eliza continued to pat the butter into shape.

"Special ships that keep the butter cold, so it arrives in perfect condition with our customers."

Eliza nodded. This did sound like a foolproof scheme.

"Good job that we have the other share milkers with us now," she said, "for we'd never be able to afford such an expensive method of transportation on our own."

"No, we wouldn't, but I can't see them objecting to putting their money into this transportation method. After all, if our customers keep refusing to pay their bills we'll all miss out. In the same way, if we fund this type of transport to ensure our butter's safe arrival then we will all make more money in the end. It's the only practical way forward."

For once Eliza agreed with her husband. They would have to pay out for transportation if they were to survive. If they didn't the business would surely go under. Fortunately, Alister managed to convince the other share milkers and the business began to thrive once more.

Many letters had passed between Eliza and Robert over the years since he and Mary had left Frampton before the letter came that almost stopped Eliza's heart beating.

January 4, 1887

My dearest Lizzie,

How strange it is that Mary's health should be improving and growing stronger each day as I decrease in strength. Indeed, I think her health is better now than it has been at any time since our marriage. What do I mean by my health decreasing? I'm not sure but I have been finding recently I cannot enjoy my food and I often vomit after meals. At first, I thought it might be the strength of my feelings for you affecting my appetite but now I find myself also in considerable pain and I think that I should seek a medical opinion. What do you think? I have been struggling to run

St George's recently and have had to seek the assistance of a minister from a nearby living. Please don't share this news with anyone, especially Kitty.

Your own,

Robert

Frightened for Robert, Eliza replied as soon as she received his letter.

February 1, 1887

My dearest Robert,

Of course, you must seek a medical opinion and at once. I am only surprised Mary hasn't suggested it. Please let me know the prognosis at soon as you can and in the meantime, I will pray for you constantly. You can of course, be assured of my secrecy in this matter.

Write soon my love.

Your own,

Lizzie

A letter came back quickly, and Eliza's breath fair caught in her throat as she glanced at the contents.

"The news of your mother isn't good I think, Eliza?" asked Alister noticing his wife's pale face.

"My mother," she said puzzled, the shock of the letter causing her to momentarily forget the little story she had concocted.

"Yes, you told me that Margaret was keeping you informed of her progress," Alister said also puzzled.

"I'm sorry, my dear," Eliza said quickly, "I was so shocked by the contents of the letter I found it hard to gather my thoughts for a moment." That at least was true.

"My dear, I hope the news isn't bad?"

"Not good," said Eliza feeling tearful. She was struggling not to sob openly.

"Not the worst I hope?"

"Yes, the worst," she said at once, beginning to sob despite her efforts to control herself. "She's died."

"My dear, I'm sorry to hear that," said Alister, taking her hands in his in an effort to console her.

"Thank you for your comfort, Alister," said Eliza, her voice visibly shaking, "but I would prefer to be alone for a while if you don't mind." She knew that this at least was something he would understand.

"Of course, I'll arrange for someone else to take on your duties today, give you some time to yourself."

Eliza felt guilty at her husband's thoughtfulness when she was, in truth, being deliberately deceptive but she did need some time to digest the contents of Robert's letter alone so didn't try to stop him from re-arranging her duties. Quite how she would explain his letters in the future was a problem she didn't think she could apply her mind to right now. She read through Robert's letter once again, this time taking in every word with its awful stark truth. The words this time, caused her to sob openly as her tears fell on the pages, blotching the ink at several places.

March 6, 1887

My dearest, darling Lizzie,

Please don't upset yourself but I have been to the doctor and I'm afraid the news isn't good. He says I have cancer of the stomach. There is nothing that can be done, and he says I should have only months to live as the cancer is well advanced. I don't grieve for myself my dear, the pain can be alleviated by strong painkillers and I know I should soon face my Maker, which gives me great joy. My only deep sadness is that we should never meet again as we once hoped against all hopes. Now I know that can never be. But perhaps it is better this way. If I cannot have you in this life perhaps we can meet and love in the next. We can surely enjoy God's wonderful presence one day knowing that we took our responsibilities seriously and didn't betray those closest to us, excepting the once, with young Kitty. May God forgive me for that, I consider myself wholly responsible my dearest, although I find I still can't be sorry. Maybe the Lord may even forgive us our clandestine correspondence? I do pray so. I will certainly beg the full forgiveness of the Lord at the end and pray for His mercy in the light of the catalogue of my many sins.

I will write again soon and love you forever.

All my love dearest, fairest Lizzie,

Robert x

However, this was to prove the last letter she ever received from him so there was no need for her to dissemble over any further letters.

Just over a month later, when Eliza was beginning to fret at having received no further news from Robert, the letter came that she had dreaded receiving. It was from Mary and addressed to them both.

April 10, 1887

My dear Alister and Eliza,

It is with great sadness I write to tell you that my dearest Robert has passed away. We were told a few weeks ago that he had just a few months to live but in the end the disease took him much quicker than was expected. It was only a matter of a couple of weeks later when he passed away peacefully in his sleep. He was unable to take on many duties at George's in the last few months anyway and the stipendiary minister who had been assisting him, the Reverend Jonathan Anderson, has now become his permanent replacement.

I know that you were good friends of ours at one time and in his last few weeks, Robert spoke of you both constantly. I can hardly believe that I have, in the end, outlived him. My health is more robust than it was in Frampton although as I get older I feel more aches and pains, but I mustn't grumble I suppose.

No, you mustn't thought Eliza, *for you are still here and my beloved Robert has gone aged just fifty-five.* She felt angry with Mary. *Here was her beloved, who had devoted most of his life to this creature, gone, and yet she still spoke more of her own ailments rather than dear, sweet Robert's sufferings.* Eliza clenched her fists in fury beneath the table. But as Alister read on she had even more reason to feel both outraged and devastated in equal measures.

We buried Robert just last week. I did think of asking you and Eliza to the funeral but then considered you would be too busy to leave the business and come all the way over to Palmerston North. The milking and butter making is, I know, an all-consuming task, not to mention the care of the children, and so I thought I would write to you instead, just to let you know of his passing. We were all close once, weren't we? Even though we haven't managed to meet up in the last few years.

She finished her letter with the usual polite greetings and saying that if they ever happened to be in the area they were very welcome to call in and see her.

"How could she not see fit to invite us to Robert's funeral?" asked Eliza both angry and upset at the same time. "We could have made the time. The children are old enough to leave now and there are plenty workers on the farm."

"But she's right, dear," said Alister in a matter-of fact tone. "Only consider, I am very busy at the survey offices at present. A trip there would have meant us being away for several days, and I'm not sure I could have spared the time. Besides, it is a while since they were a part of our lives."

A while since they were a part of their lives, Alister had said. Little did he know how much she and Robert had corresponded since they left. Robert, dead or alive, would always be a part of her life. He would be in her every waking thought and prayers until she went to be with him. As to Mary saying that they hadn't met up in the last few years, Eliza felt certain it was Mary who had made sure of that.

And what of Alister? He had said he could not have spared the time and yet for her, all time had practically stopped. Her dearest, best love taken from her. Her heart felt heavy, like a lead weight within her and she felt she could never be completely happy again. Robert, lost to her forever, at least in this life, and she had been denied the chance to even bid him goodbye. All she had was that last letter of his which declared that he would "love her forever."

Chapter Fourteen

KITTY

ALTHOUGH LIFE WENT ON, ELIZA felt in some ways as if she had died when Robert died. Then just a few months later, when she was collecting Alexander from school, her mind recalled once again the incident of the school fire and of writing to Robert to share the tale. She remembered how amused he had been by the story of the small community so tightly gathered around the school shed that the fire service struggled to reach the blaze. In remembering his amusement as she recounted the tale to him she also remembered that he wasn't there anymore to share her stories, her thoughts and dreams and it seemed as if her heart stopped within her at the thought. Not simply emotionally, as previously, but physically too, as she found herself on the ground with shooting pains in her chest before everything went black.

For one blissful moment, she imagined she'd gone to be with him, but instead as she came around she saw first the face of the doctor, then the worried faces of her dear Kitty and young Alexander gazing at her in concern. She must rouse herself. Robert might be gone but they still needed her. It took Eliza a few weeks of bed rest to recover from the enormous jolt her heart had taken, but the strength of the attack had so weakened her, that she was forced, from this point, to leave the milk and butter making to her family.

When alone on her bed she had given vent to the deepest emotions she had ever felt. The death of her dear sister Kitty had been great, but this grief was in a class of its own. At least through the darkest moments of Kitty's death, Robert had been there to hold her hand, to pray for her and now she would never feel his touch again. Lying there in bed gave her time to think about him and to miss him even more intensely. It was especially during the night hours when the house was still, that her thoughts of him almost took on a shape of their own.

One night soon after her heart attack was especially vivid. She had been dreaming of Robert yet again, only to wake up and remember that he was gone from her forever and the waves of grief again threatened to almost overwhelm her. Then glancing across towards the window she could just about make out the shape of a man standing there. "Alister," she called out, imagining it could be no other, when the figure turned towards her and she saw in that moment the face of her beloved gazing at her. "Robert? My darling how I have longed for you. But no, it cannot be you. Why are you here?"

He didn't speak but smiled, a smile of love and devotion as he seemed to beckon her towards him. "Robert, I cannot come," she whispered, "I am too weak to leave this bed."

But still the figure beckoned her to come. All at once it was as if her feet grew wings and her old strength returned to her as she sprung out of bed to go towards him. As she got nearer she saw the figure fade and her feet once again became leaden as her strength left her and she collapsed in a heap on the floor.

Hearing a loud bang, Kitty dashed into the room crying, "Mama, Mama, what on earth are you doing out of bed? You were told to rest by the doctor. Is there anything I can get you?"

Staring into the space that Robert had seemed to occupy such a short time ago, there was nothing Eliza could want apart from him. But not wishing to frighten her daughter by telling her of the apparition she shook her head as Kitty helped her to her feet and back into the bed. Whether he had really been there in some ghostly form or was just a figment of her own fertile imagination, Eliza never knew, but she felt comforted by seeing him. Now she could face the future, however long she had, and be strong, knowing that he was waiting for her on the other side of time.

* * *

She was brought back to the present with a start. It was now more than three years since his passing and yet as fresh in her mind as if it had happened yesterday. But each day it seemed as if she grew weaker. Although she had a desire to remain on the earth to see her children all settled, each day her soul and her heart seemed to grieve for him a little more and it seemed as if her desire to join him grew a little stronger. She was tired, weary of this life and now with young Alexander having left school, there seemed little to keep her here, except to see her dearest Kitty settled with a good man. Alister's civic duties took him away more and more and now that she had been bedridden for these last three years, his desire for her and her company seemed to have dwindled. She was glad really. Lying in his arms and making love to him felt like a travesty after Robert. Alister seemed frightened to tire her and she was reluctant to have much physical contact with him now that Robert had gone.

Eliza had always thought it might be her eldest Charlotte or even Annie or Belle who'd take to life at the dairy but Charlotte and Adam had moved away from Waireka to take charge of one of the other share milking farms a few years ago and Annie and Jack had moved into Frampton itself, where he was required to help with the town's expansion plans, even though Jack still saw to Waireka's building needs. Even Belle and Monty, although remaining at Waireka, were now involved solely with the care of the horses. Belle and Monty had been married for over ten years now and Annie and Charlotte longer. Even her little Jean had married a local farmer from Grantley, a cousin of Monty's and had all but deserted her these three years. Where had all the years gone? It was now Russell, David and Kitty who managed the large dairy herd and organised the butter production and distribution. Russell and David were married too, each of them living with their wives on one of the other share farms, although working at the Waireka factory for most of their time. Kitty and Alexander were her only unmarried children now.

Kitty was young and capable, growing more like Robert day by day and Eliza loved her accordingly. Life was hard in this pioneering land and it forced women to take their places alongside the men in establishing the new land. It was Kitty who had surprised Eliza the most with her independent spirit and single devotion to herself. Kitty who had declared that she would never leave Waireka and selfishly Eliza hoped she never would.

The voice of Kitty sitting beside her then broke through her thoughts, "Mama, Mama, should I go and help David and Russell with the milking or would you rather I stayed here with you?"

Eliza felt weak and listless, but she didn't want to keep her daughter with her when there was work to be done.

"I'm fine, my dear," she said reaching out her hand towards her daughter. "Just a bit weak but nothing that won't wait when there's milking to be done. You'd best be gone, or the cows will be dropping their milk." She smiled reassuringly.

Kitty marched off determinedly, assured that her mother would be fine for a while and anxious to get to her work.

Sometimes Eliza thought it was her dear children, especially Kitty, who had kept her going these few years since Robert's death. Kitty was so like him with her dark curls and fine features that took her right back to that time of indiscretion, the only time, but a time that she had lived and re-lived again in her mind. Alister had never accepted that Kitty could be anyone's but his, even if he had sometimes suspected it. Eliza supposed this to be because he could not conceive of his wife not fulfilling her marital duties to himself alone.

But as she grew Kitty seemed to take more particular care of her than the others. Kitty had been just a young girl when Robert left and since then had grown more and more like him.

As she lay there thinking of those first few years setting up the farm with Alister and building the dairy sheds, her mind moved back decades to when she, as a young seventeen-year-old girl herself, younger then than her beloved Kitty's twenty-four years, had left her home in Scotland to travel here to New Zealand. What an adventure her life had been, the good and the bad bits! Why, when they set sail in the autumn of 1850, New Zealand was still a relatively unexplored land and they were some of the first settlers. Now many more folk made the journey, which although still precarious, was safer than it had been in those days.

Then she thought of the letters, Robert's letters to her. She would never know what had become of hers to him but suspected that if Mary had found them amongst his things she would probably have burnt them. But knowing Robert and how careful he was to protect Mary's health from the truth of their relationship, she imagined that he had probably burnt them himself after reading them. But she hadn't been so strong. His letters were still tied up with a red ribbon in the drawer where she kept her undergarments, a place she knew Alister would never go. It was time to hand them on now. She would give them to Kitty, she decided, then Kitty would know about her and Robert and her true parentage. It was only right that she should know the truth that she was born of a deep, passionate love. Surely, she would know what to do with their letters. But as Eliza reasoned this in her mind she then considered the consequences of her actions. Supposing this was a complete shock to Kitty and made her despise her mother, despise her mother's betrayal of the man she thought of as her father? Eliza could hardly bear the thought of losing Kitty's high regard for her. *What should she do?*

Eliza agonised over her decision for days, but as she became weaker still, she resolved that she must disclose the letters to Kitty. They mustn't simply be discovered after her death. If that should happen, she was sure that Kitty would feel betrayed by her, upset by the fact she hadn't trusted her enough to confide in her. And what should happen if they fell into the hands of the rest of her family? Eliza shuddered to think.

The family were now caring for her around the clock as Eliza's health weakened further and the Reverend Patterson was a regular visitor. One night, when it was Kitty's watch, Eliza opened her eyes and spoke quietly and haltingly to her daughter.

"Kitty, there's something you should know. Something I must tell you."

"Hush Mama, sleep. Don't upset yourself."

"I need you to understand about Robert—Reverend Yate—about his letters, about us. Please my dear, it's important to me."

"The Reverend Yate's letters, Mama, whatever are you talking about?" Kitty thought that her mother was becoming delirious. "You must try to rest, Mama, for your own good."

"No, I cannot rest until you know everything, please."

Her mother seemed so adamant, Kitty could see she was growing anxious and wanted to avoid her becoming worse. It was probably just something trifling but perhaps she should try and humour her, people often needed to reveal things they considered important before they died.

"What is it then, Mama?" she asked gently.

"Alister is not your father," Eliza began.

Kitty's face drained of colour. Was her mother that delirious or was there some ominous truth in the words she had spoken?

"What on earth do you mean, are you saying I'm adopted?" She couldn't think of any other sensible explanation for what her mother was saying.

"No of course not. You are mine, but Robert, Reverend Yate, was your father."

"My father, whatever do you mean?" *Had her dear Mama really lost all sense of reason? Was she talking nonsense?* But something about her Mama's quiet but forthright statement convinced her that this was much more than nonsense. It had a distinct ring of truth to it. She had always wondered why she was dark and most of her brothers and sisters were fair, but her father had always assured her that her colouring must have come down the line from a distant relative, and she had always believed him, until now.

"I loved him and he, me," said Eliza her eyes misting over. "Go to the big chest and open the small top drawer. His letters will explain what we meant to one another."

"Your undergarment drawer?" asked Kitty puzzled. It was a place she had never gone into before. Everything seemed so strange, so unreal.

"Yes, just do what I say."

No one was more surprised than Kitty as she delved under the pile of her mother's undergarments and pulled out a package of letters tied with a red ribbon. She felt cold, although the day was warm.

"Bring them over here, dear and read them, all of them. I . . . I don't want to have any secrets from you before I die, my dearest Kitty."

Kitty nodded. As she sat down beside the bed and untied the ribbon, her mother's eyes were upon her. Slowly she opened the first and began to read it quietly. After reading for a few minutes she became aware that her mother had drifted off to sleep. Probably just as well as the nature of the letters surprised her greatly and the depth of the emotions once or twice caused her to gasp aloud. She had often wondered about the relationship between her mother and father. Although now it seemed he was not her father. Certainly, there was affection there, but she had never been able to see any depth of feeling between them or that romance which she herself had always dreamt of. Romance that she had sometimes caught a glimpse of between Charlotte and Adam but most particularly between Belle and Monty, united by their love of horses. Father seemed more distant these days with his civic duties, and he and Mama seemed to have grown even further apart since Mama's heart attack.

As Kitty read on she slowly began to realise that her Mama's heart condition stemmed from just a few months after the letter had come from Mary Yate telling them all that the Reverend Yate, Robert, had died. It was as if her Mama's love for Robert was so great that her heart couldn't stand the strain of being parted from him. And yet anger burned within Kitty. Where did that leave her? Part of the family and yet not a part. Her sisters and brothers not full sisters and brothers to her. She had never felt so alone.

She remembered how Mama had loved her dear sister, Kitty, her namesake, who had tragically died before reaching them at Waireka. And of how Mama had told her of Robert being sent to administer the last rites to her and her Mama when she, Kitty, was just a baby.

"They feared for the both of us, Kitty," she had said, "but Robert prayed us back to life because he loved us."

At the time, Kitty hadn't fully understood the import of her mother's words. Now she did. It seemed that her beloved Mama had had an affair with Robert Yate, the minister and she was the result of their affair.

Finally, as her mother opened her eyes again, she said quietly, "I don't understand, Mama, how long had you and Robert been having an affair before I was born?"

"Not an affair, Kitty. It wasn't really like that."

"What was it like then?" asked Kitty both angry and sad at the same time. She felt her dearest Mama had let her down as she then spluttered out, "How many times, Mama?"

"How many times what?" said Eliza not fully understanding the question.

"How many times did you lay with him?" asked Kitty in a low angry voice. She got up and walked across to the window, needing to get away, to catch a glimpse of her beloved Waireka to bring her back to normality.

"Once, just once," said Eliza gazing at her beautiful daughter's back, through a mist of tears. "And you were the result of that once, my darling. You must believe me, we wouldn't have hurt you for the world. I love you and so did Robert."

"He knew I was his?"

"Well, not at first. But as you grew and developed and had his colour of hair and his fine features, well, yes, he guessed."

"But not father?" Kitty corrected herself, "Alister?"

"No, not him."

"He always told me that my different colouring was probably from some distant relative."

"Maybe that's what he liked to believe," said Eliza carefully. She was worried that these revelations could destroy the relationship between herself and her daughter forever. She couldn't bear the thought. Kitty was all that she had left of Robert and his love for her.

"And you never thought to tell him," said Kitty angrily. She still couldn't bear to turn around and look at her mother.

"No, although I suppose I can't ask you now not to tell him. I hope you don't though, it would break his heart. He's a good man, his only fault being that I didn't love him. I shouldn't have married him really, but I felt I had no choice."

"What do you mean by no choice?"

"I was raped, Kitty."

"Are you telling me that my father," she corrected herself, "Alister raped you?"

"No, of course not. Alister is a good man and if things had been different, I might not have accepted his proposal. I knew then that I didn't love him, but I was put in an almost impossible position as a nursemaid to two young children when their father, the Reverend Reid, raped me. I couldn't stay with them and I wouldn't have got another position in any respectable household either. Alister's proposal came just at the right time and saved me from humiliation and I really believed I'd come to love him in time. That might well have happened too, if I hadn't met Robert. I guess I must tell you the whole story."

And through the hours of the night Eliza told Kitty everything from her last time in England, the ship and meeting Alister, to getting married and meeting Robert. She held nothing back. If after hearing the whole sordid story, Kitty hated her, so be it. It would break her heart, but Kitty must make up her own mind about things.

"You mean, little Alister wasn't father's, I mean, Alister's either?" Kitty said after learning about the Reverend Reid.

She was equally horrified but also as supportive as Robert had been. "Rape is a serious crime, Mama. It could never have been your fault. Surely Alister saw that?" Kitty came back from the window and sat down on the edge of her mother's bed taking her frail hands in her own.

"No, he didn't. But you must remember dearest Kitty, rape victims are often viewed as willing participants by many."

"But surely you weren't?" breathed Kitty in horror, dropping her mother's hands for a moment.

"No, of course I wasn't. I hated the Reverend Reid for what he had done. I felt violated, alone. Marrying your father was really my only way out."

Kitty balled her fists in anger. "Mother, how awful for you. I wish I could do something to put it right."

"But you can't, and it was enough that Robert believed in me, saw me as the victim too."

"You told, Robert, father?" The word applied to the Reverend Yate still seemed to stick in her throat. It seemed such a strange word to apply to him, even though she had loved him dearly and he had always been really kind to her.

"Robert, ah . . . " Again Eliza' eyes seemed to mist over as she seemed to gaze into an imaginary space. "He would have guessed if I hadn't told him I'm sure. We had no secrets between us. Robert was outraged for me. He felt the blame was all the Reverend's and wanted to apologise on behalf of all men of the cloth."

"Rightly so, too," said Kitty indignantly.

Sometimes Eliza could see so much of herself in the young girl.

But smiling through her tears, Eliza said, "The cruel irony of life is that if I had I not married your F . . . " she automatically corrected herself, "Alister, then I wouldn't have met Robert, your true Father. Oh, Kitty I know this is a nasty shock to you but please believe me, I never meant to hurt Alister. I was so young when I married him. I didn't know what else to do after what had happened to me. Alister had already proposed to me and I had to get away from the Reid family as quickly as possible. I always hoped that I would one day be able to return Alister's love. But when I met Robert, I realised what real love was and that I could never feel that for Alister. Of course, Robert had Mary. Our love could never be. He was duty bound to her in her weakness. I tried so hard to keep our love to myself and so did he. The gossip at St Andrew's was nasty, upsetting and we knew it could damage his career, his reputation. And I was conscious of my care of you, of Charlotte, Annie, Belle, Jean and the boys as Robert was of Mary. Mary, as you know, was barren and an invalid and he loved me."

"That's pretty mean of him though not to love Mary simply because she was an invalid," said Kitty in disgust.

"Oh no," Eliza gasped in horror. "That wasn't it at all. Robert told me that if he'd loved Mary he would have given her his devotion always, invalid or not, but he believed that he'd already lost any feelings he might have had for her before the marriage. A strong sense of duty and a deep fondness for her were emotions he mistook for love. The marriage was also something that deeply pleased their respective families and with all these considerations, he told me, he was determined to give Mary all the care and devotion she needed."

"Did Mary love him?"

"No, I don't think she did really. She never gave the impression that she was devoted to him and was always more concerned with her own health and needs rather than his. But she must have known that if she didn't marry him her chances of marriage would be over. I guess she was fond of him though in her own way." Eliza was determined not to bear any ill feelings towards Mary now, even though she hadn't seen her since Robert and her had left Frampton. She guessed that she and Alister probably never would now, there seemed little point.

"How very sad, for you, Robert, Mary and Alister," said Kitty thoughtfully, tears gathering in her eyes at the realisation of the struggle they had all lived through. "Love can be so cruel."

"No, Kitty not if you marry the right person, like your Aunt Kitty did. She and your Uncle Charles were blissfully happy which was why

I called you Kitty. You too were born out of a relationship of true love like theirs."

"But they died early," said Kitty sadly.

"Yes, they did, but that was just sad, unfortunate. These things happen. Life is hard."

Kitty nodded. Life could be very hard, unfair. She didn't know what to make of what her mother had told her. But at least she supposed she was a child of love. She had been loved and very much wanted.

"We never wanted to cause you pain, Kitty. I never wanted to cause you any pain, please believe me."

"And yet you have," said Kitty her unshed tears beginning to slowly make their way down her cheeks.

Eliza, even though her sight was failing, saw the tears tracing down her young daughter's cheeks and berated herself for causing such pain to the dearest person she now had on earth. "May God forgive me, us. Please also forgive us, my dearest Kitty."

Her mother grew pale and looked slightly clammy. Kitty could see the effort in telling her everything was costing her mother. Perhaps she should try and understand.

Reading through the letters again as her mother slept, in the realisation of who she really was, Kitty wept over the love her parents had had for one another. At last, drying her eyes, she re-tied the ribbon around the letters and stuffed them quickly back into the drawer concealing them again under her mother's clothes. *What was she to do? Should she tell her siblings? Or Papa? No, certainly not him. That would be to betray Mama and Robert, her true Father. And if she told Charlotte, Annie, Belle, Jean or their brothers what would they say? Would they understand?* She felt that Belle would probably be the most sympathetic but if she told just her would that be right and if she told all of them wouldn't Papa find out?

Kitty struggled with these questions most of the rest of the night that was left but as her mother opened her eyes in the early dawn, Kitty knew she must talk it over again with her mother.

"Mama," she ventured.

"Yes, my dearest."

"The letters, what do you want me to do about them, tell the others or not?"

At first her Mama seemed to look at her vacantly as if she didn't know what she was talking about. That frightened Kitty; it was as if she was somehow even less aware of her surroundings now than she had ever been, even less perhaps than the previous night.

But then her mother opened her eyes and gazed fully at her.

"I trust you, Kitty. You must do what you think is best but I'm not sure you should upset your other sisters and brothers by telling them about the letters. What do you think? Wouldn't it betray our Robert, too?"

Mama had called him "their" Robert giving them both ownership of the love and trusting her to make the right decision and she would. Would it help her sisters and brothers to know the truth about their parent's marriage? Perhaps it would only colour their marriages to know that their mother had never fully loved their father. No, it was better not to tell them. Mama had trusted her with the secret and it would live and die with her. That was best.

"I don't think it would help them to know, Mama, do you? Let it be our secret. Yours, Robert's and mine. There's no need for it to go any further. You can trust me."

"I know that Kitty," said her mother reaching out and taking her hands. How frail her mother's hands felt. Kitty wished with all her heart she could pour some of her own strength into her mother and make her well again. But perhaps that was selfish. She never wanted to be parted from her dearest Mama but then Mama longed to be reunited with her Robert from whom she had been parted these three long years. If she truly loved her Mama, she must let her go, go to Robert, her father.

"I love you, Mama, too much to hold on to you. You must go to be with your Robert when the time's right. But I will keep your letters safe always, rest assured." Kitty's tears blended with those of her mother's as they fell.

"Bless you, Kitty, my love. You live up to the namesake of my dear sister, your aunt. I know that my time here is almost done and although I love you all dearly I am anxious to go and be with my Robert again."

Kitty suddenly saw her mother stir, sit up and seemingly grasp towards a space in front of her which appeared empty to Kitty but obviously not to her mother.

"Look, he has come for me at last, my dearest Robert, I am here," she said reaching out in front of her. Then the effort of the movement having drained her of all her remaining strength, she fell back on to her pillows, her face white as a sheet and her breath coming in short, sharp bursts.

Alarmed, realising that the time was drawing near for her to leave them all, Kitty quickly summoned the household who had all been waiting anxiously for a word from Kitty. It was but a few minutes before they were all assembled by her mother's bedside.

Alister took his wife's frail hand in his own as a smile and a deep sense peace settled over her and her rasping breath quieted. After her eyelids fluttered open once more and she gave them all the semblance of a last smile, she shut her eyes and was gone.

It took Kitty a few minutes before she realised what had happened. Her dearest Mama was no more. Her soul was finally reunited with his, forever. Her tears fell quickly. She was happy for her dearest Mama but oh so sad for herself. Her Mama was her dearest friend and she would miss her forever.

After a few moments, Alister leaned forward and bestowed a kiss on the cheek that was already growing cold, saying "Ah well, she'll have an eternity now to catch up with her beloved sister Kitty. She missed her dearly after her death, I know."

But not as much as him, her beloved Robert, Kitty thought, and she smiled through her tears as she thought of the love between them that could now blossom for eternity.

Kitty determined in that moment that marriage was not for her. It seemed too cruel, too hard to bear. She would devote her life to Waireka, along with Russell and David and take it on into the next century which was just a few years away. Her dearest Mama had devoted her life to the business, leaving her home and family in Scotland and faithfully building it up along with her husband. She had also devoted herself to her family, to all of them, and sacrificed the true love of her life by doing so.

"Be happy now my dearest Mama," whispered Kitty quietly leaning down and placing a final kiss on her mother's cheek. "I forgive you everything my dearest. I know you loved me and did your best for me, for us all. It's your turn now to enjoy the love you sacrificed for us. And don't you worry about me, will you? Waireka has my heart, dearest, and it always will."

THE END

BIBLIOGRAPHY

From Tulliallan to Tarureka by Graham Donald

An Important Family by Dorothy Eden

Green Dolphin Country by Elizabeth Goudge

The Trespass by Barbara Ewing

Pioneer Families: The Settlers of Nineteenth-Century New Zealand by Angela Caughey

How to be a Victorian by Ruth Goodman

Say it in Maori: Phrase Book by Alan Armstrong

For more information about
Sheila Donald
&
Waireka
please visit:

www.journojohnson.blogspot.com
www.facebook.com/Sheila-Donald
@journojohnson
www.linkedin.com/in/journojohnson

For more information about
AE BOOKS
please visit:

www.ambassador-international.com
@AmbassadorIntl
www.facebook.com/AmbassadorIntl